A KILLING SPRING

A KILLING SPRING

A Joanne Kilbourn Mystery

Gail Bowen

M&S

Canadian Cataloguing in Publication Data

Bowen, Gail, 1942-
   A killing spring

"A Joanne Kilbourn mystery".
ISBN 0-7710-1484-8 (bound)   ISBN 0-7710-1486-4 (pbk.)

I. Title.

PS8553.08995K55   1996   C813'.54   C96-930968-6
PR9199.3.B68K55   1996

The publishers acknowledge the support of the Canada Council and the Ontario Arts Council for their publishing program.

Typesetting by M&S, Toronto

Printed and bound in Canada

McClelland & Stewart Inc.
The Canadian Publishers
481 University Avenue
Toronto, Ontario
M5G 2E9

   2 3 4 5   00 99 98 97 96

For our children,
Hildy Wren, Max, and Nathaniel.
"Every age is the best."

≈

With thanks to Carol Abbey, for her computer wizardry and endless patience; to Dr. Joan Baldwin, for being everything a family physician should be; to Dr. Bernie Selinger, for his unflagging support and friendship; and to Ted, for never having to be asked twice.

CHAPTER

1

In the twenty-five years I had known Julie Evanson-Gallagher, I had wished many things on her. Still, I would never have wished that her new husband would be found in a rooming house on Scarth Street, dead, with a leather hood over his head, an electric cord around his neck, and a lacy garter belt straining to pull a pair of sheer black stockings over his muscular thighs.

I was on my way to my seminar in Politics and the Media when Inspector Alex Kequahtooway of the Regina Police Force called to tell me that the landlady of the Scarth Street house had found Reed Gallagher's body an hour earlier and that he wanted someone who knew Julie with him when he broke the news. Although my relationship with Reed Gallagher had not been a close one, I felt my nerves twang. Alex's description of Reed Gallagher's death scene was circumspect, but I didn't require graphics to understand why Julie would need shoring up when she heard about the manner in which her husband had gone to meet his Maker.

On the Day of Judgement, God's interest might lie in what is written in the human heart, but Julie's judgements had

I

always been pretty firmly rooted in what was apparent to the human eye. Discovering she was the widow of a man who had left the world dressed like RuPaul was going to be a cruel blow. Alex was right; she'd need help. But when he pressed me for a name, I had a hard time thinking of anyone who'd be willing to sign on.

"Jo, I don't mean to rush you . . ." On the other end of the line, Alex's voice was insistent.

"I'm trying," I said. "But Julie isn't exactly overburdened with friends. She can be a viper. You saw that yourself when she paraded you around at her wedding reception."

"Mrs. Gallagher was being enlightened," he said tightly, "showing everyone she didn't mind that you'd brought an aboriginal to the party."

"I wanted to shove her face into the punch bowl."

"You'd never make a cop, Jo. Lesson one at the police college is 'learn to de-personalize.'"

"Can they really teach you how to do that?"

"Sure. If they couldn't, I'd have been back on Standing Buffalo Reserve after my first hour on the beat. Now, come on, give me a name. Mrs. Gallagher may be unenlightened but she's about thirty minutes away from the worst moment of her life."

"And she shouldn't be alone, but I honestly don't know who to call. I think the only family she has are her son and her ex husband, and she's cut herself off from both of them."

"People come together in a crisis."

"They do, if they know there's a crisis. But Alex, I don't know how to get in touch with either Mark or Craig. Mark's studying at a Bible college in Texas, but I'm not sure where, and Craig called me last week to tell me he and his new family were on their way to Disney World."

I looked out my office window. It was March 17, and the campus, suspended between the bone-chilling beauty of winter and the promise of spring, was bleak. Except for the slush that had been shovelled off the roads and piled in soiled ribbons along the curbs, the snow was gone, and the brilliant cobalt skies of midwinter had dulled to gunmetal grey. To add to the misery, that morning the city had been hit by a wind-storm. Judging from the way the students outside my window were being blown across the parking lot as they ran for their cars, it appeared the rotten weather wasn't letting up.

"I wish I was in the Magic Kingdom," I said.

"I'm with you," Alex said. "I've never been a big fan of Minnie and Mickey, but they'd be better company than that poor guy in the room upstairs. Jo, that is one grotesque crime scene, but the media are going to love it. Once they get wind of how Reed Gallagher died, they're going to be on this rooming house like ducks on a June bug. I have to get to Julie Gallagher before one of them beats me to it."

"Do you want me to come with you?"

"I know you aren't crazy about Mrs. G.," he said, "but I've been through this scene with the next of kin enough times to know that she's going to need somebody with her who isn't a cop."

"I was just on my way to teach," I said. "I'll have to do something about my class." I looked at my watch. "I can meet you in front of Julie's place at twenty after three."

"Gallagher's identification says he lives at 3870 Lakeview Court," he said. "Those are the condos, right?"

"Right," I said.

After I hung up, I waited for the tone, then I dialled Tom Kelsoe's extension. This was the second year Tom and I had co-taught the Political Science 371 seminar. He was a man whose ambitions reached far beyond a Saskatchewan university, and whenever he heard opportunity knocking, I covered his classes for him. He owed me a favour; in fact, he owed me many favours, but as I listened to the phone ringing unanswered in his office, I remembered that this was the day Tom Kelsoe's new book was being launched. Today of all days, Tom was hardly likely to jump at the chance to pay back a colleague for past favours. It appeared that our students were out of luck. I grabbed my coat, stuffed a set of unmarked essays into my briefcase, made up a notice saying Political Science 371 was cancelled, and headed out the door.

When I turned the corner into the main hall, Kellee Savage was getting out of the elevator. She spotted me and waved, then she started limping down the hall towards me. Behind her, she was dragging the little cart she used to carry her books.

"Professor Kilbourn, I need to talk to you before class."

"Can you walk along with me, Kellee?" I asked. "I have to cancel the class, and I'm late."

"I know you're late. I've already been to the seminar room." She reached into her cart, pulled out a book and thrust it at me. "Look what was on the table at the place where I sit."

I glanced at the cover. "*Sleeping Beauty*," I said. "I don't understand."

"Read the note inside."

I opened the book. The letter, addressed to Kellee, detailed the sexual acts it would take to awaken her from her long sleep. The descriptions were as prosaic and predictable as the graffiti on the wall of a public washroom. But there was something both original and cruel in the parallel the writer had drawn between Kellee and Sleeping Beauty.

Shining fairies bringing gifts of comeliness, grace, and charm might have crowded one another out at Sleeping Beauty's christening, but they had been in short supply the day Kellee Savage was born. She was not more than five feet tall, and misshapen. One shoulder hunched higher than the other, and her neck was so short that her head seemed to be jammed against her collarbone. She didn't bother with eye makeup. She must have known that no mascara on earth could beautify her eyes, which goggled watery and blue behind the thick lenses of her glasses, but she took pains with her lipstick and with her hair, which she wore long and caught back by the kind of fussy barrettes little girls sometimes fancy.

She was a student at the School of Journalism, but she had been in my class twice: for an introductory course in Political Science and now in the seminar on Politics and the Media. Three times a week I passed her locker on the way to my first-year class; she was always lying in wait for me with a question or an opinion she wanted verified. She wasn't gifted, but she was more dogged than any student I'd ever known. At the beginning of term when she'd asked permission to tape my lectures, she'd been ingenuous: "I have to get good grades because that's all I've got going for me."

I held the book out to her. "Kellee, I think you should take this to the Student Union. There's an office there that deals with sexual-harassment cases."

"They don't believe me."

"You've been there already?"

"I've been there before. Many times." She steeled herself. "This isn't the first incident. They think I'm making the whole thing up. They're too smart to say that, but I know they think I'm crazy because . . ." She lowered her eyes.

"Because of what?" I asked.

"Because of the name of the person who's doing these things to me." She looked up defiantly. "It's Val Massey."

"Val?" I said incredulously.

Kellee caught my tone. "Yes, *Val*," she said, spitting his name out like an epithet. "I knew you wouldn't believe me."

This time it was my turn to look away. The truth was I

didn't believe her. Val Massey was in the Politics and the Media seminar. He was good-looking and smart and focused. It seemed inconceivable that he would risk an assured future for a gratuitous attack on Kellee Savage.

Kellee's voice was thick with tears. "You're just like the people at the Harassment Office. You think I'm imagining this, that I wrote the letter myself because I'm . . ."

"Kellee, sometimes, the stress of university, especially at this time of year . . ."

"Forget it. Just forget it. I should have known that it was too good to last."

"That what was too good to last?"

She was crying now, and I reached out to her, but she shook me off. "Leave me alone," she said, and she clomped noisily down the hall. She stopped at the elevator and began jabbing at the call button. When the doors opened, she turned towards me.

"Today's my birthday," she sobbed. "I'm twenty-one. I'm supposed to be happy, but this is turning out to be the worst day of my life."

"Kellee, I . . ."

"Shut up," she said. "Just shut the hell up." Then she stepped into the elevator and disappeared from sight.

She hadn't taken *Sleeping Beauty* with her. I looked at the face of the fairy-tale girl on the cover. Every feature was flawless. I sighed, slid the book into my briefcase, and headed down the hall.

Class was supposed to start at 3:00, and it was 3:10 when I got to the seminar room. The unwritten rule of university life is that, after waiting ten minutes for an instructor, students can leave. I had made it just under the wire, and there were groans as I walked through the door. When he saw me, Val Massey gave me a small conspiratorial smile; I smiled back, then looked at the place across the table from him where Kellee Savage usually sat. It was empty.

"Sorry," I said. "Something's come up. No class today."

Jumbo Hryniuk, a young giant who was planning a career hosting "Monday Night Football" but who was saddled nonetheless with my class, pushed back his chair and roared with delight. "Hey, all right!" he said. "We can get an early start on the green beer at the Owl, and somebody told me Tom Kelsoe's publishers are picking up the tab for the drinks at that party for him tonight."

Val Massey stood and began putting his books into his backpack. He imbued even this mechanical gesture with an easy and appealing grace. "Tom's publishers know how to court students," he said quietly. He looked at me. "Are you going to be there?"

"Absolutely," I said. "Students aren't the only people Tom's publishers know how to court." Then I wrote a reading assignment on the board, told them I hoped I'd see them all at the launch, and headed for the parking lot.

There was a cold rain falling, and the wind from the north was so fierce that it seemed to pound the rain into me. My parking spot was close, and I ran all the way, but I was still soaked to the skin by the time I slid into the driver's seat. It was shaping up to be an ugly day.

As I waited for the traffic to slow on the parkway, I looked back towards the campus. In the more than twenty years the new campus of the university had existed, not many politicians had been able to resist a speech praising their role in transforming scrub grass and thin topsoil into a shining city on the plain. I had written a few of those rhetorical flourishes myself, but that day as I watched the thin wind-driven clouds scudding off the flatlands, I felt a chill. Set against the implacable menace of a prairie storm, the university seemed insubstantial and temporary, like a theatre set that could be struck at any moment. I was glad when there was a break in the traffic, and I was able to drive towards the city.

Wascana Park was deserted. The joggers and the walkers and the young mums with strollers had been forced indoors by the rain, and I had the road that wound through the park to myself. There was nothing to keep me from thinking about Julie and about how I was going to handle the next few hours. But perversely, the more I tried to focus on the future, the more my mind was flooded with images of the past.

Julie and I shared a quarter-century of memories, but I would have been hard pressed to come up with one that warmed my heart. C.S. Lewis once said that happy people move towards happiness as unerringly as experienced travellers head for the best seat on the train. In the time I'd known her, Julie had invariably headed straight for the misery, and she had always made certain she had plenty of seatmates.

Craig Evanson and my late husband, Ian, had started in provincial politics together in the seventies. In the way of the time, Julie and I had been thrown together as wives and mothers. From the first, I had found her brittle perfection alienating, but I had liked and respected her husband. So did everyone else. Craig wasn't the brightest light on the porch, but he was principled and hardworking.

When we first knew the Evansons, Julie had just given birth to her son, Mark, and she was wholly absorbed in motherhood. The passion with which she threw herself into making her son the best and the brightest was unnerving, and when the unthinkable happened and Mark turned out to be not just average but somewhat below average, I was sure Julie's world would shatter. She had surprised me. Without missing a beat, she had cut her losses and regrouped. She withdrew from Mark completely, and threw herself headlong into a campaign to make Craig Evanson premier of the province. It was a fantastic effort, and it was doomed from the beginning, but Julie's bitterness when her plans didn't work out came close to poisoning Craig's relationship with everyone he cared for. The Evansons' eventual divorce was a relief to everyone who loved Craig. At long last, we were free of Julie.

But it turned out that Julie had some unfinished business with us. Two months before that blustery March day, several of Craig's friends had found wedding invitations in our mailboxes. Julie was marrying Reed Gallagher, the new head of the School of Journalism, and the presence of our company was requested. For auld lang syne or for some more complicated reason, most of us had accepted.

Julie had been a triumphant bride. She had every right to be. She had married a successful man who appeared to be wild about her, and the wedding, every detail of which had been planned and executed by Julie, had been textbook perfect. But as I turned onto Lakeview Court and saw Alex's Audi parked in front of 3870, I felt a coldness in the pit of my stomach. Five weeks after her model wedding, Julie Evanson-Gallagher was about to discover the cruel truth of the verse cross-stitched on the sampler in my grandmother's sewing room: "Pride goeth before destruction, and an haughty spirit before a fall."

As soon as I pulled up behind the Audi, Alex leaped out, snapped open a black umbrella, and came over. He held the umbrella over me as I got out of the car, and together we raced towards Julie's porch and rang the doorbell. There was a frosted panel at the side of the door, and Julie's shape appeared behind it almost immediately, but she didn't hurry to open the door. When she finally did, she wasn't welcoming.

"This is a surprise," she said in a tone which suggested

she was not a woman who welcomed surprises. "I was expecting the caterers. Some people are dropping in before Tom Kelsoe's book launch, and I'm on a tight schedule, so, of course, I've had nothing but interruptions." She smoothed her lacquered cap of silver-blond hair and looked levelly at Alex and me. She had given us our cue. It was up to us to pick it up and make our exit.

"Julie, can we come in out of the rain?" I asked.

"Sorry," she said, and she stepped aside. She gave us one of her quick, dimpled smiles. "Now, I'm warning you, I don't have much time to visit."

Alex's voice was gentle. "This isn't exactly a visit, Mrs. Gallagher. We have some bad news."

"It's about Reed," I said.

Her dark eyes darted from me to Alex. "What's he done?"

"Julie, he's dead." I said. "I'm so very sorry."

The words hung in the air between us, heavy and stupid. The colour drained from Julie's face; then, without a word, she disappeared into the living room.

Alex turned to me. "You'd better get out of that wet coat," he said. "It looks like we're going to be here for a while."

From the appearance of the living room, Julie's plans had gone well beyond some people dropping in. Half a dozen round tables covered with green-and-white checked cloths had been set up at the far end of the room. At the centre of each table was a pot of shamrocks in a white wicker basket with an emerald bow on its handle. It was all very festive, and it was all very sad. Less than an hour before, Kellee Savage had sobbed that her twenty-first birthday was turning out to be the worst day of her life. It was hard to think of two members of the sisterhood of women who had less in common than Reed Gallagher's new widow and the awkward and lonely Kellee Savage, but they shared something now: as long as they lived, they would both remember this St. Patrick's Day as a day edged in black.

Julie was standing near the front window, staring into an oversized aquarium. When I followed the line of her vision I spotted an angelfish, gold and lapis lazuli, gliding elegantly through a tiny reef of coral.

Julie was unnaturally still, and when I touched her hand, it was icy. "Can I get you a sweater?" I asked. "Or a cup of tea?"

She didn't acknowledge my presence. I was close enough to smell her perfume and hear her breathing, but Julie Evanson-Gallagher was as remote from me as the lost continent of Atlantis. Outside, storm clouds hurled themselves across the sky, wind pummelled the young trees on the lawn, and rain cankered the snow piled beside the walk. But in the silent and timeless world of the aquarium, all was serene. I understood why Julie was willing herself into the peace of that watery kingdom; what I didn't understand was how I could pull her back.

Alex was behind us. Suddenly, he leaned forward. "Look," he whispered. "There, coming out from the coral. Lionfish – a pair of them." For a few moments, the three of us were silent, watching. Then Alex said, "They're amazing, Julie."

They were amazing: large, regal, and as dazzlingly patterned as a bolt of cloth in a street market in Jakarta. They were also menacing. Spines radiated like sunbursts off their sleek bodies and, as they drifted towards us, I instinctively stepped back.

"They're my favourites," Julie said.

"Have you ever been stung?" Alex asked.

Julie dimpled. "Oh yes, but I don't care. They're so beautiful they're worth it. Reed doesn't like them. He wants a dog. Imagine," she said, "a dog." For a moment, she was silent. Then she said, "Was he alone?"

It seemed an odd first question, but Alex was unruffled. "He was when the landlady found him."

Julie flinched. "Where was he?"

"At a rooming house on Scarth Street."

"I want to see him," she said. Her voice was lifeless.

"If you want, I'll take you to him," Alex said. "But I need to know some things first. Could we sit down?"

Julie gestured to one of the tables that had been set up for the party. Alex took the chair across from her. He was silent for a moment, watching her face, then he said, "When did you last see your husband?"

Julie's answer was almost inaudible. "Last night. Around eight-thirty."

"Was it usual for you to spend the night apart."

She looked up defiantly. "Of course not. We'd just had a disagreement."

"What was the disagreement about?"

Julie shrugged. "I don't remember. It was just one of those foolish quarrels married people have."

"But it was serious enough that your husband didn't come home. Weren't you concerned?"

"No . . . Reed was angry. I thought he'd just gone somewhere to cool off. I went to bed."

"Did you try to locate him today?"

Suddenly Julie's eyes blazed. "Of course I did. I called his office, but he wasn't there."

"And that didn't surprise you?"

"He's an important man. He doesn't have a silly little job where he sits at a desk all day." She leaned forward and adjusted the green bow on the wicker basket. When the ribbon was straight, she looked up warily. "Why are you asking me all these questions?"

"The circumstances of your husband's death were unusual."

Alex's tone was matter-of-fact, but I could see Julie stiffen. "What are you talking about?"

"Well, for one thing, he was dressed oddly."

Julie's eyes widened. She was wearing a silk shirt, a cardigan, slacks, and sandals, all in carefully co-ordinated shades of taupe. She glanced reflexively at her own outfit as if to reassure herself that, whatever her husband's eccentricities, her own clothing was beyond reproach.

Alex leaned towards her. "Was your husband a transvestite?" he asked softly.

Julie leaped up so abruptly that her legs caught the edge of the table. The crystal wine goblet in front of her leaned crazily, then fell. "You don't know what you're talking about," she snapped. "I don't know why they'd send someone like you out here in the first place. What are you, some sort of special native constable?"

"I'm not a special anything, just a regular inspector who happens to be Ojibway."

"I don't care what kind of native you are," she said.

She disappeared down the hall, and when she came back she was wearing a trenchcoat and carrying an over-the-shoulder bag. "You can leave now," she said. "I'm going down to the police station to find someone who knows what he's doing."

As he zipped his windbreaker, Alex's face was impassive. "I'll give you a lift," he said. "I don't think you should be driving right now."

"I've got my car here," I said. "I can take her, Alex."

She shot me a venomous look. "So you can relay all the details to your friends? No thanks."

She headed back into the hall, and I followed her. There was a mirror near the front door and she stopped and checked her makeup.

"Julie, there has to be something I can do," I said.

Her mirror image looked at me coldly. "Always the girl guide, aren't you, Joanne? But since you're so eager to serve, why don't you phone my guests and tell them the party's cancelled. The list is by the phone in the kitchen." Beneath the mirror there was a small bureau. Julie opened its top drawer, took out a key and handed it to me. "Lock up before you leave," she said. "There was a break-in down the street last week. Put the key through the letter slot when you go."

"I'll make sure everything's safe," I said.

She laughed angrily. "You do that," she said. Then she opened the door and vanished into the rain.

Alex turned to me. "I'll call you," he said. "Right now I'd better get out there and unlock the car before Mrs. G. gets soaked."

I drew him towards me and kissed him. He smelled of cold rain and soap. "My grandmother used to say that every time we turn the other cheek, we get a new star in our crown in heaven."

Alex raised an eyebrow. "Let's hope she's right. I have a feeling that before Reed Gallagher is finally laid to rest, his widow is going to give us a chance to build up quite a collection."

CHAPTER

2

Julie's kitchen was the cleanest room I had ever seen. Everything in it was white and hard-scrubbed: the Italian tile on the floor, the Formica on the counters, the paint on the walls, the handsome Scandinavian furniture, and the appliances, which shone as brightly as they had the day they'd come out of their packing boxes. That morning my fifteen-year-old son had taped a sign above our sink: "Kitchen Staff No Longer Required to Wash Their Hands." Somehow I couldn't imagine Angus's sign eliciting any chuckles in Julie's kitchen.

The telephone was on a small desk in the corner. Beside it, in a gold oval frame, was Julie and Reed Gallagher's formal wedding portrait. They had been a handsome bridal couple. The week before the wedding, Reed had been invited to speak at a conference in Hilton Head. Judging from their tans, he and Julie had logged some major beach time in North Carolina. Against her white-blond hair and dark eyes, Julie's bronzed skin had looked both startling and flattering. She had worn an ivory silk suit at her wedding. She had made it herself, just as she had sewn the ivory shirt Reed wore, dried the flowers that decorated the church, tied the bows of ivory satin ribbon at the end of each pew, and smoked the salmon for the hors-d'oeuvres. She had been attentive to every detail, except, apparently, her new husband's appetite for unusual bedroom practices.

I picked up the photograph. Reed Gallagher didn't seem the type for kinky sex. He was a tall, heavy-set man, with an unapologetic fondness for hard liquor, red meat, and cigars. I'd met him only a few times, but I'd liked him. He took pleasure in being outrageous, and in the careful political climate of the university, his provocations had been refreshing. I tried to remember the last time I'd seen him. It had been in the Faculty Club at the beginning of the month. He'd been in the window room with Tom Kelsoe and my friend Jill Osiowy. They'd been celebrating Reed's birthday with a bottle of wine and, as people always do when they're celebrating, they had seemed immortal. I put down the photograph and started reading the names on Julie's list.

Twenty-four people had been invited to the party, and the first name was that of the guest of honour. I dialled Tom Kelsoe's office number. There was still no answer. There was no one at his home either. I hung up and dialled the next number. I drew a blank there, too, but there was an answering machine, and I left a message that was factual but not forthcoming. As the hour wore on, I had plenty of opportunities to refine my message. Out of the seven couples and ten singles on the list, I was able to talk to only three people.

One of those people was Jill Osiowy. She was an executive producer at Nationtv, but her concern when she heard the news of Reed's death was less with getting the story to air than with making certain that she found Tom Kelsoe so that he would hear the news from her rather than from a stranger. Her anxiety about Tom's reaction surprised me. In the years I'd known her, Jill had had many relationships, but none of them had ever reached the point where a blow to the man in her life was a blow to her.

Until she met Tom Kelsoe, Jill's romantic history could be summarized in one sentence: she had lousy taste in men, but she was smart enough to know it. The fact that the deepest thing about any of the men who paraded through her life was either their tan or the blue of their eyes never fazed her. When she came upon the term "himbo" in a magazine article about the joys of the shallow man, Jill had faxed it to me with a note: "Thomas Aquinas says, 'It's a privilege to be an angel and a merit to be a virgin,' but check this out – there are other options!"

For the past six months, it seemed Jill had decided that Tom Kelsoe was her only option. At the age of forty, she was as besotted as a schoolgirl. At long last, she had found Mr. Right, but as I hung up the phone I wondered why it was that Jill's Mr. Right, increasingly, seemed so wrong to me.

It was 4:30 when I crossed the last name off Julie's list. I could feel the first twinges of a headache, and I leaned back in the chair, closed my eyes, and ran my forefinger along my temple until I found the acupressure point I'd seen a doctor demonstrate on television the week before. I was so absorbed in my experiment with alternative medicine that I didn't hear the doorbell until whoever was ringing apparently decided to lean on it.

All I could see when I opened the door was someone in a yellow slicker hunched over a huge roasting pan, trying, it seemed, to keep the wind from tearing the lid off. I couldn't make out whether my visitor was a man or a woman. The hood of the slicker had fallen forward, masking individual features as effectively as a nun's wimple, but when the person at Julie's front door began to speak, it was apparent that I was not dealing with a Sister of Mercy.

"Holy crudmore," she said. "Are you all deaf? There's a monsoon going on out here in case you hadn't noticed."

She pushed past me into the house, and I glimpsed her profile: determined chin, snub nose, and skin rosy with cold and good health. She kicked off her shoes and headed for the kitchen.

"Just a minute," I said. "What's going on?"

"Catering's going on," she snapped. "At least it's supposed to be unless you've changed your mind again." She tossed her head, and her hood fell back. She glanced towards me and her mouth fell open. "Oh, my lord, you're not her. Sorry. I should have checked before I snarled."

"You may still want to snarl," I said. "I've got some bad news. There isn't going to be any party."

"You mean she gave into him after all?" She struck the palm of her hand against her forehead. "And what," she groaned, "am I supposed to do with that old-country trifle of hers with all those barfy kiwi shamrocks?"

"Mrs. Gallagher has had some bad news," I said. "She's just found out that her husband died. That's why I'm here. We just heard about what happened."

Her young face grew grave. "Bummer," she said, stretching out the last syllable in anguish. "Bummer for him, of course, but also for me." She looked thoughtful. "I guess I could make sandwiches out of the corned beef, and you can always do something with potatoes." She slumped. "But the Lunenburg cabbage! And the old-country trifle! No way I can hold that trifle over till tomorrow."

"You won't be out anything," I said. "Just send the bill to Mrs. Gallagher. She'll understand."

"She's not the understanding type." The girl's eyes filled with tears. "I'm sorry. It's just I've had such an awful week. Trying to please Mrs. Gallagher was about as easy as putting socks on a rooster. Then last night when she called to re-book, she told me that, if there were any extra costs, I'd have to swallow them because it was her party, and it was unprofessional of me to cancel the party without consulting her. I mean, wouldn't you figure that if a husband calls you and says 'Cancel the party,' you should cancel the party?"

"Yes," I said, "I would. Did Mr. Gallagher explain why he was changing their plans?"

"No, he just said the dinner was off, but at least he was nice about it. Told me he was sorry for the inconvenience and he'd pay the bill. Not like her. She'd squeeze a nickel till the Queen screamed. Trust me, this is going to cost me big time." She wiped her nose with the back of her hand. "Have you got a Kleenex?" she asked.

I opened my purse, found a tissue and handed it to her.

"Thanks," she said. "I never even told you who I am, did I? I'm Polly Abbey." She fumbled in the pocket of her slicker, pulled out a business card and handed it to me. "Abbey Road Caterers. Like you'd ever hire me after seeing me like this."

"I understand," I said. "My name's Joanne Kilbourn, and my daughter owns a catering business. I know what these last-minute cancellations do to her cash flow. Look, why don't I buy some of the meat. I haven't got anything started for dinner tonight, and my kids love corned beef."

Polly brightened. "You can have the Lunenburg cabbage too," she said. "I'll even throw in some potatoes. Now if I could only find a home for that stupid trifle."

I thought of Julie's poisonous dismissal of Alex. "Polly, do you know where the Indian-Métis Friendship Centre is?"

"Sure," she said. "It's on Dewdney. Actually, it's not far from my shop."

"Good," I said. "Why don't you drop the old-country trifle off there on your way back? Tell them it's a gift from an admirer."

Her eyes widened. "Not Mrs. Gallagher?"

I nodded.

"Cool," she said, and for the first time since she'd come in out of the rain, Polly Abbey smiled.

When I opened the front door to our house, Benny, my younger daughter's ginger cat, was waiting. He looked at me assessingly. As usual, I didn't pass muster, and he wandered off. Somewhere in the distance the Cranberries were singing, but theirs were the only human voices I heard.

"Hey," I shouted. "Anybody home?"

Taylor came running. She was wearing the current costume of choice for girls in her grade-one class: jeans, a plaid shirt, and a ponytail anchored by a scrunchy.

"Me. I'm home, and Angus and Leah are downstairs," she said, reaching her arms out for a hug. Benny, who had a sixth sense for the exact moment at which Taylor's affections wandered from him, reappeared and began rubbing against her leg. She picked him up, and he shot me a look of triumph.

"Guess what?" Taylor said. "I lost a tooth, and I'm going to draw a mural for the Kids Convention." She shifted Benny to the crook of her arm, and pulled her lip up with her thumb and forefinger. "Look!"

"The front one," I said. "That's a loonie tooth."

"Serious?"

"Serious," I said. "Now tell me about the Kids Convention."

"All I know is it's after Easter holidays and I'm making a mural about the Close-Your-Eyes Dance."

"The story Alex told you. He'll be pleased."

"I'm going to do it in panels. The first one's gonna be where that hungry guy . . ."

"Nanabush," I said.

". . . where he sees those ducks. Then I'm going to show him singing and drumming, so he can trick them. You really think Alex will like it?"

"I know he will," I said. "Now, come on, let's get cracking. We have to eat early because I'm going out."

Taylor's face fell. "I hate it when you go out."

I put my arms around her. "I know, T, but we've talked about this before. I'm never gone for long. And Leah and Angus are staying with you. If you like, you can invite Leah for supper."

Taylor's gaze was intense. "You promise you'll come back?"

"I promise," I said. "Now, I'm going to go change into something warm. Why don't you go find Leah and ask her if she likes corned beef and cabbage. If you guys play your cards right, I might even throw in green milkshakes."

Reassured, at least for the time being, Taylor ambled off towards the family room. In the past few months she'd become troubled when I left at night. Her fearfulness was something I'd been half-expecting since her mother died suddenly and Taylor had come to live with us. Even before her mother's death, Taylor's life had been tumultuous, and at first, when she had come to us, she had seemed relieved just to know that, when she woke up in the morning, the day ahead was going to be pretty much like the day before. But when her best friend's father died shortly before Christmas, Taylor had been shaken. As she watched Jess grieve for his father, she grieved too, and she grew anxious. At six and a half, the awareness that we are moored to our happiness by fragile threads had hit her hard. I was doing my best to reassure her, but some nights my best just wasn't good enough. As I changed into jeans and a sweatshirt, I was hoping this particular night wasn't one of them.

When I brought Polly Abbey's dinner in from the car,

Taylor was sitting at the kitchen table, drawing. Benny was on her lap, and she looked so content I uncrossed my fingers. Maybe my going out wasn't going to be a problem after all.

When she heard me, Taylor glanced up. "I almost forgot. A lady called you," she said.

"Do you remember her name?"

Taylor's face pinched in concentration, then she lit up. "It's Kellee," she said. "Her name is Kellee and today's her birthday, and she's going to call back."

"Swell," I said. Then I took down the butcher knife and began slicing the corned beef. When I had the platter filled, the phone rang. I picked up the receiver without much enthusiasm, but I was in luck. It wasn't the birthday girl on the line; it was Alex.

"How are you doing?" he asked.

"Fine," I said. "I'm just slicing up the funeral baked meats."

"I don't get it."

"The caterer came when I was at Julie's, and I bought some of the corned beef they were going to have at the party. Any chance you can join us?"

"Nope. We're still searching this place for evidence, so I'm not going anywhere for a while. Anyway, there's something about a crime scene that takes away the appetite."

"At least you're free of Julie. Did she ever find her white knight?"

He laughed. "No. She decided to stick with me."

"Is she there now?"

"No, but she was. I tried to talk her out of coming. I thought it would be easier on her if she waited until they took her husband down to pathology at the hospital, but the lady was insistent."

"So she saw him there."

"Yeah, in all his glory."

"How did she take it?"

"Weirdly. Not that there's any rule about how to react when you see your dead husband decked out in leather and lace, but I would have thought it'd be a sight to grab a wife's attention."

"And it didn't grab Julie's?"

"Not for long. Jo, did you notice this afternoon how quickly she zeroed in on the question of whether Gallagher was alone when he died?"

"Yes."

"What did you make of it?"

"The obvious. I thought Julie was afraid Reed was having an affair."

"That seemed to be her focus while she was here, too. We'd already sealed the scene, so she couldn't get past the threshold, but she kept leaning in, looking around. One of the ident officers asked if he could help, but she just shook her head and kept on looking."

"What do you think she thought she'd find?"

"Given her concern this afternoon about whether Gallagher was alone when his body was discovered, I would guess that she thought she might find some evidence of his sexual partner."

"Poor Julie," I said. "She and Reed seemed so happy at the wedding, but apparently they really did have problems. The young woman they'd hired to cater their party told me Reed called her last night and said the dinner was cancelled."

Alex's voice was tight with interest. "Did she give you the time when he called?"

"No, but you can check. Her name is Polly Abbey and her company's called Abbey Road Catering – it's on Dewdney."

"Got it," he said. Then he paused. "Jo, am I missing something here? When we were at the Gallaghers' today, didn't you get the impression that the party was still on?"

"Yes, because it was. Polly Abbey said Julie called her last night to re-book. Maybe that's what Julie and Reed fought about."

"Maybe," he said wearily. "Or maybe they fought over the fact that she didn't share his sexual tastes. When it comes to domestic disputes, causes are never in short supply."

"Do you know anything more about what happened to Reed?"

"Splatter says that, judging from the condition of the body, Gallagher died last night."

"Who's Splatter?"

"Sorry, he's our M.E. – the medical examiner. His real name is Sherman Zimbardo. The guys call him Splatter because he's got this uncanny ability to interpret blood patterns at a crime scene."

"I'm sorry I asked."

"Actually, I think the guys see the nickname as a kind of compliment. Anyway, Zimbardo says he should have more solid information about how Reed Gallagher died after he's completed the autopsy. Till then, we're just calling it a suspicious death."

"Which means . . . ?"

"Which means that we don't know what happened, but there are enough loose ends to keep us interested for a while. Zimbardo says he's seen a couple of cases like this."

"You mean with the hood and the cord?"

"Yeah. Apparently, they indicate a particular type of auto-eroticism."

"Sex play on your own."

"Right. How did you know that?"

"I took Greek and Latin at school."

"Fair enough. Anyway, this particular variation of auto-eroticism is called . . . wait a minute, the name's in my notes . . . it's called hypoxyphilia. Did you cover that in class?"

"I don't think so."

"Good. It's a dangerous business. The people who practise it apparently find sex more interesting when they cut off their oxygen. Every so often the fun and games get out of hand, then we have to cut them down."

"That doesn't make sense to me."

"It doesn't appeal to me much either."

"I didn't mean the kinkiness. I meant that I don't understand why a man like Reed Gallagher would have a fight with his wife and decide that the next step was to hop in the car, drive downtown to a rooming house, and go through some sort of bizarre masturbation ritual."

"Zimbardo's done some reading on the subject. He says people who are into hypoxyphilia claim that it's a great stress-reliever."

"I think I'll stick to single-malt Scotch." I said. "And from what I'd seen of Reed Gallagher, I would have thought that would be his solution, too."

"The leather and lace doesn't sound to you like something he'd do?"

"No," I said, "Reed always struck me as a man who coped with life head-on."

"But you didn't know him well."

"No," I said. "Not well at all." Just then I heard the call-waiting signal. "Alex, could you hang on? I've got a beep."

At first, all I heard on the other line was music and party sounds. Then there was giggling, and Kellee Savage said, "Can you hear them singing? Well, they don't have as much reason to sing as I do." Her words were slurred. It was obvious that she'd been drinking, but I'd had enough. Birthday or no, Kellee Savage was going to have to find somebody else to play with.

"Kellee, I'll have to talk to you later. I have an important call on the other line."

"This is an important call," she said belligerently. "I've figured it all out. Exactly why he's after me all the time. Here's what's happening . . ."

"Kellee, I really have to go. If you want to talk to me, come to my office Monday morning." I clicked off, but not before I heard someone in the bar begin to sing "Danny Boy."

When I apologized for keeping him waiting, Alex's voice was easy. "It's okay," he said. "I was just remembering the Gallaghers' wedding."

"I would have thought you'd want to excise that from your memory."

"It wasn't that bad, Jo. At least nobody called me Chief. Anyway, the whole thing just seems so sad now. I keep thinking about those birds they had on the wedding cake."

"The doves," I said. "They were made of sugar. It's been years since I've seen any that weren't made of plastic."

"Julie Gallagher made them herself," Alex said. "She told me she couldn't find a store in town that sold them."

"That's Julie for you. Always gilding her own lily."

"I don't think it was that," Alex said softly. "Mrs. Gallagher told me there was an old wives' tale that every sugar dove on a wedding cake brought a year of happiness, and she wanted to make sure that she and her husband had a lifetime-full."

Despite my sad mood, dinner that night was fun. Angus's new girlfriend, Leah Drache, had a good head on her shoulders and a knack for smoothing over raw edges. Leah also had, according to Taylor, who had asked, thirteen separate body piercings. I'd seen the seven on Leah's ears, the two on her left eyebrow, the one through her right nostril, and the one in her navel. As we drank our green milkshakes and listened to Toad the Wet Sprocket, I tried not to think about the location of the other two.

When we started to clear off the table, Taylor stayed at her place, staring out into the night. I went back and sat beside her. "Penny for your thoughts, T," I said.

Her voice was small and sad. "I wish you didn't have to go out tonight."

"So do I. But a book launch is a special thing. It's a lot of work to write a book, and the man who wrote this one is Jill's boyfriend."

"Is he nice?"

I pointed towards the garage. "Look at the size of that branch the wind blew down. I'll bet Angus could cut it up and make a good scratching post for Benny."

Angus, who knew I didn't like Tom Kelsoe, turned from the sink where he was scraping his plate and gave me a side-long smile. "Nice feint, Mum."

"Thanks," I said. "That means a lot coming from the master-feinter." I gave Taylor a quick hug. "Okay, kiddo, it's time for me to grab a shower and get dressed. The sooner I get there, the sooner I get home."

The phone on my nightstand rang just as I'd finished undressing. I ignored it and continued into the bathroom. As soon as I turned on the shower, Angus hollered, "It's for you!" I grabbed a towel and swore. The law of averages that day pointed towards a bad-news phone call.

Kellee Savage didn't even bother to say hello. "I've got proof," she said. "I wasn't supposed to say anything till it was all checked, but I can't find him, so what's the point of waiting?" She enunciated each syllable carefully, confirming to herself and to the world that she was still sober. In the background I could hear laughter, but there was no mirth in Kellee's voice.

"Kellee, I don't understand what you're talking about. Who is it that you can't find?"

"That's confidential, and a good journalist honours

confidences." For a beat she was silent, then she said sulkily, "And a good journalist knows when to get the story out. I don't care if he thinks I should wait. It's my story, and I'm getting it out. In fact, I'm coming to your house right now to tell you what's happening. You'll be sorry you didn't believe me."

"Kellee, it's a rotten night. You'll feel a lot better tomorrow if you just go back to your own place and go to bed."

"I don't wanna go to bed. It's my birthday. I'm s'posed to get my way. I have a birthday song. My mum made it up when I was little. 'Oh Kellee girl, today is your birthday and smiles and fun will last the whole day long.'" She fell silent. "I forget the rest."

"Kellee, please. Call a cab and go home."

"Can't," she said. "I'm a journalist. Got to get the story out. Besides I used up all my quarters phoning you."

"I'll call the taxi for you. Just tell me where you are."

She snorted. "Oh no, you don't. I know what you're trying to do. You're trying to stop me. He probably called and warned you that I'm dangerous." She giggled. "Well, I am dangerous. You know why? Because I'm a journalist, and if we're good, we're dangerous." There was a long silence, and I wondered if she'd passed out. But as luck would have it, she rallied. "Stay tuned," she slurred, then she slammed down the receiver so hard, it hurt my eardrum.

I walked back to the bathroom, stepped into the shower stall, lifted my face towards the shower head and turned the water on full force. It was going to take a real blast to wash away the last three hours.

CHAPTER

3

Tom Kelsoe's book launch was being held at the university Faculty Club on the second floor of College West. I'd been to some great parties there, but as I walked through the door that night, I knew this wasn't going to be one of them. Real shamrocks and shillelaghs that looked as if they could be real were everywhere, but the mood was sombre. The lounge to the right of the entrance area was jammed. Ordinarily, guests picked up their drinks at the bar and drifted into one of the larger rooms; that night, people weren't drifting. It was apparent from their pale and anxious faces that the news of Reed Gallagher's death had spread, and that the rumours were swirling.

Several of the people I'd left messages for that afternoon spotted me in the doorway and came over. They were full of questions, but I hid behind Alex's statement that, until the police had finished their investigations, Reed's death was being classified as accidental. It wasn't a satisfactory answer, but no one seemed to have the heart to press me.

I made my way through to the bar and ordered Glenfiddich

on the rocks. When it came, I took a long sip; the warmth spreading through my veins felt so good, I took another.

"There are times when only single-malt Scotch will do." The voice behind me was throaty and familiar.

"And this is one of them," I said. "Care to join me?"

Jill Osiowy scrutinized my glass longingly. "Tom and I are off hard liquor," she said.

I turned to face her. There was no denying that the abstemious life agreed with her. I'd hedged when Taylor asked me about my feelings for Tom, but even I had to admit that the effect he was having on her lifestyle was a positive one. In the years I had known her, Jill had been a workaholic: routinely putting in fourteen-hour workdays, subsisting on junk food, too busy to exercise, and too tense at the end of the day to unwind without a couple of stiff drinks.

Tom Kelsoe had changed all that. He was into vegetarianism and weight training, and now so was she. She had never been heavy, but now she was very lean and muscular. Her auburn hair was cut in a fashionable new way that made her look ten years younger. She was wearing black lace-up boots, form-fitting black velvet pants, and an extravagantly beautiful jade jacket with a black mandarin collar and elaborate black fastenings.

"You look like about seven million dollars," I said.

"I feel like homemade shit."

"Where's Tom?"

"At the gym," she said. "He says he has a lot of stuff to get through. Reed was his first boss when he got out of J school. He was like a father to Tom."

"How much does Tom know about what happened?"

"Just what I told him, and I got that from you." She shook her head in a gesture of disbelief. "Jo, what did happen?"

I started to tell her what I knew. Then, over her shoulder, I saw Ed Mariani bobbing towards us. He was a portly and pleasant man, my favourite, by far, of the faculty at the School of Journalism. Earlier in the semester, I'd sat in on his lectures on the Politics of Image, and I'd understood why there were always waiting lists for the courses he taught. He was passionate about his subject, and while he was demanding with his students, he was genuinely excited about their response to what they were learning. In and out of class, Ed was fun, and, under normal circumstances, he would have been exactly the man I wanted to chat to at a party. But these were not normal circumstances.

I grabbed Jill's arm. "Come on," I said. "It'll be easier to talk in the hall."

Ed Mariani's face fell when he saw us leaving, but I didn't relent. Julie Evanson-Gallagher had leached me of charity. Jill and I walked to the end of the corridor and found an alcove where we wouldn't be spotted by latecomers. There, I told her everything I knew about Reed Gallagher's death.

Jill had worked in the media for twenty years; she had more than a nodding acquaintance with the tragic and the bizarre, but she stiffened as I described the scene the police had found in the room on Scarth Street. When I finished, she seemed dazed. Finally she said, "I have to get back inside. When Tom comes, he'll want me there."

"What about what you want?"

The harsh institutional light above her shone directly on her face, knifing in the years. "What I want doesn't matter. Tonight, Tom is all that matters. Jo, I've never been a very giving person, but I'm trying, and I've finally reached a point where Tom knows he can trust me absolutely. I can't let him down. There've been so many betrayals in his life."

"And I'll bet he's told you about every one."

"That was cruel."

"I'm sorry. It's just that I hate to see you acting like a Stepford wife, especially with Tom Kelsoe."

She moved towards me. "Tom has suffered so much, Jo. His father was a real horror show – bullying and abusive – but whenever Tom's mother threatened to leave, his father would force Tom to beg her to stay. You just don't know him. He is so vulnerable."

"And so manipulative. Jill, I do know Tom. I've worked with him for two years. I've seen him in action."

For one awful moment, I thought she was going to hit me; then, without a word, she turned and walked back down the hall. When she disappeared into the Faculty Club, I followed her. I couldn't afford to lose any more points with her by being late for Tom's party.

Inside the club, it looked as if the main event was finally about to begin. People were moving out of the lounge and finding places at tables which had been set up to face a lectern at the end of the room. On a table a discreet distance from the lectern, copies of Tom's new book were stacked beside a cloisonné vase of white freesia. Everything was ready for the reading, but the man behind the microphone wasn't Tom Kelsoe. It was Ed Mariani.

There was a certain logic in his being there. It was no secret that Ed had wanted to be head of the School of Journalism. In fact, his appointment had been considered a sure thing until Reed Gallagher applied, and Ed withdrew from the competition. His decision to take his name off the list of candidates had been as abrupt as it had been inexplicable, but whatever his reason for withdrawing, Ed had rapidly become Reed's staunchest ally. He had moved quickly to make sure that department members who had supported his own candidacy threw their support behind Reed, and he had spoken out against those who feared that Reed's plans for the school were too ambitious. That night, we had gathered to honour a member of the School of

Journalism; with Reed gone, Ed Mariani was the one to take charge.

But as he adjusted the microphone, it was apparent there was no joy in it for him. Ed had features made for smiling, but his face was crumpled with sorrow. "This is an evening to be with friends," he said, and his voice broke. He took a handkerchief from his pocket, mopped his eyes, and began again. "As you have no doubt heard, Reed Gallagher died last night. We're only now beginning to comprehend the depth of our loss. He was our colleague, our friend, and, for those of us in the School of Journalism, he was our example of what a journalist should be. Rudyard Kipling called what we do 'the black art,' but as Reed Gallagher practised it, journalism was a shining thing – incisive, compelling, and humane. It's hard to know where we go from here, but I think those of us who counted Reed as a friend know that he would have wanted . . ."

Before Ed Mariani had a chance to finish, a door behind and to the left of the lectern flew open. Suddenly, all eyes were focused on the man in the doorway. Tom Kelsoe hesitated long enough to take in the situation, then he strode towards the podium and pushed Ed aside. It was a gesture so gratuitously rude that people gasped.

Tom didn't seem to notice or care. "Talking about what Reed would have wanted us to do is a waste of time," he said, and his voice was cutting. "And he despised wasting time as much as he despised anything that was fake or second-rate." He shot a furious look at Ed Mariani, who was standing by the window with his partner, Barry Levitt. Ed lowered his eyes, but Barry took a step forward. His face was flushed with anger, and Ed grabbed his arm and drew him back.

I moved to Jill. She didn't acknowledge my presence. Her

attention was wholly focused on her man. I didn't blame her. As he stood gripping the edges of the podium, Tom Kelsoe was enough to grab anybody's attention. He wasn't a big man, no more than five-foot-ten, but that night, in a black stressed-leather jacket, black turtleneck, and jeans, his body had a kind of coiled spring tension that was almost palpable. There was always an admixture of woundedness and anger about Tom; grief seemed to have distilled the mix into an essence as potent as testosterone. As he leaned into the microphone, he looked, as Lady Caroline Lamb is reputed to have said of Byron, "mad, bad, and dangerous to know."

Without preamble, Tom picked up his book. "This is about the people who will never be in this room or even at this university. It's about the charter members of the permanent underclass in our country – the ones who've never read Hobbes but who don't need Philosophy 101 to know that life is nasty, brutish, and short.

"The title of this book is *Getting Even*. The words come from some advice a woman who's dead now gave her sons. The woman's name was Karen Keewatin, and I met her boys on the corner of Halifax and Fourteenth shortly after midnight on April Fool's Day last year. The date was appropriate. I *was* a fool to be in that area at night, but I was also more desperate than I can ever remember being."

At the table nearest Tom, a group of students from our class sat transfixed. Hearing your instructor publicly admit frailty is riveting stuff.

"I'd been given a substantial advance to write a book about life in the streets," Tom said. "The previous month I'd finished a manuscript and sent it to my publishers. I'd given it my best shot. I'd spent months researching life in the meanest areas of Vancouver, Toronto, and Winnipeg. I'd recorded and transcribed the stories of murderers, thieves,

34

pimps, prostitutes, junkies, pushers, and street kids, but the book wasn't alive. I knew it, and my publishers knew it, but nobody knew how to fix it. Luckily for me, Reed Gallagher had just accepted the job here, and I called him and told him I needed help."

For a beat, Tom seemed overcome with the pain of his memory. Then he smiled ruefully. "Reed went through the manuscript that night, and he was brutal. He told me that what I'd given him was voyeurism not journalism and that I should throw out everything I'd written and start again. 'This time,' he said, 'get it right. Leave your tape-recorder at home. Give these people a chance to be something more than research subjects. Give them some dignity, and give your readers a chance to come to some sort of deeper understanding about what it feels like to be used and abused and choking with rage.'"

"So that rainy April night when I was standing on the corner of Halifax and Fourteenth Street, I'd left my tape-recorder at home, which was just as well because, when those two kids jumped out from behind the bushes and started beating me with their baseball bats, I wouldn't have had time to push *record*. The next thing I remember is a nurse who looked like Demi Moore bending over me and asking me if I knew what day it was. Lovely as that nurse was, I didn't want to hang around Regina General. I wanted to find those kids with the bats and beat the shit out of them.

"Reed Gallagher had a better plan. He agreed that I should find the kids, but he said that, instead of killing them, I should try to win their trust. He said if I could get to a point where I understood what made two kids attack a person they'd never seen and from whom they took nothing, I might have something to write about." He shrugged. "So I did. It took a while, but I found them. I don't think I can read tonight. I just want to talk. I just want to tell you a story: the story of Karen Keewatin and her sons, Jason, who's eleven now, and Darrel, who just turned ten."

It was a brilliant performance. The room was filled with emotion, and Tom Kelsoe seemed to feed off it. It was as if he took the pain we were feeling and channelled it into his account of the pain that had fuelled the lives of Karen and her sons.

As he told their story, despite my distrust of Tom, I felt my throat burn. Karen was a reserve girl from the north who came to Regina in search of the good life. She had no plans beyond the next party, and she ended up on the street. She started working as a prostitute when she was fourteen; by the time she was nineteen, she had a significant police record and two babies. One frigid night, she got into the wrong car. The john took her down an alley, beat her, threw her out and left her for dead. When she regained consciousness, she crawled down the street till she found a girl she knew. Tom said Jason Keewatin told him his mother was afraid that if she went to the hospital, Social Services would take her boys away.

It took her six weeks to recover. Girls she knew from the street took turns caring for her and her children. Six weeks is a long time to stare at the ceiling and, for the first time in her life, Karen Keewatin started thinking about how she'd come into this world and how she was going to leave it. She made up her mind that, if she got better, she was going to change her life. And she did. She applied for social assistance and subsidized housing, and she enrolled in an upgrading program. School was agony. In the north, she had attended class sporadically, and the schooling she did receive was abysmal. In her upgrading placement exam, she tested at a grade-four level.

Karen Keewatin had a lot of catching up to do, but she was

determined. Her boys told Tom Kelsoe that the most vivid memory they had of their mother was of her sitting at the kitchen table, trying furiously and often futilely to understand what was written in the books in front of her. But she never gave up. She told her sons, "You guys aren't gonna have to go through this, because if it's the last thing I do, I'm going to make sure you're even-Steven with everybody else right from the start."

It took her five years, but Karen finally graduated from high school and enrolled in a dental hygienists' program. After she got her diploma, she got a job, a "respectable job, with nice people." When she brought home her first paycheque she told her sons, "We're even now. You guys got nothing you have to prove." Six months later, she was diagnosed with AIDS. She was fired; she tried to find other "respectable" work, but her medical record followed her. Finally, she went back on the streets. Early one morning, she picked up a bad trick, and this time, after the beating, she didn't crawl back.

On the night Tom Kelsoe met them, Karen's boys were doing what they had done most nights since their mother's death. They were getting even with the men who lived in the world that killed their mother.

When he finished, Tom Kelsoe bowed his head. Then he picked up a copy of his book from the table beside him. "I'm proud of every page of this book," he said softly. "I'm proud because Darrel and Jason Keewatin have read their story and they tell me I've got it right. I'm proud because in here you'll discover what it feels like to live inside the skin of those who live without hope." His voice cracked. "And I'm proud because in the dedication I'm able to make a first payment on the immeasurable debt I owe to the man who was my teacher and my friend." He opened the book and read. "For Reed Gallagher, with respect and thanks."

There was silence; then Tom did a curious thing. He turned towards Ed Mariani, and held out his hand. After a moment that seemed to last forever, Ed walked over to Tom and shook his hand. It was a gesture as generous as it was characteristic. Everyone liked Ed, and the memory of Tom's rudeness to him was fresh. By his handshake, Ed made it possible for people to respond openly to Tom's reading, and they did. It was as if a breach had been made in the wall of emotion that had been held in check since we heard about Reed's death. People stood and applauded. More than a few of them wept; when I looked across the room, I was surprised to see the future Frank Gifford, Jumbo Hryniuk, crying lustily into his handkerchief. Beside him, dry-eyed but transfixed, was Val Massey. Even from where I was standing, I could see the glow of hero worship. At that moment, Tom Kelsoe was everything Val Massey dreamed of becoming.

A bookseller appeared and hustled Tom to the table of books. *Getting Even* was launched, and from the way people were jostling one another to get in line to buy a copy, it appeared that the evening was going to be a commercial triumph.

I walked to the end of the line to take my place, but as I queued up, a wave of tiredness washed over me. I had had enough. I looked around to see if I could find Jill, so I could apologize. I spotted her in the corner talking to Barry Levitt. There were reconciliations all around.

As I walked past the bar to get my coat, old Giv Mewhort spotted me. Giv was a professor emeritus of English and as much a fixture of the Faculty Club as the grand piano in the corner. Rumour had it that he raised his morning glass of Gilbey's when the Faculty Club staff were still laying out the breakfast buffet, but Giv was always a gentleman.

That night, as he came over to help me on with my coat,

he was courtly. When I thanked him, he smiled puckishly. "My pleasure," he said. "In fact the whole evening has been a pleasure." He glanced towards the table where Tom Kelsoe was signing books. "I haven't enjoyed a performance this much since I saw the young Marlon Brando play Mark Antony in *Julius Caesar*." He waved his glass in Tom's direction. "That boy over there is good."

It was 9:00 when I pulled into my driveway. The wind had stopped, but it was still raining. It seemed to me I had been cold and wet the whole day. The dogs met me hopefully at the breezeway door.

"Not a chance," I said. "I promise we'll go for a walk first thing tomorrow. But right now, the best I can do for you is let you out for a pee."

When I came into the kitchen, Alex Kequahtooway was sitting at the kitchen table, smearing mustard onto a corned beef sandwich. He looked up when he saw me. "I had an hour clear, so I took a chance that you'd be home early. Angus told me to help myself."

"Good for Angus," I said. "But I thought we were out of mustard."

"I carry my own."

"You're kidding."

"That's right," he said, "I'm kidding. I thought you looked like you could use a joke."

"Actually, I think what I could use is you."

He put down his sandwich, came over, and put his arms around me. His shirt was fresh and his hair was wet.

"You smell like lemons," I said.

"It's the shampoo," he said. "When you spend much time in the room with a body, the smell kind of soaks in. Lemon's the only thing I know that takes it out." He smiled. "Would you like me to change the subject?"

"Maybe just switch the focus. How's the investigation going?"

"Okay. The M.E.'s finished, and the landlady was co-operative. I bet she doesn't weigh eighty-five pounds, but she's a tough old bird. Most people would be pretty shaken if they'd walked in on the scene she walked in on, but her big gripe seems to be that Gallagher died in a room she was trying to rent. She'd just finished cleaning."

"The room was vacant?"

"Apparently. Come on. Let's sit down, and I'll tell you about it. Want some milk?"

"I think what I would like is a pot of Earl Grey tea."

"I'll put the kettle on," he said. "Anyway, the room was vacant, and at seven o'clock last night it was as presentable as a dump like that would ever be. Alma Stringer – that's the landlady – said she hauled the vacuum up herself because she'd shampooed the rug. Of course, with one thing and another, her shampoo job is pretty well shot now."

"Wasn't the door locked?"

"The doors on the main floor were. Alma has more locks on those doors than the government has on the Federal Mint, but she'd left the door to the room Reed Gallagher ended up in open; she wanted to give the rug a chance to dry. Anyway, the room's on the third floor, and there's a fire escape just a couple of steps down the hall. Alma says if she finds the tenant who left the door to the fire escape open, she'll kill him with her bare hands, and I believe her."

The kettle started to sing. I warmed the pot, then measured in the Earl Grey. "None of this makes sense, Alex. Reed Gallagher had money, and I'll bet he had a wallet full of credit cards. Why would he risk breaking into a rooming house when he could have just gone to a hotel?"

Alex poured the tea. "Zimbardo's theory is that with this

kind of masochistic sex, the danger of the surroundings is part of the kick. You'll have to admit, Jo, it's not exactly the type of act you want to pull off at the Holiday Inn. And another thing, we found drugs at the scene. Street drugs. Gallagher might have been down there making a buy and just decided to stay in the neighbourhood."

"What kind of drugs?"

"Amyl nitrites. The street name is poppers. They dilate the blood vessels. They were originally used to treat angina."

"But you don't think Reed was using them for medicinal reasons."

"Not with the hood and the rest of the paraphernalia. Poppers are also supposed to prolong and intensify orgasm. Splatter figured that's what Gallagher was doing, but it was a bad choice. Amyl nitrites cause a sharp decrease in blood pressure. The current theory is that Gallagher blacked out, and wasn't able to extricate himself from his bondage."

"What an awful way to die."

"It's not the best, that's for sure." Alex studied the tea in his cup, then he looked up. "Jo, was Reed Gallagher bisexual by any chance?"

"I don't know. Why?"

"Because poppers are primarily used by gay men. It's odd to see a straight guy with them."

"The whole thing is odd," I said.

"It is that," he said. "And I think we've both had enough of it. Let's talk about something more pleasant. How was your evening?"

"Actually, not much better than yours." I started to tell him about the launch. I skipped the ugly exchange I'd had with Jill, but I did tell him about Tom Kelsoe's rudeness to Ed Mariani.

When I finished, Alex shook his head in disgust. "Why would a terrific woman like Jill put up with a prick like that?"

"She's in love," I said. "Or she thinks she is. But that was a pricky thing to do, wasn't it? I'm glad to have some objective corroboration. My instincts weren't very trustworthy tonight."

"You've got great instincts."

"When it comes to Tom Kelsoe, I'm not exactly impartial. You know, I'm embarrassed even to say this, but at the book launch I realized that, in addition to everything else, I'm jealous of him."

"Because of all the attention he's getting?"

"Partly, I guess. When my book came out, my publisher didn't lay on a launch. I just invited all my friends over for a barbecue and made them buy a copy."

"I didn't know you'd written a book."

"Neither did anybody else. It was a biography of Andy Boychuk. It's been almost five years since he died, but I still think how different this province, maybe even the country, would have been if he'd lived."

"Do you really believe one person can make a difference?"

"Sure. Don't you?"

"I used to. That's why I joined the force. I was going to show the public that a native cop could be as smart and as reliable as a white cop, and I was going to show the native community that the law was fair and impartial." He laughed. "In those days, I thought of myself as a force for change."

"And you don't think of yourself that way any more?"

He shook his head. "No," he said. "I don't."

I looked at him. Even in the softly diffused light from the telephone table, the acne scars of his adolescence were apparent. The first time we'd made love, he'd recoiled when I touched his face. The more I came to know Alex Kequahtooway, the more I believed the acne scars were just the beginning.

"We're wasting our hour talking," I said.

He came and put his arms around me. "So we are," he said. "So we are."

Angus's stage cough was discreet. "Sorry to interrupt, but Leah and I are going to 7-Eleven, and I wanted to make sure Alex was still going to give me a driving lesson tomorrow."

"I'll be here at nine a.m.," Alex said.

"With your Audi," Angus said.

"With my Audi."

"Was a driving lesson the price you paid for that corned beef sandwich?" I asked.

"I volunteered." He looked at his watch. "And I've got to get back."

Angus's eyes widened. "A break in a case?"

"Paperwork," Alex said, and he stood and zipped his jacket. "I'll see you tomorrow morning. Both of you."

I walked him to the door. Then the dogs and I headed for bed. I almost made it. I'd already checked on Taylor, brushed my teeth, and discovered that all my nightgowns were in the clean laundry in the basement when Angus yelled that there was a lady at the door who had to see me.

I pulled on my jogging clothes and sweatsocks and padded downstairs. Julie Evanson-Gallagher was standing in the hall. She was wearing the London Fog trenchcoat she'd put on to go down to police headquarters that afternoon, but she'd added gold hoop earrings, a paisley silk scarf, a tan leather bag and matching gloves. She was immaculate, but her careful grooming couldn't hide the tension in her body or the anguish in her eyes.

I stepped aside. "Won't you come in, Julie?" I said.

"No," she said. "I just wanted to give you the keys." She

fumbled with her purse. When the clasp finally opened, she took out a set of keys.

"I'm leaving for the airport to catch a flight to Toronto. I'll need somebody to look after the house when I'm away. I don't know who else to ask."

I took the keys from her. "I'll be happy to help."

"I didn't mean you had to go over there. I thought I could pay one of your children. There's not much to do – just feed the fish and take in the mail. But someone should clean out the refrigerator. My cleaning lady quit last night." She shook her head in bewilderment. "Why does everything have to go wrong at once?"

"Julie, this has been a terrible day for you. Why don't you come in and have a drink, and when you're ready, I'll drive you to the airport."

"I can't take a chance on missing my plane," she said. "I don't want to be here when people find out how he died."

"Did you tell Alex you're going? The police should know."

"They know," she said dully. Then the implication of what I'd said seemed to dawn on her, and for a flash she was the old Julie. "Surely you're not suggesting that the police think I was connected with what went on in that room." Her voice rose dangerously. "How could they? How could anybody believe that, if I had a choice, I'd let the world see my husband like that?"

I touched her arm. "Julie, all I meant was that the police might need your signature for something."

"They can find me at my sister's," she said tightly. "She lives in Port Hope. The police have the address, and I've left it by the phone in my kitchen in case you need to get in touch with me. Everything's taken care of." Suddenly her composure cracked. "I don't deserve this," she said. "I did everything right, and I had such hopes."

As I watched her cab drive up my road towards the airport,

44

I thought of Julie's epitaph for her marriage. The words were heartbreaking, but tonight wasn't the first time I'd heard her use them. Years before, I'd run into Julie outside our neighbourhood high school. It was late June, and she had just learned that her son, Mark, had failed every class in grade ten and the counsellor was recommending a non-academic program for him. She had been devastated. "He's never going to do anything that matters," she'd said, miserably. "And I don't understand. I did everything right, and I had such hopes." Then, having absolved herself of blame and purged herself of hope, Julie Evanson had closed the door on her only child forever.

CHAPTER

4

When I woke up Saturday morning, the sun was shining, the sky looked freshly washed, the birds were singing, and the phone was ringing. I picked up the receiver, heard Jill Osiowy's familiar contralto and felt my spirits rise.

It wasn't unusual for Jill to call on a Saturday morning. She produced Nationtv's political panel, and I was one of the regulars. The show was telecast live on Saturday nights, and if Jill spotted a provocative item in the morning paper, she'd often call to see how I felt about leading with it. But after my Stepford-wife crack the night before, I was anticipating a chill, and it was a relief to hear her sounding cordial.

"Jo, are you up for a whole change of topic for the call-in segment tonight? It seems there's been some major-league vandalism at the university."

"Where at the university?"

"I don't know. I haven't been to the campus yet, but one of our technicians, Gerry McIntyre, was out there for his morning run, and he saw squad cars over by the Education building. When he went over to ask what was going on, the cops told him the place had been vandalized."

"Jill, I hate to shoot down a story idea, but a certain amount of vandalism is one of the rites of spring at any university. It's ugly, but it doesn't usually amount to much beyond kids getting drunk and deciding to leave their mark on the world. Last year some Engineering students decided they weren't getting the respect they deserved, so they spray-painted 'Engineers Rule' on every blank wall they could find."

"This wasn't quite that sophomoric. Gerry says it looks like a hate crime."

"A hate crime?" I repeated. "Who was the target?"

"Homosexuals," Jill said. "Apparently, the graffiti the vandals left behind is homophobic, and, Jo, the reason I think this particular vandalism may be worth talking about is that it's not unique. I've been watching the wire services, and gay-bashing seems to be enjoying a certain cross-country vogue again. Anyway, what do you think about the change of topic?

"My stomach is already churning at the thought of the phone-ins."

"We'll screen the callers so we know everything about them but their blood type, and I'll keep my finger on the cut-off button . . ."

I laughed. "Okay. You're on."

"You're going to have to do some digging. There've been several rulings on sexual orientation lately, and you should have that stuff at your fingertips. Are you sure I'm not crowding you?"

"I'm sure. I try to keep up on the major rulings that come out of the Charter, and I have a file folder stuffed with articles on gay and lesbian rights."

Jill laughed. "Still clipping newspapers. Jo, you're a dinosaur."

"Maybe," I said. "But I like the way newspapers feel in my

hands. Anyway, don't worry about giving me enough lead time. All I've got on today is taking Taylor to her class – oh, and feeding Julie's fish. She's going to her sister's in Port Hope till this blows over."

"When the going gets tough, the tough get going," Jill said mildly.

I laughed. "You know Julie. She's never liked a mess."

"I guess she's not alone in that," Jill said. "See you tonight."

She sounded more like her usual self than she had in months, and I felt the relief wash over me. "Jill, I'm so glad you called. And Springtime for Homophobes is a great topic."

"Thanks," she said, "but actually, it was Tom's idea."

After I hung up, I pulled out the telephone book, checked the university's listings, and dialled the number opposite the office of Physical Plant. I got a recorded message telling me when the regular office hours were and giving me a number to call if I deemed my concerns to be of an emergency nature. They weren't, but I *was* curious. I looked at my watch. If I hurried, I could drive up to the campus and be back before the demands of Saturday morning made themselves felt.

When I started for the bathroom, I caught a glimpse of myself in the mirror over my dresser and cringed. I'd slept in the clothes I'd greeted Julie in the night before. I was getting worse than Angus. I grabbed clean underwear and a fresh sweatshirt and jeans, then I went into the bathroom and splashed water on my face. As I began brushing my teeth, my mind drifted. The night before I had told Alex that Tom Kelsoe's new celebrity was only part of the reason for my jealousy. Most of the reason, although I hated to admit it, was Jill.

We had always been close. The day after she graduated

from J school, she'd started working for my husband, Ian. He was the youngest attorney general in the history of our province, but he'd been in politics long enough to be both bemused and touched by Jill's fervent idealism. After he died, Jill kept working for the government, but she said the spark was gone. She moved to Ottawa, did a graduate degree in journalism, and started working for Nationtv. When she came back to Saskatchewan, one of the first things she did was hire me for the political panel. I'd never thought of doing television, but Jill had faith and patience; she shepherded me through the gaffes and panics of the early days, and it had worked out. Personally and professionally, Jill and I were a nice mix. Her relationship with Tom Kelsoe had changed all that, but as I rinsed my toothbrush I decided that, even if it meant holding my nose and learning to love Tom Kelsoe, I was going to change it back.

"Jo, look. I've started the drawings for my mural."

Taylor was standing in the bathroom door with her sketchpad under her arm.

I put my toothbrush back in the cup. "Okay," I said, "show me."

She pushed past me, flipped down the toilet seat and settled herself on top of it. After she had balanced her sketchpad on her knees, she began explaining. "Alex said nobody ever gets close enough to Nanabush to take his picture, but this is how I think he looks."

As Taylor's index finger danced across her sketchpad, pointing out details, lingering over problems, I was struck again by the gulf between the little girl perched on the toilet seat, legs dangling, and the gifted artist who had made the pictures of Nanabush on the pages in front of me. At the age of six, Taylor's talent was already undeniable. It was a question of nature not nurture. Taylor's mother had been a brilliant artist, and Taylor had inherited the gift.

When we'd looked at the last sketch, Taylor hopped off the toilet. "I'm hungry," she said.

"I wouldn't be surprised," I said. "You've already done a lot of work today. Why don't I get you some juice and cereal. I have to go up to the university for a few minutes, but as soon as I get home, I'll make pancakes."

When I put the dogs on their leashes and led them to the garage, they looked dubious, and when I opened the back gate of the Volvo our aging golden retriever, Rose, sat down defiantly. "Come on, Rosie," I said. "Get in. We'll have our run out at the bird sanctuary. The paper says the bluebirds are back. It'll be an adventure." She cocked her head and looked at me sceptically. I moved behind her and pushed her until she finally lumbered into the car. Sadie, our collie, who was beautiful but easily led, bounded in after her.

By the time I pulled into the parking space at the university, the dogs had perked up, and they jumped out, eager to follow me, as I headed for the Education building. The red-white-and-blue police cars were still there, as was the vandals' handiwork. The long glassed-in walkway that linked College West and the Lab building was dripping with all the ugly anti-gay invective the wielder of the spray-paint canister could think of. I was cheered to see that the vandal had crossed out the extra *s* that had initially been in "cock-sucker." Maybe literacy was on the rise after all.

The dogs and I walked towards the Education building. A young police officer with a blond braid was standing by a squad car making notes.

"What's up?" I asked.

Her look was noncommittal. "Everything's under control," she said coolly. "Why don't you and your dogs finish your walk?"

"I'm not rubbernecking," I said. "I teach here."

"I hope for your sake that your office isn't in this building."

"Can I go in?"

"Not with your dogs."

I walked them back and put them in the car. First seduced and now abandoned, they began to bark, furious at the betrayal.

When I came back, the blond-braided police officer had been replaced by a young constable who looked as if he could bench-press two hundred kilograms without breaking a sweat. I flashed my faculty ID at him and said, "I teach here."

He waved me through. "Go ahead," he said. His voice was surprisingly high and sweet as a choirboy's. "Stay away from the areas marked by crime-scene tape, and if an officer asks you to leave, please obey."

I went into the building, turned left, and walked towards the cafeteria. It looked as it always did after hours: the accordion security gates were pulled across, the tables were wiped clean, and the chairs were stacked in piles against the far wall. Someone had suspended cutouts of Easter rabbits and of chicks in bonnets from the ceiling above the empty food-display cases, and by the cash register there was a sign announcing that Cadbury Easter Creme Eggs were back. Everything seemed reassuringly ordinary, but when I continued along the hall and pushed through the double doors that led to the audio-visual department of the School of Journalism, I stepped into chaos.

I was ankle-deep in paper: computer printouts, dumped files, books with pages torn and spines splayed. The walls around me were spray-painted with the same snappy patter I'd seen on the walkway between College West and the Lab building. It was slow going, but finally I made it past the photography department and turned down the hall that led to the Journalism offices.

As I walked towards Ed Mariani's office, I was reassured to see that whoever had done the trashing was an equal-opportunity vandal. The offices of straight and gay alike were destroyed. Through open doors, I could see books and pictures heaped on desks, plants overturned, keyboards ripped from their terminals. On Ed's door was a sign: "Of all life's passions, the strongest is the need to edit another's prose." Beside it somebody had spray-painted the words "Fairy-Loving-Bum-Fucker." I closed my eyes, but I could still see the words, and I knew Ed's sign was right: at that moment, I hungered for a paint canister of my own and a chance to do a little judicious editing.

Sick with disgust, I turned and doubled back towards the front door of the building. I wanted to be outside where my dogs were waiting; the air was sweet and the bluebirds had come home.

When I pulled up in front of our house, Taylor was sitting on the top step of the porch, with Benny on her knee. She was still wearing her nightie, but she'd added her windbreaker and her runners. "Winter's over," she said happily.

"It certainly feels like it," I said. "Now let's go inside and get something to eat. I'm starving." I made coffee and pancake batter. Taylor, who had already eaten a bowl of cereal and a banana poured batter in the shape of her initials onto the griddle; when she'd polished off her initials, she made Benny's initials. I was watching her devour these and waiting for my own pancakes when Alex came.

"I haven't even had a shower yet," I groaned.

"You look good to me," he said. "After yesterday, you deserve to laze around."

"I wish," I said. "I feel like I've already put in a full day." I took the pancakes off the griddle. "Do you want these?"

"You take them, but if there's plenty . . ."

I handed him the bowl and the ladle. "Taylor makes hers in the shape of her initials."

He smiled. "She's such a weird little kid." He went over to the griddle and poured. "Okay. Fill me in on your day."

I watched his face as I told him about the vandalism at the university. He listened, as he always did to whatever the kids and I told him, seriously and without interruption or comment.

"I guess it could have been worse," I said. "At least whoever did it vented their spleen in words. Nobody was hurt."

"Sticks and stones may break my bones but names will never hurt me," he said, and there was an edge of bitterness in his voice that surprised me. "Did Mrs. Gallagher get in touch with you last night?" he asked.

"She made a house call. She brought her keys over because she's going to her sister's in Port Hope."

"She told me she might do that."

"So she did talk to you."

"Of course. She's a good citizen. She wouldn't leave town without telling us where she'd be. Anyway, I was glad she called. I had some questions; she answered them."

"What kind of questions."

"Just tidying-up-loose-ends questions. I wanted her to go over again what she knew about where her husband was in the twenty-four hours before he died. She didn't have much to add except . . ."

"Except what?"

"Except I still don't think she's told us everything. For one thing, I have a feeling that yesterday wasn't the first time she'd been in that rooming house on Scarth Street. When I took her there, she started down the hall on the main floor as if she knew where she was going."

"But Reed's body wasn't on the main floor."

"No. It was upstairs, on the top floor. Actually, we have a witness who thinks he saw Gallagher going up the fire escape at the back at around quarter to nine."

"I don't understand how you can let Julie go when you think she might be holding something back."

"Jo, when someone dies suddenly, everybody who knew them holds things back. There are a hundred reasons why the living don't choose to disclose everything they know about the dead, but as long as those reasons don't have a direct bearing on our case, we don't push it."

"So Julie doesn't have to stay in Regina."

"There's no legal reason why she should. Her husband's dead, and human decency might suggest that she hang around till he's in the ground, but there's nothing to indicate that Gallagher's death was anything other than accidental. They're doing an autopsy this afternoon, but with the hood and the garter belt and all the other paraphernalia, I think we know what they'll find."

"Which is?"

"Which is that Reed Gallagher died of a fatal combination of bad judgement and bad luck."

"It still doesn't make sense to me."

"Jo, a lot of sexual practices don't have much to do with common sense, but that doesn't mean they don't happen. Sherman Zimbardo had coffee with a couple of doctors from the E.R. at the General last night; he says some of the stories those women had about what they've removed from there would curl your hair." Alex deftly slid his pancakes onto his plate and smiled at me. "And it's all in the name of love."

I passed him the butter. "'"Thank goodness we're all different," said Alice.'"

Alex looked quizzical. "Who's Alice?"

"Someone who stepped through the looking-glass," I said.

Alex picked up the maple syrup. "I know the feeling," he said. "Now, what's on your agenda today?"

"Nothing but good works," I said. "I'm going to take Taylor to her art class and get ready for tonight's program. How about you?"

"I'm taking Angus for his driving lesson."

I winced. "Talk about good works. Can I reward you by taking you to a movie after we do our show?"

"Sounds great, but I'll have to take a rain check."

I felt a sting of disappointment. "More paperwork?"

He looked away. "No, family matters." His voice was distant. "I've got a nephew out on the reserve who seems to be in need of a little guidance."

"How old?"

"Fifteen."

"Angus's age."

"Yeah, but he's not **Angus**." The edge was back in his voice, and I could feel the wall going up. Alex talked easily about his life on Standing Buffalo when he was young, but never about life there now, and I tried not to pry.

Angus appeared in the doorway. For once, his timing was impeccable, as was his appearance: slicked-back hair, earring in place, faded rock shirt, and jeans so badly torn I wondered how he kept them on. He went over and slapped Alex on the back. "So," he said, "are you ready to rip?"

It was only six blocks from our house to the Gallaghers' condo on Lakeview Court, but because we were going straight to Taylor's lesson after we were through at Julie's, we drove. When I opened the front door, Taylor slipped off her boots and ran inside to find the aquarium. Before I'd even hung my coat up, she was back in the hall, breathless.

"Oh, Jo, they're beautiful, especially the striped ones.

We've got to get some. We could stop at the Golden Mile after my lesson. They've got fish in the pet shop – all kinds of them. And we'll need some of that pink stuff that looks like knobby fingers."

"Coral," I said.

"And a castle. These fish have a castle in the corner of their tank, and they swim right through the front door."

"Do you know who would really love it if we got some fish?" I asked her.

"Who?"

"Benny," I said.

Her eyes widened with horror. Then a smile played at the corner of her lips. "No fish, right?"

"No fish," I said.

After I showed Taylor how much food to put in the aquarium, I turned to the rest of my tasks. There wasn't much to do. The dishes and the checked cloths were off the rental tables, and the extra chairs had been stacked, ready for pickup. Julie had left the rental company's business card on the kitchen table with a note asking me to arrange a time when I could be there to let them in. The only hints of the evening before were the pots of shamrock that had been in the white wicker centrepieces. The plants were lined up neatly on a tray where they could catch the light from Julie's kitchen window. When I touched the soil, it was moist. She had taken care of everything, but those must have been bleak hours for her, alone in her house, dismantling the evening she'd planned with such care while her new husband lay dead in the morgue at Regina General.

The refrigerator didn't take long to clean. There were no nasty surprises mouldering in old yogurt containers, just perishables that had obviously been intended for the party: two quarts of whipping cream, unopened; two large plastic bags of crisp salad greens; three vegetable platters that looked as if they could still make the cover of Martha Stewart's *Living*. I boxed up everything for the Indian-Métis Friendship Centre. Julie was moving into contention for their award as Benefactor of the Year.

After I dropped Taylor off at her art lesson, I drove Julie's food donation to the Friendship Centre, and then headed downtown to check out the sales. Angus had been hinting about a new winter jacket, and Taylor needed rubber boots.

Cornwall Centre was in its spring mode. Hyacinth, daffodils, and tulips bloomed beside the water fountains, and winter clothes marked 60 per cent off bloomed on the racks in front of stores. At Work Warehouse, I discovered that the jacket Angus had admired loudly and frequently before Christmas had at last reached my price range, and I bought it. Then I went to Eaton's basement and found a pair of rubber boots in Taylor's favourite shade of hot pink. As the salesclerk was wrapping them up, I remembered my early-morning resolve to get back in Jill's good graces by cosying up to Tom Kelsoe. From what I'd seen of Tom, the surest way to his heart was through his ego. I went to City Books.

There was a single copy of *Getting Even* beside the cash register. When I handed it to the woman behind the counter, she groaned. "That's the last copy. I was going to buy it myself." She eyed the author picture on the back and sighed. "He is attractive, isn't he? He was on the radio yesterday morning. I didn't hear him, but people have been coming to the store in tears because of a story he told about a mother and her two sons – right here in Regina." She shrugged. "Well, I'll just have to order more. Cash or credit?"

I hadn't planned to drive by the rooming house where Reed Gallagher died, but as I headed along my usual route to pick Taylor up at her class on the old campus, I ran into a construction detour. The next street that would take me south was Scarth Street, and there was no way I could drive along Scarth without seeing number 317. It was a house straight out of an Edward Hopper painting: a Gothic spook with a mansard roof, a widow's walk, and a curved front porch. In summer, the porch was filled with vacant-eyed women in rockers and wiry men with wicked laughs who would taunt passers-by with insults and invitations; in winter, the tenants took to their rooms, and you could see their shadows, dark and shifting, behind the blinds that separated their blighted existence from the lives of the lucky.

A block past number 317, I yielded to impulse, pulled into a parking spot and started back towards the house. The porch was empty, but the blinds in every window were raised. Eyes that had seen it all were peering out to seek further proof, as if they needed it, that people were no damn good.

The spectacle in the front yard must have offered them proof aplenty. The rain had turned the grassless yard to gumbo, but it hadn't kept any of us away. The gawkers and misery-seekers were quite a group: media people with cameras; young couples with kids; teenagers with Big Gulps and cigarettes, and middle-aged, respectable people like me who should have known better but who came in response to stirrings as dark as they were ancient. As I walked towards the back of the building and the fire escape Alex had told me Reed used to get to the third floor, I heard snippets of conversation: "hookers with whips . . . ," "mirrors all around so he could watch himself . . . ," "wearing a dress and a Dolly Parton wig . . ."

After these fevered images of Sodom and Gomorrah, the actual fire escape seemed disappointingly mundane. It was a rickety metal affair that zigzagged from the back alley to the third floor, an eyesore that had been added on as a sop to some busybody at City Hall who took fire regulations seriously. Utilitarian as it was, it had done the job. It had taken Reed Gallagher where he wanted to go. I walked over to the foot of it, and for a few minutes I stood there looking up through the dizzying height of steps into the pale March sky. When I started back across the yard, I met an old man with a walker. He was moving with exquisite slowness, but as I passed him, he stopped and grabbed my arm. His voice was raspy whisper. "Did you hear what happened in there?"

"Yes," I said, "I heard."

He pulled me so close I could feel his breath on my face. "Men who don women's clothing are an abomination to God," he said, then he continued his methodical passage towards the site of the abomination.

After such a chilling insight into how a fellow being saw the heart of God, an afternoon reading the dry legal language of the Canadian Charter of Rights and Freedoms was a relief. When Angus came home at 4:00, I told him that, as a reward for babysitting on a Saturday night, he could choose the dinner menu. He decided on sandwiches from the Italian Star deli, an easy call for me, so after I picked up the mortadella and provolone, I had time for a quick nap before I showered and dressed. I was just fastening the turquoise and silver necklace Alex had given me for Christmas when Taylor came in and sat on my bed. Benny was in her arms, but her eyes were anxious.

I sat down beside her. "Taylor, in all the time since you came to live with us, have I ever not come home?"

"No," she said. "But what if . . . ?"

"What if what?" I asked.

She shook her head dolefully. "I don't know," she murmured.

I drew her close to me. "Taylor, life is full of what-ifs, but if you spend all your time being afraid of them, there's not much time left over for being happy, and I want you to be happy."

"I am happy," she whispered. "That's why I'm scared of what if . . ."

Twenty minutes later as I walked through Wascana Park towards the Nationtv studios, Taylor was still at the forefront of my thoughts. She'd come to the front door to wave to me when I left. She'd been hugging Benny to her, and doing her best. It was a worry, but it was a worry that was going to have to wait. I took a deep breath and started mentally running through the clauses relating to sexual orientation in the Charter. I was trying to remember the three key points of a bill on homosexual rights that had been defeated in the Ontario legislature when I realized I'd turned onto a path that had a degree of fame in our city.

The old campus of our university is on the northern edge of the park. It's a serene setting for the handsome pair of buildings that once housed our entire university, but which are now given over to the departments of Music, Drama, and Art. The path I walked along ran behind the buildings. By day, it was a place where students gravitated for a smoke, young mums wheeled strollers, dog-walkers walked dogs, and joggers jogged. But at night, the path changed character. After dark, it was a cruising park for gay men. The students at the university called it "the Fruit Loop." So, in my private thoughts, did I. More sticks and stones.

When I got to Nationtv, I went, as I always did, to makeup, where Tina, who had taught me that if I wanted a clean lip-line after the age of forty, I had to use lip-liner, and that I would be insane to buy any eye shadow more expensive than Maybelline, was waiting for me. As she swept blush along my cheeks, I looked at my reflection in the mirror. Despite my nightly slatherings of Oil of Olay, it was clear that Father Time was undefeated. I shrugged, turned away from the mirror, and asked Tina to tell me about her wedding. The week before, she'd been agonizing about how to tell her future mother-in-law that, since the wedding dinner was catered, she wouldn't need to bring the jellied salads in the colours of the bridesmaid's dresses that she had made for all of her other children's weddings. I was eager to hear if Tina had brought it off.

When Tina was done with me, I went, as I always did, to the green room to wait until Jill came out to talk me through the first question and walk me into the studio. But that night, Jill didn't come. Five minutes before airtime, I took matters into my own hands. As I pushed the door into the studio open, a young man I'd never seen ran into me. He glanced at my face, then grabbed my arm and pulled me into the studio.

"They're waiting," he said.

"I've been here all along," I said.

He looked right past me. "Whatever," he said. "Let's just say there's been a screwup."

It wasn't the last one.

When she'd first set up the weekly panel, Jill had decided to cover the ideological spectrum rather than have repre-sentatives from specific political parties. From the outset, Keith Harris, who had once been my lover and was now my friend, spoke for the right, Senator Sam Spiegel articulated the view from the centre, and I was there for the left. Over the years, the images of Keith and Sam on the television monitor had become as familiar as my own. But that night as I glanced towards the screen, I saw a face I'd never seen before in my life. The woman on screen appeared to be in her mid-thirties; she had a head of frosted curls, cerulean eyes, and a dynamite smile.

The young man who'd dragged me into the studio was kneeling in front of me, trying to fasten my lapel mike. I touched his shoulder. "Who's that?" I asked.

He glanced quickly at the monitor. "Didn't anybody tell

you? That's Glayne Axtell. She's the new voice for the right." He leaped out of camera range.

"What happened to Keith Harris?" I asked.

He looked irritated and moved his fingers to his lips in a silencing gesture. Through my earpiece, I heard the familiar "Stand by," and we were on the air.

By the time the last caller had been thanked and the moderator in Toronto was inviting people to join us next week, my back was soaked with sweat. It had been a rough evening. Keith's mysterious disappearance had been a blow. I had to admit that Glayne Axtell was good. She was far to the right of Keith, but she was witty and crisply professional. The problem wasn't with her; it was with me. I couldn't seem to adjust to the new rhythm, and for the first time, I let the callers on our phone-in segment of the program get to me. Usually, I dealt with the crazies by reminding myself that the law "every action has an equal and opposite reaction" governs physics not politics. In politics, most of the time, you got back pretty much what you handed out, and if you were lucky, reason would beget reason.

That night I seemed to be beyond both luck and reason. As the torrent of hate and fear poured through my earpiece, I couldn't seem to stop myself from lashing back. I kept wondering where Jill was with the cut-off button. But as the red light went black, and we were finally off the air, I had to admit that, as exhausting as it had been, the panel on homophobia had been good television.

Jill came down from the control booth almost immediately. She was wearing jeans, a black turtleneck, and a hounds-tooth jacket, and she didn't look happy.

I unclipped my mike and went over to her. "I thought you were going to keep the mad dogs at bay tonight. But maybe you were right to let them yelp and foam. It was an exciting show."

Jill gave me a tight smile. "Do you have time for a drink?"

"Sure," I said. "Angus is with Taylor. He has plans, but I've got time for a quick one. I wanted to ask you about Keith. Did he quit or what?"

"Let's talk about it later," Jill said.

It was a mild night, but when I told Jill I'd left my car at home and suggested we walk downtown to our old standby, the Hotel Saskatchewan, she said she'd rather drive to the Chimney. It was an odd choice. The hotel bar was a place for grown-ups to unwind: elegant surroundings, deep soft chairs, and discreet bartenders. The Chimney was a family restaurant in a strip mall not far from where I lived. They made good pizza, and my kids liked the open fireplace, but it wasn't Jill's kind of place.

As we drove up College Avenue and turned onto Albert Street, she was uncharacteristically quiet. In fact, she didn't say anything until we'd found a table and ordered two bottles of Great Western.

When the waiter left, Jill glanced around the room as if she were seeing it for the first time. "This is nice, isn't it?" she said absently.

"I've always like it," I said. "But it must be thirty degrees in here tonight. Somebody should have told whoever's in charge of the roaring fire that spring has sprung." I leaned towards her. "But listen, I've been dying to know what happened with Keith. I know he's been busy since he moved back to Ottawa. Did he just have too much on his plate?"

"It was more of a mutual decision," Jill said. "We've been looking at the demographics – thinking we should try to hook a younger audience."

She wouldn't meet my eyes, and I knew the truth without

63

asking. "And so you decided to replace Keith with Glayne Axtell."

"She did a good job tonight," Jill said defensively.

"Keith's done a good job ever since the show started," I said, and my voice was so loud the people at the next table turned and looked at us.

Jill winced. "Jo, please. Don't make this any worse than it already is."

The waiter brought our beer, and I took a long sip. The heat in the restaurant and the turn in the conversation were beginning to make my head spin.

Jill's voice was guarded. "I know Keith's done a good job, Jo. The panel just needed – I don't know – a fresh look."

"Spring cleaning?" I said. "Jill, we're not talking about a piece of furniture here. We're talking about a friend."

Suddenly, Jill looked furious. "Christ, Jo, it's never easy with you, is it? All right, here it is. We think it's time you considered other options, too."

I felt as if I'd been kicked in the stomach. "You mean I'm out as well? What about Sam?"

Jill was icy. "He's staying. Sam has an avuncular quality. We thought he'd be a nice mix with Glayne and . . . the other new panellist."

"Who is it?" I asked. And then, I knew. "Oh fuck, Jill. Is it Tom? Are you getting rid of me so you can hire your boyfriend?"

She didn't say anything. I stood up and grabbed my coat. As I pulled it on, I knocked my beer over. I was beyond caring. It had been a long time since I'd made a scene in a restaurant. I headed for the front door, but before I opened it, I turned and looked back at Jill. She was sitting, looking numbly at the mess I'd left behind.

The Chimney was less than four blocks from my house. Even in the state I was in that night, I was home in less than ten minutes. The Chimney's proximity to my house was, I suddenly realized, the reason Jill had chosen it in the first place. Once we had been as close as sisters. I guess she figured she owed me an easy exit. But I wasn't grateful; the thought of her planning the logistics of my firing made me sick to my stomach.

When I got home, Taylor was already in bed, and Angus was so full of news about an '85 Camaro he'd seen for sale up the street that he was oblivious to my mood. Leah, who was sensitive to emotional currents, looked at me with concern, but I told her it had been a tough show, and she said that she had tuned in for the phone-in segment and she understood.

When she and Angus finally left for the late movie, I felt the relief an actor must feel at the end of a bad performance. The audience was gone. I could wail, rend my clothing, or gnash my teeth to my heart's content. But as I walked into the living room and began searching aimlessly through my CDs, I was overwhelmed with self-pity.

I wanted to talk, but the three people I counted on most were busy with their own lives: Alex was out at Standing Buffalo; my friend Hilda McCourt was in Europe with her new beau; and, as the old saw had it, Jill was no longer part of the solution, she was part of the problem.

I selected a disc Keith Harris had once given me: Glenn Gould playing the Goldberg Variations. As I listened to the shimmering precision of Gould's performance, I felt my pulse slow, and, for the first time since I left the restaurant, I found myself able to think. Being fired from the show was not the end of the world. I still had family. I still had Alex. I still had friends and my job at the university. Summer was coming. Without the show, there would be no reason to be in town on Saturdays. We could rent a cottage and drive out there on weekends. Taylor could use the extra time with me.

I could teach her to canoe. We could get Benny a life jacket. I had just convinced myself that it was all for the best, when the phone rang. I leaped to answer it. I was certain it was Jill, apologizing and making everything right again.

But the voice on the other end of the line wasn't Jill's. It was a man's.

"Is this Joanne Kilbourn?"

"Yes."

"Joanne, it's Ed Mariani. I just wanted to thank you for the things you said on your show. They were all the things I would have said, or I hope I would have said, if I'd been there. Barry and I were very moved."

"Your timing couldn't have been better," I said. "I just got fired."

"Not because of what you said tonight?" His voice was full of anger.

"I wish that were the reason," I said. "At least that would have a little dignity."

"What was it, then?"

"Ed, I'm sorry. I shouldn't have said anything. I'm just upset."

"Do you want to talk about it?"

"No. I'll handle it. I'm a big girl."

"Even big girls need a chance to vent once in a while."

"Thanks," I said. "I'll be okay."

"I know you will," he said. "But let's speed up the process. Come for dinner tomorrow night. Barry's making paella. It's his best dish, and he loves to show it off. You're welcome to bring whomever you like: significant other, kids, pets . . . Barry's paella is endless."

"All right," I said. "I accept. But there'll just be my youngest daughter and me. My son has a basketball game tomorrow night."

"We'll send you home with a doggy bag for him. Six-thirty?"

"Six-thirty would be great. And, Ed, thanks."

When I hung up, I felt better. Then I remembered the scene in the restaurant and I felt worse. I put some ice cubes in a glass, took down the Glenfiddich, poured myself a generous shot, and went back into the living room. Glenn Gould was still playing. I kicked off my shoes, collapsed on the couch, and took a long sip of my drink. It was terrific. As someone who had once been a good friend had told me not that long ago, there are times when nothing but single-malt Scotch will do.

CHAPTER

5

At church Sunday morning, we used the old Book of Common Prayer. When Angus pulled out a pencil and began drawing basketball strategies on the back of the bulletin, I opened the Prayer Book to the Service for Young People and pointed to the line "Lord, keep our thoughts from wandering." But my thoughts were wandering too: to Jill, to the end of my work on the political panel, to the scene I'd made the night before at the Chimney. When the rector read out, "Come unto me all that labour and are heavy laden, and I will refresh you," I knew it was the best invitation I'd had all week. An hour later, I left church, not yet in a state of love and charity with my neighbours, but at least in a state where I could contemplate the possibility.

The weather was so warm by noon that we took our egg-salad sandwiches and iced tea out to the deck. Angus, who was always quick to spot a mellow mood, asked if we could drive out to the valley after lunch, and I agreed. Alex had been letting him take the wheel for almost a month now, and it seemed churlish not to take my turn.

My son was already in the driver's seat when Taylor and I came out of the house.

"Hurry up," he yelled. "I want to open up this old junker and see how fast she can go."

"Don't even think about it," I said, as I buckled up.

I turned to make sure Taylor had her seatbelt on. She did, but she looked grim.

I tried to sound confident. "T, there's nothing to worry about. Alex says your brother's a good driver, and I know that Angus is going to be especially careful with you in the car." I looked hard at my son. "Aren't you?"

He gave me a mock salute. "Yes, ma'am," he said, and we were off.

He was as good as his word. I was boggled by the transformation that took place the minute the key was in the ignition. Angus drove through the city streets as prudently as the proverbial little old lady who only took a spin on alternate Sundays. Alex had obviously been an inspired teacher. It was as pleasant an uneventful a drive as a mother could expect from a fifteen-year-old with a learner's permit. Lulled by the absence of catastrophe, Taylor began to read aloud the roadside signs: "Big Valley Country"; "Stella's Pies, We-Bake-Our-Own"; "Langenegger's: All-Vegetarian/All-U-Can-Eat." As we turned off the highway and drove through the Qu'Appelle Valley, I felt my nerves beginning to unknot. In a month, the hills would be green, and the valley would be filled with birdsong. Other years, the demands of the political panel had kept us in town on weekends. A summer of freedom to enjoy these hills would not be hard to take.

We turned at the cutoff for Last Mountain Lake and drove till we came to Regina Beach, at the heart of cottage country. Regina Beach is one of those towns which spring to life on the May long weekend, rock all summer, and sink back into quiescence after Thanksgiving. That balmy March day, the town was still sleeping: the streets were empty, the playgrounds were forlorn, and the beach was deserted. Taylor ran down the hill to the playground, took a few desultory swings, then caught up with Angus and me. We walked out on the dock, and as we sat on the end, with our feet dangling over the edge, and watched the seagulls swooping towards the sun-splashed water, I tried to figure out how I could stretch our budget to include rent for a cottage. Then Angus took Taylor to the beach and showed her how to skip stones over the surface of the lake, and I knew that, even if I had to take in laundry, I'd find a way to get us all out here by summer.

When Taylor began skipping her stones farther than his, Angus realized he needed to rest his arm for basketball that night, and we walked back up into town. It was too early for Butler's Fish and Chips to be open for the season, but there was an ice-cream stand with waffle cones and a dazzling variety of flavours and toppings. We got cones and walked up one side of the town and down the other till we discovered a little shop that sold crafts and homemade jams and jellies. Angus zeroed in on a lethal-looking hunting knife in a hand-tooled leather sheath, but we settled on a basket of preserves: saskatoon berry, choke cherry, and northern blueberry for Taylor and me to take with us when we had dinner with Ed Mariani and Barry Levitt that night.

As we started up the hill, the Volvo's engine began to cough. I looked at the gas gauge. "Cruising on empty there, Angus," I said. "I hope you've got your credit card handy." He gave me a withering look. "I'm just trying to prepare you for the realities of life with an '85 Camaro." I said.

There was a station at the top of the hill, and we sputtered up beside the gas tank. The station was a low-slung Mom-and-

Pop type of place with a garage on one side and a café on the other. What appeared to be fifty years' worth of hubcaps had been nailed into the wooden face of the garage, but except for two curled and faded cardboard photographs of ice-cream sundaes, the front of the restaurant was bare. It was not, however, without adornment. Suspended by chains from the frame of the café's front window was a jumbo-sized plaster wiener with the words "Foot Long" written in mustard-coloured script along its side.

Angus gave me the thumbs-up sign. "Check it out, Mum – wheels and weenies."

"You'd better hope wheels and weenies is open," I said. "Otherwise, you're going to have to haul out the gas can and walk."

Angus drew up next to the gas tank and turned off the ignition. "Relax, Mum. It'll be open. You always say I was born lucky."

It was true. When it came to the vagaries of day-to-day life, my youngest son always had seemed blessed. But as the minutes ticked by and no one who worked at the gas station appeared, I was beginning to wonder if Angus's run of luck was over. I was just about to remind him of the location of the gas can when Taylor pointed towards the station and said, "Look, here comes the gas boy."

His fine-chiselled features were grime-covered, and he was wearing greasy coveralls, not GAP, but there was no disguising the angular grace or the smile.

"What are you doing out here?" Val Massey asked.

"Looking for a summer cottage," I said. "At least, we're thinking about looking for one."

"We are?" Taylor asked.

"Yeah," I said, "we are." I turned to Val. "I didn't know you worked out here. Is it a weekend thing?"

He looked down at his feet. "Unfortunately, no. This job is permanent. It's the family business. I live back there." He gestured over his shoulder towards a small bungalow behind the station. As if on cue, the door opened and a squat muscular man wearing the twin of Val's coverall stepped outside. The man had a cigarette and an attitude.

"Step on it, Valentine," he shouted. "I don't pay you to charm the customers."

Val flushed. "Yes, Dad," he said softly. He tried a smile. "Well, Professor K., what'll it be?"

As Val filled the tank and wiped our window, his father smoked and watched, alert to any possible transgression. It was only after Val took my credit card inside that the older man seemed to relax. When his son was out of sight, he threw his cigarette down, ground it into the cinder path, and headed back to the bungalow. Val's face was stony when he came back to the car, and his hands trembled as he passed me my receipt. "I apologize for my father," he said, and he turned away.

Angus rolled up the window and started the engine. "I'd go nuts if I had a father like that," he said. "Why does he put up with it?"

"No option, I guess."

As we waited for a camper to pass, I glanced out the back window. Val hadn't moved, but his father had come out of the bungalow and started to walk towards him. When his father got close, Val said something to him; then, without breaking stride, the older man raised his hand and cuffed Val across the side of the head.

I was the only one who saw. Angus was busy checking for traffic on the road, and Taylor was back to looking for signs. Suddenly, she crowed with delight. "Hey, there's one I missed." The sign she'd spotted was handmade, an arrow pointing back to the station from which we'd just come.

Taylor read the words on the arrow carefully. "Masluk & Son, Gas, Food, Friendly Service."

We got home around 4:00. There were no messages on the machine, and given the chaotic state of my feelings about Jill, I was unsure whether that was good news or bad. Angus took the dogs out for a run, then went off to the 7-Eleven, pregame hangout of choice among the sportsmen in Angus's circle. Taylor got out her sketchpad and drew pictures of Regina Beach for a while, then she wandered off to choose her outfit for the dinner party. When she came up to my bedroom for inspection, I was stunned. Left to her own devices, Taylor was a whimsical dresser, but that night she was right on the money: a plaid ruffle skirt, a white pullover with a plaid diamond design, dark green leotards, and her best mary-janes. She'd even brushed her hair. It was obviously a rite-of-passage day.

Ed and Barry lived on a quiet crescent near the university. Their house overlooked the bird sanctuary and the campus, and it was clear when Ed shepherded us inside that they had designed their split-level to take full advantage of the view. The house was built into a rise so that you entered on one floor, but immediately moved up a short flight of stairs to the airy brightness of a large room that seemed to be made up entirely of floor-to-ceiling windows.

Ed led us down a short corridor to the kitchen. Barry Levitt was waiting for us. He was a small man with a receding hairline he made no effort to hide and a trim body he obviously worked hard to preserve. Ed had told me that he and Barry were the same age, forty, but Barry had the kind of charm that would be described as boyish until the day he moved into the seniors' complex. That night he was wearing an open-necked sports shirt the colour of a cut peach and a black denim bib apron. He didn't look up when we came in. All his attention was focused on the steaming pot of seafood he was dumping into a mixing bowl of rice.

When the pot that had held the seafood was empty, Barry stepped back and gestured for us to move closer so we could peer into the bowl.

Taylor stood on tiptoe and looked down. "Mussels," she said happily, "and shrimp and scallops and some things I don't know."

"Well, let's see," said Barry. "I remember throwing a squid in there, and some clams, and chicken, and a very succulent-looking lobster. I think that's the final tally."

"Paella," I said, inhaling deeply. "One of the great dishes of the world. If you can bottle that aroma, I'll be your first customer."

Barry grinned and waved his stirring spoon in the air. "Somebody get these discerning women a drink."

"We have a pitcher of sangria," Ed said, "and we have a cabinet of what Barry's father's bar book called 'the most notable potables.'"

"Sangria will be fine," I said.

He turned to Taylor. "And for you, we have all the ingredients for a Shirley Temple. Even the umbrella."

There is something ceremonial about a drink with an umbrella, and Taylor accepted her Shirley Temple gravely and waited till she was safely seated at the kitchen table before she took a sip. For a few moments, she basked in sophistication, then her eyes grew huge and she leaped up and grabbed my arm.

"Look at that," she said, pointing towards the living room, "they have a Fafard bronze horse! In their house! Jo, you told me real people could never afford to buy those horses because they cost fifteen thousand dollars."

Barry raised an eyebrow. "How old is Taylor?"

74

"Six, but she's pretty serious about art. Her mother was Sally Love."

Barry and Ed exchanged a quick glance. "We have a painting your mother did," Ed said gently. "Would you like to see it?"

Taylor put down her drink, then she went over to Ed and took his hand. "Let's go," she said.

The Sally Love painting Barry and Ed owned was an oil on canvas, about three feet by two and a half. It was a spring scene. Two men wearing gardening clothes and soft shapeless hats were working in a back yard incandescent with tulips, daffodils, and a drift of wild iris. The colours of the blossoms were heart-stoppingly vibrant, and the brushwork was so careful that you felt you could touch the petals, but it was the figures of the men that drew your eye. In painting them, Sally had used muted colours and lines that curved to suggest both age and absolute harmony. You couldn't look at the painting without knowing that the old gardeners were among the lucky few who get to live out a life of quiet joy.

"She was an amazing artist," Ed said.

"She was an amazing woman." I said.

Taylor turned to me. "I dream about her, but I can't remember her. Not really."

"Go up and touch the painting," Ed said.

"Jo says you're not supposed to . . . ," Taylor said.

"Jo's right," Ed agreed. "But this is a special circumstance. I think your mother would want you to touch her painting. After all, she touched it all the time when she was making it."

Taylor approached the painting slowly. For a few moments, she just looked up at it, taking it in. Finally, she reached out and traced the petals of an iris with her fingertips. When she turned back to Ed, there was a look on her face that I'd never seen before.

"Is it okay if I just stay here for a while?"

Ed bowed in her direction. "Of course," he said. "I'll bring your Shirley Temple." He gave me a quick look. "Why don't we grab our jackets and take our drinks outside. Taylor might enjoy some time alone, and it is a lovely night."

When Ed suggested that Barry join us, he waved us off. He was brushing focaccia with rosemary oil, and he said he'd enjoy our company more when everybody had finished eating and he could relax. So it was just Ed and me on the deck. We moved our chairs so we could look out at the university, and the view was worth the effort. The air was heavy with moisture, and in the late afternoon light the campus shimmered, as pastoral and idyllic as its picture in the university calendar.

For a few minutes we were silent, absorbed by our separate thoughts. Finally, Ed said, "Would you rather I hadn't suggested that Taylor look at her mother's painting?"

I shook my head. "No, I'm glad you did. Sally gave me a painting not long before she died. It's in my bedroom, but for the first year Taylor came to us, she refused to look at it. Lately, she's been spending quite a bit of time there."

"A way of being close to her mother."

"So it seems."

Ed nodded. "My father was killed in a car accident before I was born. He was a trumpet player. When I got old enough, I used to spend hours with his old trumpet. Holding something he had held was the only way I knew to bring him close."

"I hope Taylor can feel that connection," I said. "Her mother's death came at the wrong time for her."

Ed looked thoughtful. "Is there a right time to lose a parent?" he asked.

"I guess not," I said. "But the timing in Taylor's case was

particularly savage. I think when Sally died, she had just begun to realize how good it could be to have a daughter."

"Motherhood didn't come easily to her?"

"I don't think Sally had a maternal bone in her body, but at the end, there was a bond." I sipped my sangria. "It had a lot to do with art. Taylor has real talent. When she saw that, Sally was determined to give Taylor the best beginning an artist could have."

"That sounds a little cold."

I shook my head. "It wasn't. It was the only way Sally had of loving. I guess love comes in all shapes and sizes."

Ed smiled. "Tell me about it."

"I don't think I have to," I said. "But it took Sally a long time to realize that there was room in her life for something besides her work. In a lot of ways, Taylor was her second chance."

Ed's face darkened, and he looked away. "That's the merciless aspect of death, isn't it? The taking away of all our second chances." He paused, then he turned to face me. "Reed Gallagher called me the night he died. I wouldn't talk to him."

"That doesn't sound like you."

"Oh, I can be a real prima donna, and a real ass. Just ask Barry. Anyway, that night I was both."

"What happened?"

"It was all so stupid. That morning Reed had come to my office with some terrific news. You know about our Co-op Internship Program, don't you?"

"Sure," I said. "The kids in the Politics and the Media class have been agonizing over where they're going to be placed for months."

Ed shrugged. "You can't blame them. It's a big step. They can't graduate until they've done their internship, and it's a great chance for them to make some connections. We have support from some pretty impressive potential employers. But that week we'd scored a real coup. The *Globe and Mail* had agreed to take one of our students."

"That was a coup," I said. "The grande dame."

"It was all Reed's doing. Of course, we knew as soon as we heard that we'd have to rearrange all our placements."

"You couldn't just bump everybody up a notch?"

Ed shook his head. "No. There are always personal considerations: kids with family obligations, or just a gut feeling that intern A and placement C might be a bad mix. Reed suggested we meet at the Edgewater to hash it all out. He said we needed privacy and perspective, so it was better to meet off campus. We arranged to meet at three. When I got there, the hostess said Reed had left a message that he had a student to see, but he'd be there by quarter after. I waited till four-thirty, but he never showed."

"So you were mad because he stood you up."

Ed winced. "It sounds so childish when you put it that way, but that's about it. My only excuse is that I'd had a lousy day, and by the time I got home, I was fuming. Reed called the house just before dinner, and I told Barry to tell him to go to hell. Of course, Barry just said I was unable to come to the phone." Ed shook his head in disgust. "It was so petty. Anyway, that was it. The next night I heard he was dead."

I walked over and stood beside him. Across the road, some students ran out of the classroom building and began to throw a ball around on the lawn. They were wearing shorts and T-shirts. They must have been cold, but they were Prairie kids and it had been a long winter. Exams were still three weeks away, and spring and hormones were working their magic. As I watched them, I felt a sharp pang of envy.

Ed Mariani seemed to read my mind. "Remember when the biggest problem in our lives was Geology?"

"It was Physics for me." I touched his arm. "Don't be too hard on yourself. It sounds to me as if Reed just wanted to apologize for not showing up at the Edgewater."

"I hope you're right, Joanne. I'd hate to think I'd failed him. He was always good to me." Ed balanced his glass carefully on the rail. "The first day he was here, he sought me out. Of course, my ego was smarting, because he'd gotten the job I thought was going to be mine. Reed picked up on how wounded I was. He told me how much he admired my work, and how glad he was, for his own sake, that I'd withdrawn my name from consideration. Then you know what he did?" Ed smiled at the memory. "He said he thought it would be a good idea if we got drunk together."

"And you did?"

Ed shuddered. "Did we ever. I felt like the inside of a goat the next day, but it was worth it."

"That good, huh?"

"Yeah, it was fun, but it was useful too. There'd been some ugliness when I'd put my name into contention for the director's job."

"The kind of ugliness you could have taken to the Human Rights Commission?"

"No. I'm used to dealing with overt prejudice; this was more insidious, but from a couple of things Reed said that night, it was pretty apparent he hadn't anything to do with it. That was such a relief. And, to be fair, Reed really was a better choice for the job. The school needed somebody who had significant connections and strong administrative skills, and that wasn't me."

"Sounds like your boys' night out really cleared the air," I said.

Ed's expression was sombre. "It did. It was a good evening; unfortunately it wasn't the last one." He took a long swallow of his drink. "We spent some time together the Wednesday before Reed died. I must have replayed the evening a hundred times, wondering if there was something I could have said or done that might have changed what happened. But, at the time, it just seemed like an ordinary evening. We'd been working late on the budget for next year, and we went back to the Faculty Club for a drink. Reed was in a strange mood. He was always a serious drinker, but that night he was drinking to get drunk. I wouldn't have cared, except that whatever the problem was, the liquor wasn't helping. The more he drank, the more miserable he seemed to get. Finally, I asked Reed if he wanted to talk about whatever it was that was troubling him."

"And he didn't?"

"No . . . so, of course, I resorted to the usual bromides – told him that anytime he wanted to talk, I was there, and he could trust me not to betray his confidence." Ed looked perplexed. "It was just one of those things people say when they don't know what else to say, but Reed picked up on it. Joanne, he was so angry and so bitter. He said, 'I'll give you some advice: don't ever tell people they can trust you, and don't ever believe for a moment that you can trust them.'"

"I didn't know Reed well," I said, "but he never struck me as a cynic."

"He wasn't. Something had happened."

"Do you have any idea what?"

"My guess is it was his marriage."

"Did he say anything?"

"No. But he didn't have to – all that business about trust. Doesn't that sound as if there was a betrayal?"

I thought of Julie's wedding cake and of the sugar doves

she'd made so that her new marriage would be blessed with years of happiness. She and Reed had only made it to a month and two days. What could have happened in so brief a time to turn hope to despair?

It was a question I didn't want to dwell on, and I was relieved when Barry Levitt opened the deck door, stuck out his head, and invited us to join Taylor and him for dinner.

The table was beautifully set: cobalt-blue depression ware and a woven cloth as brightly coloured as the Italian flag. Barry had pulled the tables close to the window so we could watch the sunset. Taylor was uncharacteristically quiet, and when Ed asked her to light the candles, she performed the task without her usual brio. But she perked up when Barry brought in the paella dish and placed it in front of her.

"Did Jo tell you this is my favourite?" she asked.

"She didn't have to," Barry said. "Creative people love seafood. Everybody knows that."

For the next hour we sipped sangria, sopped up paella with the focaccia, and talked about summer plans as Puccini soared in the background. By the time we'd moved to Act III of *Turandot*, the paella dish was empty, and Ed brought out chocolate gelato and cappuccino.

Taylor was a great fan of gelato, and Ed's gelato was home-made. After she'd finished her dish, she turned to Barry. "This is really a nice party," she said. "I'm glad I wore my good clothes."

Barry raised his glass to her. "Whatever you choose to wear, you're always welcome at this table."

"Thank you," said Taylor.

"I'm afraid that has to be the last word, T," I said. "School tomorrow, and we're already past your bedtime."

As we stood at the doorway, saying our goodbyes, Taylor said, "Can I look at the painting one more time?"

"Sure," said Barry. "I'll come with you."

I turned to Ed. "It really was a lovely evening. Thanks for asking us. I needed some fun tonight."

"So did I," he said. "And I needed to talk about Reed. Barry doesn't want me to dwell on it, but I do. It was such a terrible ending to a good life. What's even more terrible is the possibility that the way Reed died will eclipse everything he accomplished – especially here at the university. He was so committed to the School of Journalism. Even on the night he died. Look at this." Ed reached into his inside jacket pocket, pulled out a single sheet of paper and handed it to me. "This was in the mailbox when I went out to get our paper Friday morning."

I unfolded the paper. On it, handwritten, were sixteen names. I recognized them as the students who were just completing the term before their placement. Opposite each name, Reed had written in the name of the media organization where the student would intern.

"Can you imagine what he must have been going through that night? But he still made sure the kids were taken care of. He must have dropped the list off after Barry and I had gone to the symphony." Ed swallowed hard. "Well, life goes on. I'll set up interviews with the students tomorrow to tell them the news."

"Would you like to use my office?" I said. "From the way yours looked yesterday morning, I think it'll be a while before you can even find your desk."

Ed frowned. "You should think carefully before you make an offer like that, Joanne. You know what Clare Boothe Luce said. 'No good deed goes unpunished.'"

"I'm not worried," I said. "I'll get a key made for you tomorrow morning. Consider it settled. But, Ed, there's one thing I don't understand . . ."

I never got to finish my sentence. Taylor was back, toting

an armload of art books that Barry was lending her. As she showed her collection to Ed, I glanced again at Reed Gallagher's placement list. The class Tom Kelsoe and I taught was mandatory for Journalism students in their final year, so I was familiar with the work of the people Reed was assigning as interns. Most of the students on Reed's list were ranked just about where I would have placed them, but there was one surprise, and it was right at the top. The student Reed Gallagher had chosen for the plum internship with the *Globe and Mail* was Kellee Savage.

The clock in the hall began to chime. It was 9:00. I handed the list back to Ed. The mystery of Kellee Savage would have to wait.

"Okay, Taylor," I said, "now it really is past your bedtime. Say goodnight, Gracie."

"Goodnight, Gracie." Taylor said and roared with laughter the way her mother would roar when she made a joke. It had been quite an evening: paella, Puccini, and a reprise of an old Burns and Allen routine. I'd hardly thought about Jill at all.

Taylor didn't need a bedtime story. As she was telling me about how her mother swirled her brushstrokes, she fell asleep in mid-sentence. I tucked her in and started downstairs, but when I heard the ricochet of adolescent jokes and insults coming from the kitchen, I stopped and headed back up to my room. Angus and his buddies were in the kitchen, and his friend Camillo had just decided they should make nachos. Dinner with Ed and Barry had boosted my spirits but I knew my limits. I wasn't ready for a kitchen full of teenagers and the aroma of processed cheese warming in the microwave. I needed peace and I needed time to think, and one of the things I needed to think about was Kellee Savage.

She had been in two of my classes, but I had never seen anything in her work to indicate that someday she would be the one to catch the brass ring. My briefcase was on the window seat. I pulled out the folder of unmarked essays and sorted through till I found Kellee's. It was an analysis of how a councillor from the core area used the alternative press to get across his message that the city had to start listening to the concerns of the prostitutes who lived and worked in his ward. Like everything else Kellee had done for me, it was meticulously researched, adequately written, and absolutely without a spark. I curled up on the window seat and began leafing through some of the other essays. Jumbo Hryniuk had written about how J.C. Watts, the brilliant quarterback for the University of Oklahoma and the Ottawa Rough Riders, had parlayed fame on the football field into a seat in the U.S. House of Representatives and special status as one of Newt Gingrich's boys. As always, Jumbo was almost, but not quite, on topic. Linda Van Sickle, the young woman Reed had ranked second, had submitted a case study of a civic government that showed how the city council's political timidity was growing in direct proportion to the increasingly adversarial nature of local media outlets. It was a brilliant paper, good enough to be published. So, I discovered, was Val Massey's essay, "The Right to Be Wrong: The Press's Obligation to Protect Bigots and Bastards." Reed's decision simply didn't make sense. I skimmed through the rest of the essays. Of the sixteen people in our seminar, I would have ranked seven ahead of Kellee Savage.

When Alex called, I was still mystified, but the words on the page were starting to swim in front of me, and I knew it was time for bed. Alex sounded as tired as I felt.

"Glad you went home?" I asked.

"I don't know. I'm glad I was there, but I wish it hadn't been necessary."

"How's your nephew?"

"Immortal," he said. "Like all kids his age are. That's why

they can drink and sniff and snort and speed and screw without protection."

"You sound as if you've had enough."

"That doesn't mean there's not more coming. Jo, sometimes I get so goddamn sick of these little pukes. I don't know. Maybe it's just that I'm sick of going to their funerals."

"Is it that bad with your nephew?"

"I hope not. Jo, I'd really rather not talk about this."

"Okay," I said. "Come over, and we don't have to say a word. That's the advantage real life has over telephones."

He laughed. "It's a tempting offer, but I'd better not. Even without words, I'd be lousy company tonight."

"Then come tomorrow morning," I said. "I don't have to teach till ten-thirty, and the kids leave for school at eight."

"I'll be there," he said. "Count on it."

CHAPTER

6

When I first met Alex Kequahtooway, there was nothing to suggest that he would be a terrific lover. He was knowledgeable and passionate about serious music, but he was guarded in his response to everything else. We went out for three months before we were intimate, and during that time of coming to know one another, he was kind but almost formally correct with me. After we became lovers, the kindness continued, but it was allied with an eroticism that awed and delighted me. Alice Munro differentiates between those who can go only a little way with the act of love and those "who can make a greater surrender, like the mystics." Alex was one of love's mystics, and that morning as I lay in bed beside him, breathing in the scent of the narcissi blooming in front of the open window, listening to Dennis Brain play the opening notes of a horn concerto on the radio, I was at peace.

He took my hand, leaned over and kissed me. "Mozart," he said. "The second-best way to start the day."

It was a little after 10:00 when I nosed into my parking spot at the university. The test I was about to give was on my desk, and I checked it to make sure it was typo- and jargon-free, then I went down to the Political Science office. I needed exam booklets, and I wanted to make copies of a hand-out for my senior class. As I counted out the exam booklets, I was still humming Mozart.

When Rosalie Norman, the departmental admin assistant, saw me at the copying machine, she hustled me out of the way. "I'll do that. Every time you faculty use it, something goes wrong, and I'm the one who has to call the company and then try to figure out whose secretary I can sweet-talk into doing your photocopying until the repairman decides to show up."

On the best of days, Rosalie was not a sunny person, but that morning, even the most casual observer would have seen that she had a right to be cranky. Over the weekend, she had got herself a new and very bad permanent. Her previously smooth salt-and-pepper pageboy was now tightly coiled into what my older daughter, Mieka, called a "Kurly Kate do," after the girl on the pot-scrubber box.

I tried not to stare. "Rosalie, if you have a spare minute later on, would you mind getting me an extra key for my office?"

Her blackberry eyes shone with suspicion. "What do you need an extra key for?"

"I'm going to be sharing with Professor Mariani until the Journalism offices are straightened around."

She sighed heavily. "I'm going to have to go over to Physical Plant in person, you know. They don't just give out those keys to anybody. More sweet-talking. I'll probably be there half the morning."

I considered the situation. Rosalie Norman had a choleric disposition, and for the foreseeable future, she was stuck with the permanent from hell. Chances that her day would ever begin as mine just had, with world-class love-making, were slim to nil.

I patted her hand. "I'll go over to Physical Plant," I said. "No use wasting your morning sucking up to an office full of sourpusses."

A smile flickered across her lips so quickly that I was left wondering if I'd just imagined it. "Thanks," she said, then she leaned over the copier, scooped up my copies and slid them into a file folder. "The next time you need copying done, put it on my desk in the tray marked 'copying.' We have a system around here, you know."

The phone was ringing when I got back to my office. It was Ed Mariani.

"I've told our admin assistant you're moving in," I said, "and I'm just about to phone Physical Plant for your key."

He laughed. "And I pride myself on being a Virgo. I really do appreciate your generosity, Joanne. I know it's not going to be easy having somebody else lumbering around your office. Now, I'm afraid I have another favour to ask."

"Ask away. You've already softened me up with your Clare Boothe Luce allusion."

"Thanks," he said. "It's about Kellee Savage. She wasn't in my class this morning. Normally, I wouldn't give it a second thought, but I want to get these interviews started, and Kellee's the logical person to start with. If she shows up for Politics and the Media, would you get her to give me a call at home?"

"Sure," I said. "And, Ed, don't worry about the lumbering. I'm looking forward to having you around." I hung up, called Physical Plant, arranged to pick up an extra office key later in the morning, and set out for class.

After I'd got my Poli Sci 100 students started on their test, I opened my briefcase to take out the senior class's papers. That's when I noticed I still had the copy of *Sleeping Beauty* that Kellee Savage had thrust into my hands on St. Patrick's Day. As it turned out, there had been more truth than poetry in the image of Kellee Savage as Sleeping Beauty. Her story might have lacked a handsome prince, but she had certainly nabbed the prize that would awaken all her possibilities. When Ed Mariani told her that she had been chosen to live happily ever after, or at least for a semester, in the big city, Kellee was going to be one triumphant young woman.

That afternoon, when I walked into the Politics and the Media seminar and saw that Kellee's place at the table was still empty, I felt a shiver of annoyance. Kellee had been made the recipient of a shining gift; the least she could do was stop pouting and show up to claim it.

As soon as class got under way, Kellee was banished from my thoughts. It was a spirited hour and a half, not because of the questions I'd prepared for discussion, but because of an item that had dominated the weekend news. Late Friday afternoon, an Ottawa reporter, faced with the choice of revealing the source of some politically damaging documents that had been leaked to her or of going to jail, had revealed her source. Early Sunday morning, the senior bureaucrat the reporter named had jumped off the balcony of a highrise on rue Jacques Cartier. The argument about whether a journalist ever had the right to put self-interest above principle was fervent. Even Jumbo Hryniuk, who usually cast a dim eye on the doings of the non-jock press, grappled vigorously with the ethics of the case. Only one student was not engaged. As the passions swirled about him, Val Massey remained preoccupied and remote. Remembering his father's casual act of brutality the day before, I was worried.

When the seminar was over, I handed back the essays I'd graded, and as always when papers were returned, I was soon surrounded by a knot of students with questions or complaints. Linda Van Sickle waited till the room had cleared before she came up to me. She was a sweet-faced young woman with honey hair and the glowing good looks that some women are blessed with in the last weeks of pregnancy. In her Birkenstocks, Levi's, and oversized GAP T-shirt, she was the symbol of hip fertility, a Demeter for the nineties.

I smiled at her. "If you're here to complain about your grade, you're out of luck," I said. "I think that's the highest mark I've ever given."

She blushed. "No, I'm very pleased with the mark. I just wanted to ask you about Kellee. I know I should have done something about this sooner, but I did try to call her a couple of times, and I was sure by now I would have run into her."

"Back up," I said. "You've lost me."

Linda shook her head in annoyance. "Sorry. I'm not usually this scattered." She smoothed her shirt over the curve of her stomach. "I'm a little distracted. This morning my doctor told me it's possible I'm carrying twins."

"Twins!" I repeated. "That would distract anybody."

She shrugged. "When we get used to the idea, we'll be cool with it, but the doctor wants me to have an ultrasound Friday, so I'm going to miss your class, which means it'll be another week before I can get Kellee's tape-recorder to her. She left it in the bar Friday night. I picked it up after she left. She was pretty . . . upset."

"I know she was in rough shape," I said. "She phoned me. Linda, I'm aware that Kellee was drinking pretty heavily that night."

"Then you know why she hasn't been coming to class or answering her phone."

"You think she's ashamed of her behaviour," I said.

"Yes, and she should be," Linda said flatly. "I like Kellee, but she wasn't just blitzed that night at the Owl; she was mean. She was sitting next to me, and I thought if I let her ramble on, she'd give it up after a while, but she never stopped. The worst thing was that the person she was accusing wasn't there to defend himself."

"Val Massey," I said.

"She told you!" Linda's normally melodic voice was sharp with exasperation. "That really was irresponsible. It's totally ludicrous, of course. Val could have any woman he wanted on this campus. He's not only terrific-looking; he's bright, and he's sensitive, and he's kind. There'd be no reason in the world for him to come on to Kellee Savage."

"That was pretty much my feeling too," I said. "When Kellee talked to me, I tried not to leap to Val's defence, but she knew I didn't believe her."

Linda looked at me levelly. "No rational person would believe her."

"That night at the Owl – didn't anybody realize Kellee needed help?"

"At first we all just thought it was sort of funny. That was the first time any of us ever remembered seeing her in the bar, and there she was, sucking back the Scotch." Linda wrinkled her nose in distaste. "I don't know anybody under the age of forty who drinks Scotch, but Kellee said she was drinking it because Professor Gallagher told her that once you acquire a taste for Scotch, you'll never want anything else. I don't know whether she acquired the taste that night, but she sure got hammered."

"Why didn't somebody take her home?"

"As a matter of fact, I'd just about talked her into letting me drive her back to her place, when Val walked in. That's when everything went nuts. Kellee ran over to him and started pounding him on the chest and saying these crazy things; then Meaghan Andrechuk discovered Kellee's tape-recorder whirring away on the seat in the booth where we'd been sitting. Can you believe it? Kellee had been recording the private conversations of people she was in class with the whole evening . . ."

"Did Kellee ever explain what she was doing?" I asked.

"She didn't get a chance." Linda gnawed her lip. "Did you ever read a story called 'The Lottery'?"

I nodded. "In school. As I remember, it's pretty chilling."

"Especially the ending," Linda agreed, "when everybody in town starts throwing stones at the woman who is the scapegoat. There were no stones Friday night, but there might as well have been. Everybody had had too much to drink, and Kellee didn't help matters. Instead of apologizing, she started shouting that she was the only one of us who was doing real journalism, and she was going to show us all. She was so loud the manager came over and threatened to throw her out."

I closed my eyes, trying to shut out the image. "It must have been awful."

Linda's gaze was steady. "It got worse. Kellee started arguing with the manager. He was really patient, but she kept pushing it. Finally, he gave up and asked one of the women who worked in the bar to help him get Kellee into a cab. They were trying to put Kellee's coat on her when Meaghan came back from the bathroom and said there'd been a bulletin on TV: Professor Gallagher was dead. Kellee went white and ran out of the bar. She left this." Linda opened her knapsack and took out the tape-recorder that I recognized from class as Kellee's. "You'll make sure she gets it, won't you?"

"Of course," I said. "And thanks for bringing it in. It'll give me an excuse to call her. I know Kellee's behaviour was pretty rotten, but it's so close to the end of term. I'd hate to see her lose her year."

"So would I," Linda said. "But, Professor Kilbourn, when

you talk to Kellee, make sure she understands that she has to stop hounding Val. You saw what he was like in class today. That was Kellee's doing. I'm sorry that she's disturbed, but that doesn't give her licence to ruin Val Massey's life."

I thought of Val's face, pale and expressionless, and the words seemed to form themselves. "You're right," I said. "She has to be stopped."

On my way back to the department, I made a quick trip to Physical Plant and picked up the extra key I needed for Ed Mariani. The woman who handed it to me was friendly and obliging, and I wondered, not for the first time, whether Rosalie Norman would take it amiss if I suggested her life would be smoother if she weren't so prickly.

When I got back to my office, Val Massey was waiting outside. I was relieved to see him there. I unlocked my door and Val followed me inside. I was grateful that he was giving me a chance to confront the Kellee Savage quandary head on.

"I was just about to make coffee," I said. "Would you like some?"

"No, thanks," he murmured.

"Well, at least sit down," I said, gesturing to the chair across from mine.

He didn't seem to hear me. He walked over to the window and stood there, wordless and remote, until the silence between us grew awkward.

"You have to be department head before they give you a view of anything other than the parking lot," I said.

Val turned and looked at me uncomprehendingly.

"That was a joke," I said.

He smiled and moved towards my bulletin board. I'd filled it with campaign buttons from long-ago elections and with pictures of my kids.

"How many children do you have?" he asked.

"Four," I said. "The two you met when we came out to Regina Beach, a daughter who's married and running a catering business in Saskatoon, and a son who's at the vet college."

"Have any of your children ever got themselves into a real mess?" he asked.

"Of course," I said. "I've got into a few real messes myself. It seems to come with living a life."

He looked so miserable that I wanted to put my arms around him, but I knew that the most prudent course was simply to give him an opening. "Val, you don't need to be oblique with me," I said. "I know about Kellee Savage."

At the sound of her name he recoiled as if he'd taken a blow.

"It's all right," I said quickly. "I don't believe what she's saying about you. In fact, I've decided to talk to her about the damage she's doing, not just to you but to everybody, including herself."

"Don't!" he shouted. The word seemed to explode in the quiet room. Val winced with embarrassment. When he spoke again, his voice was barely a whisper. "Don't talk to her . . . please. Don't get involved." He raked his fingers through his hair. "I'm sorry," he said. Then he ran out of the room.

I went after him, but by the time I got to the door, he was already out of sight. The hall was empty. I was furious: furious at myself for handling the situation badly and furious at Kellee Savage for creating it in the first place.

Ten minutes later, when Ed Mariani stuck his head in, I was still upset.

"Ready for an office-mate?" he asked.

"Am I ever," I said. "Make yourself at home." I pointed to the bookshelf nearest the window. "There's the kettle and the Earl Grey, and, as you can see, the cups and saucers are right next to it."

"Since everything's so handy, why don't I make us some tea?" Ed said. He picked up the kettle and padded out of the office. When he came back, he plugged the kettle in and eased into the student chair across the desk from me. He was such a big man, it was a tight fit.

"Do you want to trade?" I asked.

As he raised himself out of his chair, he smiled at me gratefully. "I'll try not to be here when you are."

"Don't worry about it."

Ed put a bag in each cup, poured in boiling water, then settled happily into my chair.

"So was Kellee Savage in class today?" he asked.

I shook my head. "No."

Ed raised an eyebrow. "I think I'd better just go ahead and tell the students about their placements. They've waited long enough."

"Yes, they have," I said, and I was surprised at how acerbic I sounded. "Ed, do you understand why Kellee Savage was the one who got the internship with the *Globe*?"

"No," he said, "I don't, and believe me, ever since I saw her name heading up that list, I've wondered what Reed saw in her that I didn't."

"She works hard," I said.

He laughed. "No disputing that," he said. "But there's no imagination in her work, nothing that takes you into any deeper understanding of what she's writing about."

"How well do you know her?" I asked.

"The J school is small," he said, "so we're a lot tighter with our students than you are in Arts. By the time the kids graduate we've usually had them in a couple of classes, we've helped them with practical skills like interviewing, we've supervised their independent projects, and we've spent time with them socially. Not that Kellee has ever been exactly a party girl." He picked up my mug. "Weak or strong?" he asked.

"Strong."

"A woman after my own heart," he said. "What's that old Irish saying? 'When I makes tay, I makes tay, and when I makes water, I makes water.' Anyway, what I remember most about Kellee Savage is the obituary she wrote."

"Of whom?"

"Of herself. It's an exercise most J schools assign in Print Journalism I. It's partly to teach students how to make words count, and partly to help them focus on their goals. Most of the obits the kids write are depressingly Canadian. You know: 'his accomplishments were few, but he was always decent and caring.' Kellee's was different. The writing was predictably pedestrian, but she had such extravagant ambitions, and she did have one glorious line. 'Kellee Savage was a great journalist, because although no one ever noticed her, she was there.'"

I shuddered, "That's certainly gnomic."

"Isn't it?" he said. He put a spoon into my mug, pressed out the last of the tea and fished out the bag. "I believe your tea is ready, Madam."

After I'd picked Taylor up from her friend Jess Stephens's house, we drove to Lakeview Court to feed Julie's fish. For Taylor, most chores were obstacles to be dispatched speedily, so she could get on with the real business of her life, but Julie's fish intrigued her, and she gave her full attention to feeding them. She had developed a routine, and I watched as she pulled a needlepoint-covered bench close to the tank, kicked off her shoes, climbed up on the bench, and shook the fish food carefully over the surface of the water. When she was done, she jumped down, pressed her face against the glass, and watched as the minute particles drifted down through the water, driving the fish crazy.

We watched for a few minutes, then I said, "We have to boogie, T. I haven't even thought about dinner yet."

"I have," Taylor said. "Why don't we have paella?"

"Why don't we have fish and chips?" I said. "I think there's a coupon for Captain Jack's at home." I looked at my watch. "Angus has a practice at six-thirty, so I might as well call the Captain from here."

When I went into the kitchen to use the phone, the light from the answering machine on Julie's desk was blinking. I hit the button, and a woman's voice, pleasantly contralto, filled the quiet room. "Reed, it's Annalie. It's Sunday, ten p.m. my time, so that's nine yours. My husband and I were at our cabin for the weekend, so I just got your message. It was such a shock to hear your voice after all these years. It's funny, I thought I'd feel vindicated when you finally figured out the truth, but all I can manage is a sort of dull rage." She paused. When she spoke again, her voice was tight. "I guess Santayana was right: 'Those who cannot remember the past are condemned to repeat it.' But Reed, remembering isn't enough. Now that you know what happened, you have an obligation to make sure there are no more repetitions. If you want to talk, my number is area code 416 . . . ," she laughed. "Of course, you have my number, don't you?" There was a click and the line went dead.

I rewound the tape and played it again. It still didn't ring any bells for me, but while Annalie's message was perplexing, her voice was a pleasure to listen to: musical and theatrically precise in its pronunciations. It was a professionally trained voice, and as I archived her message, I found myself wondering what part the enigmatic Annalie had played in the past that Reed Gallagher had chosen not to remember.

When we got home, Alex was there. I asked him to stay for dinner, but he insisted on paying.

"If I'd known you were picking up the tab," I said, "I would have ordered Captain Jack's world-famous paella."

Taylor was placing knives and forks around the table in a pattern that a generous eye might have seen as a series of place settings. When she heard the word "paella," she swivelled around to face me. "We could still order some." She narrowed her eyes. "That was one of your jokes, wasn't it, Jo?"

"It was," I said, "and you fell for it."

After Taylor sailed off, I poured Alex a Coke, made myself a gin and tonic, and we sat down at the kitchen table to exchange the news of the day. When I told Alex about the message on the Gallaghers' answering machine, he tensed with interest.

"That was the whole thing?"

"I archived it, if you want to hear it yourself. What do you make of it?"

Alex centred his Coke glass carefully on the placemat. "It doesn't sound good. All that talk about dull rage and vindication and making sure there are no more repetitions of history sounds like Reed Gallagher was getting hit with some pretty heavy stuff from the past."

"I wonder if that's what he and Julie quarrelled about the night before he died."

He whistled softly. "Could be. Then to relieve tension after their fight, Gallagher went down to Scarth Street, broke into a rooming house, pulled on his pantyhose, opened the poppers, and tried his hand at erotic strangulation." He shook his head in a gesture of dismissal. "This still doesn't feel right to me, Jo. But we haven't got anything else. We've talked to everybody we can come up with. We've gone over that room on Scarth Street with the proverbial fine-tooth comb, and Splatter's spent so much time on Gallagher's body that we're telling him it must be love. Still, all we've got is what we started with – accidental death."

"So what's next?"

Alex shrugged. "Nothing. That's it. No leads. No evidence. No case. They're ready to release the body, so we'll need a signature. I'll have to phone Mrs. G. – unless, of course, you want to volunteer."

"You're buying dinner," I said. "I'll call."

Alex raised an eyebrow. "I got the best of that deal."

"I know you did," I said. "But I'm keeping track."

After dinner, Angus talked Alex into letting him drive the Audi over to his basketball practice. As I watched the Audi lurch onto Albert Street, I decided if Alex could be heroic, I could too. I squared my shoulders, marched back inside, and dialled the number where Julie said she could be reached.

The listing was in Port Hope, a pretty town of turn-of-the-century elegance on Lake Ontario. I'd spent a summer there when I was young. Luckily, my memories were happy ones, because I had plenty of time to recollect summers past before Julie finally picked up the phone.

She did not sound happy to hear from me, and I didn't waste time on pleasantries. When I told her that the police were releasing Reed's body, she was curt. "I'll take care of it," she said. Then, mechanically, like a child remembering an etiquette lesson, she added, "Thank you for calling."

I thought of the last time I'd seen her. She had seemed so alone the night she dropped her keys by my house. "Julie, wait," I said. "Call me when you know your flight time. I'll pick you up at the airport."

Her tone was incredulous. "Why would I go back there? Hasn't he already humiliated me enough?"

"You can't just leave him," I said. "Somebody has to sign for the body and make funeral arrangements."

"There isn't going to be a funeral." She laughed bitterly. "What could people possibly say about the dear departed?"

The next morning, Ed Mariani and I had tea together in the office before class, and I told him about Julie's decision to bury Reed without any formal ceremony. Ed was furious.

"Damn it, Joanne, I never liked that woman, and it turns out I was right. Reed was a good man. He needs to be remembered, and the people who cared about him need to take stock of what they've lost."

"I suppose if Julie doesn't want to handle it, Reed's colleagues at the university could organize a memorial service."

Ed nodded agreement. "We could, and we should. But you and I aren't the colleagues who were closest to Reed."

"Tom Kelsoe," I said. "He's the one whose history with Reed goes back the farthest. He was Reed's student. Reed gave him his first job, and from what I heard at the time, Tom was the real mover and shaker in getting Reed appointed as director of Journalism."

Ed cocked an eyebrow. "So they say."

I felt my face go hot with embarrassment. "I'm sorry, Ed. You didn't need to be reminded of that."

"No," he said, "I didn't, but it wasn't your doing. Now come on. Let's get back to the memorial service."

"Somebody should call Tom, so we can get some people together and make the arrangements," I said.

Ed looked away. "Joanne, I'll help in any way I can, but I don't want to have anything to do with Kelsoe."

I waited, but Ed didn't elaborate, and I didn't ask him to. Instead, I reached for the phone and dialled Tom's office number. When an operator came on and told me the line was no longer in service, I remembered the chaos in the Journalism offices, and dialled Tom's apartment.

I had just about decided he wasn't there when Jill Osiowy picked up the phone. She sounded distracted, and for a beat I worried that I'd got her at a bad moment, then I remembered the scene at the Chimney Saturday night, and I hoped, childishly, that her morning had been filled with bad moments.

"How are you, Jill?"

"I'm okay," she said. "How are you?"

"Never better," I said. "But I need to speak to Tom. Is he there?"

"I'll see if he can come to the phone."

When Tom Kelsoe picked up the receiver, he barked his name in my ear, and I felt my gorge rise. But this wasn't about me. I tried to make my voice civil.

"Tom, Julie Gallagher has decided against a funeral for Reed, but some of us at the university have been talking about a memorial service. You and Reed were so close. I thought you'd want to be part of the planning."

He cut me off. "I don't get off on primitive group rituals, Joanne. I think the idea sucks. I won't help and I won't be there." He slammed the receiver down.

I turned to Ed Mariani. "Tom declines," I said. "And without regrets."

Ed put his hands on the arms of his chair and pushed himself up heavily. "Then I guess it's up to us," he said.

CHAPTER

7

Reed Gallagher's memorial service was held at the Faculty Club on Friday, March 24, a week to the day after his body had been discovered in the rooming house on Scarth Street. In every detail of the planning, Ed Mariani's watchword had been dignity; the service seemed to become his way of reclaiming for Reed the respect and regard which his bizarre death had stolen from him. The rooms I walked into that afternoon were an invitation to celebrate civility and the pleasures of the senses: simple bowls of spring flowers touched the tables with Japanese grace. At the grand piano in the bar, Barry Levitt, trim in a cream cable-knit sweater and matching slacks, was leafing through his sheet music, and in the club's window room, a buffet with hot and cold hors-d'oeuvres had been set up beside a well-stocked bar. Ed Mariani had done Reed Gallagher proud, but as I picked up a glass of champagne punch at the bar, I was edgy. I'd been tense all week, made restless by the deepening mysteries in the lives of two people I didn't really know. One of those people was Reed Gallagher.

Ed Mariani and Barry Levitt had volunteered to organize Reed's memorial service, but they had entrusted one job to me. Because I had keys to the Gallaghers' condominium, I was to find photographs and memorabilia for the display celebrating Reed's life. At first, I burrowed through the boxes of memorabilia I found in his closet as dispassionately as an archaeologist on a dig, but as the man Reed Gallagher had been began to emerge, Annalie's cryptic allusion to Santayana took on a haunting resonance. Try as I might, I could not reconcile Reed Gallagher's sad and tawdry death with the life that was emerging from the boxes and cartons that surrounded me. As Mr. Spock would say, it didn't compute. Nonetheless, the more I dug, the more I became convinced that the answer to the enigma of Reed Gallagher's last hours lay somewhere in his past.

By any standards, his life had been extraordinary. Before he had turned his hand to teaching, he had covered wars and political campaigns and natural disasters. He had been present at many of the events that had defined our history in the past quarter-century. He had known famous people, and he had, if one could judge from the affectionate inscriptions on plaques and photographs, been liked and respected by those who worked with him and knew him best. Everything I came up with reflected a life lived with gusto and commitment. Perhaps more significantly, my burrowing uncovered no evidence of the negligence Annalie's message had suggested, nor did it bring to light even a hint of an ache so ferocious that it would someday drive Reed Gallagher up a flimsy fire escape to his appointment in Samarra.

But, as I kept reminding myself, my job wasn't to analyse; it was to gather together what Barry Levitt called my Gallagher iconography, and that afternoon, as I stood in the Faculty Club looking at the graceful mahogany table that held my handiwork, I was pleased with the job I had done. Reed Gallagher had not been badly served by his iconographer.

Scattered among the awards and testimonials were pictures of Reed flanked by two prime ministers, of Reed gripping the hand of an American president, of Reed conferring with media figures like Knowlton Nash, Barbara Frum, Peter Newman, and Richard Gwyn, people who come as close to being legendary as our country permits anyone to be. But my real coup was a picture of Reed with a woman who, in all likelihood, would be of no significance to anyone in the room but me.

I had searched hard for a photograph of Annalie, but in the end I had almost passed it by. My aim had been to balance photos of the public Reed Gallagher with some that captured his private moments, and I had found some lovely and evocative snapshots: Reed as a teenager, taking a chamois to a shining convertible with fins while two middle-aged people beamed with parental pride; Reed as a college boy in a bathing suit, exulting in the pleasure of holding a sweetly curved young woman in his arms; Reed as the very young editor of a small-town newspaper, proudly showing off his twin proofs of authority, a shining brass nameplate on his desk and a brand-new moustache on his upper lip.

By the time I came upon the carton that Reed, in his large and generous hand, had labelled RYERSON – DESK STUFF, I thought I'd made all my choices. But remembering Reed's affinity for the students at our J school, I decided to see if I could ferret out something from his early days as an instructor. The yellowed newspaper clipping of the photograph of Annalie and Reed was in an envelope with a clutch of odds and ends: a dry cleaner's receipt, an old press pass from a PC leadership convention, a ticket stub from a Leafs-Blackhawks game. In the photo, Annalie, in her capacity as editor of the

Ryersonian, was presenting Reed with a bound copy of the past year's issues. Both she and Reed were smiling.

Her full name was Annalie Brinkmann. On the phone, her voice had been filled with lilt and magic, but the picture showed a plain girl, heavy-set and wearing horn-rimmed glasses which had apparently failed to correct an outward-turning squint. Twenty years can change many things, and the girl of twenty is often barely discernible in the woman of forty, but I was hoping the picture might jog the memories of some of Reed's friends from the Ryerson days. There was even an outside chance that Annalie herself would appear. Ed had written an elegant obituary of Reed for the *Globe and Mail*, and placed a notice of Reed's death in the *Toronto Star*. Both had mentioned the time and place of the memorial service. If Annalie was a newspaper reader, chances were good she would know about what Ed Mariani had come to call Reed's last party. It was a slim straw to cling to, but if I was lucky, one way or another, the memorial service would link me and the woman who had left such a troubling message for Reed Gallagher three days after his death.

The newspaper clipping was unmounted, and I would need a frame. Fortunately, there was a small silver one at hand that was just the ticket. I didn't feel the smallest pang as I replaced the photograph of Tom Kelsoe with the one of Reed and Annalie Brinkmann. Tom had made it clear that he didn't want to be part of Reed's last party, and it was a pleasure to honour his request.

As the guests started arriving at the club, it seemed that Tom and Julie were the only people who had chosen not to come. Twenty minutes before the farewells were scheduled to begin, the room was packed, but newcomers were still appearing. I scanned the door eagerly, looking for two faces: one was Annalie's; the other was Kellee Savage's.

Kellee still hadn't shown up. As acting head of the School of Journalism, Ed had checked with all her instructors. Their reports had been the same: Kellee Savage hadn't been in class all week. Ed and I had taken turns calling the number Kellee listed as her home number, but we'd never connected. When I told Alex I was growing uneasy, he was reassuring. Kellee Savage was, he said, a white middle-class twenty-one-year-old who had got drunk and humiliated herself in front of her friends. Nothing in her life pointed to a fate worse than a bad case of embarrassment. In his opinion, when she screwed up her courage, she would be back.

Alex's logic was unassailable. Even I had to admit that Kellee's disappearance fell well within a pattern I knew. It was not uncommon for university kids to disappear from classes for a while, especially this close to the end of term. Sometimes the triple burden of a heavy workload, parental expectations, and immaturity was just too much, and the kids simply bailed out. Among themselves, the students called the syndrome "crashing and burning," but the image was hyperbolic. Most often, after a week or so, they came back to class with a stack of hastily completed term papers or a doctor's note citing stress and suggesting mercy.

The rational part of me knew that in a small Prairie city, a twenty-one-year-old woman should be able to drop out of sight for a week without setting off tremors of concern. But we are not ruled by reason alone, and that morning I'd made a decision. Ed had put a large announcement of Reed's memorial service in our local paper, and he'd posted notices all over campus, inviting students to come and pay their final respects. If Kellee Savage was in town, she would know about the service. Given her apparent closeness to Reed, if Kellee Savage had one decent bone in her body, she would be at the memorial service that afternoon. I had decided that, if she didn't put in an appearance, the time had come to find out why.

As the Faculty Club filled to overflowing, I began to circulate, looking for someone whose age suggested they might have known Reed in the Ryerson days. The group through which I made my way was an oddly festive one. Ed had let it be known that he didn't want to see anyone wearing a scrap of black at Reed's last party. The weather had continued mild and sunny, and both women and men had broken out their spring best. The swirl of pastel dresses and light suits made the rooms look like a garden party. When Barry Levitt sat down at the grand piano, and the bass player and the drummer took their places and began to play "Come Rain or Come Shine," the party took off. People had drinks, filled plates at the buffet, and visited. As the afternoon wore on, I exchanged pleasantries with many very pleasant people, but although a handful of them had known Reed Gallagher when he was at Ryerson, none of them displayed a shock of recognition when I mentioned Annalie Brinkmann's name.

There were more than a few famous faces in that room. For much of his career, Reed Gallagher had worked in the major media markets of New York and Toronto, and as I wandered, I saw some of our students in earnest conversation with people they could have known only by reputation. Success is a magnet, and our students were drawn to that small band of the elect who by anyone's criteria had succeeded: Americans who anchored television newsmagazines and supper-hour news; Canadians who wrote regular columns in Canadian newspapers that mattered or books that topped the best-seller list. But as had been the case since I was an undergraduate, the celebrities that no student could resist were the Canadians who had made it big in the U.S.A. When Ed Mariani went to the microphone to announce that the formal part of the afternoon was about to begin, he had to make his way through a group of J-school students jostling one another for a place in the circle that surrounded Peter Jennings. His manner held the implicit promise that, while the Holy Grail could only be found south of the border, it was waiting for their Canadian hands.

Ed didn't speak long, perhaps five minutes, but he touched on all the essentials: Reed Gallagher's integrity as a journalist, his commitment as a teacher, and his steadfastness as a friend. In closing, Ed said that perhaps the most fitting epitaph for Reed Gallagher could be found in H.L. Mencken's catalogue of the characteristics of the man he most admired: "a serene spirit, a steady freedom from moral indignation, and an all-embracing tolerance."

I glanced at the table near the windows where the Media class had congregated; from the rapt expressions on their faces, it was apparent that Mencken's words still had the power to inspire. It was an emotional afternoon for the J-school students. Ed concluded his remarks by inviting people to come up and share their memories. As Reed's friends and colleagues walked to the microphone, drinks in hand, to speak with tenderness about Reed Gallagher's passionate curiosity or his decency or his fearlessness, the students were visibly moved. They were young, and they had not had much experience of death; for many of them, the eulogies for a man who had been laughing with them the week before were an awakening to mortality. Linda Van Sickle was fighting tears, and when Val Massey put his arm around her, she buried her head gratefully in his chest. Then Jumbo Hryniuk, who was sitting next to Val, reached over and gently stroked Linda's hair, and I was struck again by the cohesion that existed among the students in that particular class.

As the afternoon wore on, I found myself tense with the effort to catch Annalie Brinkmann's characteristic lilt in the voice of one of the eulogists, but I never did, and by the time Ed Mariani joined me, I'd resigned myself to the prospect that Annalie was a no-show.

When the last speaker left the microphone and the jazz trio struck up "Lady Be Good," Ed leaned towards me. "Come on," he said, "there's someone I want you to meet. My one famous acquaintance. You'll like him – I promise." I followed Ed across the room, and he introduced me to a journalist from Washington, D.C., whom I recognized at once as a regular on the "Capitol Gang." Ed's friend had some riveting stories and some even more riveting gossip, and I was enjoying myself until I noticed that suddenly all the pleasure had vanished from Ed Mariani's face.

"What's the matter?" I asked.

Ed pointed towards the memorabilia table. "Look over there," he said.

Tom Kelsoe and Jill Osiowy were standing in front of the display. They had ignored Ed's edict about wearing black, and they were dressed in outfits that were almost identical: black lace-up boots; tight black pants; black shirts. Standing side by side, so close together that their bodies appeared fused, they seemed more like mythic twins than lovers. As soon as Tom Kelsoe saw me looking, he leaned down and whispered something to Jill. Then, in the blink of an eye, they were gone.

Beside me, Ed Mariani shuddered. "What do you make of that performance?"

"I don't know," I said, "but I'm glad it's over. I hate seeing Jill like that, and I'm not in the mood for a rerun of Tom as the suffering hero."

Ed's expression was bleak. "I'm never in the mood for

Tom as anything." Then he shook himself. "I'd better get over and thank people for coming. Barry used to be a camp counsellor and he says you should always kill an event before it dies on you."

It didn't take long for the Faculty Club to clear. The painful ritual of saying goodbye was over, and people were anxious to get back to the concerns of the living. When the last guest had left, the Faculty Club staff began clearing off the buffet table and carrying dishes towards the kitchen, and I went over to the memorabilia table and began to pack up.

As I worked, I remembered the warmth of the eulogies, and the question that had been troubling me since I'd heard about Reed's death floated to the top of my consciousness: given the fulfilment and the promise of his life, how could Reed Gallagher have had such a death? It was a question for a philosopher, and as I closed the last carton, I knew that it would be a long time before I had an answer. I was just about to tape up the box when I realized that I didn't remember putting in the photograph of Annalie and Reed. I checked, but the mahogany table was bare. It was obvious I was mistaken, that I'd wrapped the photo and absent-mindedly stuck it in the box with the rest. The prospect of unwrapping everything and checking didn't thrill me, but the idea of losing the picture appealed to me even less. Reluctantly, I pulled everything out and began to search. The photograph wasn't there.

I was baffled. There had been signed pictures of celebrities that were rare enough that they might have tempted a light-fingered mourner, but an old newspaper picture of Reed Gallagher and a girl nobody knew hardly qualified as a collectible. The only logical possibility was that someone had picked up the photograph, wandered off, and put it down somewhere else. I went back to the Faculty Club office and asked the manager, Grace Lipinski, to ask the cleaning staff to keep an eye out for the photograph. Then I went back to my repacking.

I'd just about finished when old Giv Mewhort came out of the bar. He was wearing a vintage white suit that would have been the very thing for one of Gatsby's parties, and his face was pink with gin and emotion. He picked up one of Reed's photos and said, " 'The noblest Roman of them all' – too famous doubtless to be cut." He smiled sardonically. "Although, from what I hear, Reed Gallagher hardly died a stoic's death. Still, he was the best of a sorry lot and a good man to drink with." He replaced the photograph carefully in the box. "I shall miss him."

The carton was unwieldy, and Barry and Ed offered to carry it down to the car for me. When we'd stowed it safely in the trunk, the three of us stood for a moment in the sunshine. I started to tell them about the missing photograph, but they both looked so weary I decided to give them a compliment instead.

"It was a terrific afternoon," I said. "I know how much work goes into making an event seem that effortless. You both did a great job."

Ed frowned. "I supposed you noticed that Kellee Savage wasn't there."

"I noticed," I said, "and I'm worried."

When I parked in front of our house, Angus was shooting hoops, and Leah was trying to teach Taylor how to skip rope. Benny, who, in repose, was beginning to look uncannily like a fox stole, was curled up on the step, watching.

When she saw me, Taylor held out her skipping rope. "Do you want a turn, Jo?"

"At the moment, I'd rather have my toenails ripped out one by one," I said, "but thanks for asking, and thank you, Leah, for giving T a hand with the womanly arts." Leah was wearing shorts, and I noticed she had a Haida tattoo of a fish on her calf.

I pointed to it. "Is that new?" I asked.

She smiled. "So new that even my parents haven't seen it."

"How do you think they'll take it?"

Leah grinned. "Oh, they'll probably want to rip my toenails out one by one, but my dad always says that as long as my grades are good, and my name doesn't end up on the police blotter, they'll adjust."

"Sounds like a wise father," I said, and I headed for the house. When I got to the porch, Taylor called out, "Don't forget. I've got a birthday party."

"Since when?" I said.

"Since Samantha gave me the invitation."

"I didn't see any invitation."

"It's been in my backpack all week." She squinted as if she was envisioning the missing invitation. "The party's from four-thirty till eight o'clock."

I looked at my watch. "Taylor, it's already twenty to five, you can't just . . ." I shrugged. "Never mind. Come on, let's drive out to Bi-rite. What does Samantha like?"

"Horses."

"Fine, we'll get her a flashlight."

Taylor ran to the porch, scooped up Benny, then came running after me. "Why are we getting her a flashlight?"

"Because they don't sell horses at Bi-rite. Now come on. Let's go."

Benny was not a happy passenger – he yowled all the way to the drugstore – but we did find a flashlight, a card that had a horse on it, and, on the clearance counter, a gift-wrap pack in what appeared to be the Old MacDonald motif. Close enough.

When we got back to the house, Taylor dumped our booty

from the drugstore on the kitchen table and began wrapping. I pulled some turkey soup from the freezer, put it on to heat, and started to make dumplings. Within five minutes, Samantha's present was ready, dinner was under way, and the phone was ringing. It was Alex, and I invited him to join us for dinner. Half an hour later, Taylor was cleaned up and at the birthday party, and Angus and Alex and I were sitting in candlelight eating soup. Once in a while, I just have all the moves.

As soon as he'd finished his second bowl, Angus jumped up. "I've got to go down to the library. Can one of you drive down with me?"

"Take your bike," I said. "We'd like a chance to talk. Besides, I'm too old to jump up from the dinner table."

"You're not old," he purred.

"Thank you," I said, "but you're still taking your bicycle."

After Angus left, Alex and I carried the candles and our coffee into the living room, and traded our news for the day.

When I told Alex about Reed and Annalie's picture disappearing, he raised an eyebrow. "You think someone stole it?" he asked.

"I don't know," I said. "Probably not. It's just that I was already on edge when I discovered the photograph was missing."

"On edge about what?"

"About all the things that don't make sense about Reed's death. Alex, I wish you could have been there this afternoon. That memorial service would have given you a very different perspective on the Reed Gallagher case."

Alex's eyes were troubled. "There is no case, Joanne. Not any more. It's all wrapped up. The death certificate will read 'accidental death due to cerebral anoxia' – lack of oxygen to the brain."

"You sound as if you don't think that's what he died of."

Alex shook his head. "Oh, I know that's what he died of. Splatter Zimbardo worked this case hard, and he's as good as they come. The question marks aren't with the pathology reports; they're with our part of the investigation. It's not that we haven't done our stuff. We have, and the physical evidence is solid: we've got the bottle of Dewar's that Gallagher was drinking from that night; we've got the tumbler he was using; we've got the glass ampoules that held the amyl nitrite he inhaled; we've got the seduction outfit he was wearing, and the hood he had on and the electric cord that was around his neck. Gallagher's fingerprints are exactly where they should be on every single item, and there were no signs of a struggle. All the evidence points in one direction."

"Except you don't believe the direction it's pointing in."

"I believe it. I just don't understand it." He leaned forward. "You know, Jo, cops don't talk much about the role imagination plays in police work, but it's essential. When an investigation into a sudden death starts moving in the right direction, it's like watching a movie playing backwards. You can see what happened in those last hours and, crazy as it sounds, you can feel the emotion. We've put all the pieces of the puzzle together on this one, but I still can't see the pictures. And I can't feel whatever it was that Reed Gallagher was feeling when he tied that cord around his neck." Alex picked up his coffee, took a sip, and turned to me. "Tell me about the memorial service, Jo."

As I told Alex about the tributes Reed's friends and colleagues had paid him, and about the sense of loss that had been in the Faculty Club that afternoon, his dark eyes never left my face. When I finished, he said, "Not a stupid man."

"No," I said, surprised. "Not at all."

"And yet that's what Zimbardo says Gallagher died of.

Stupidity. He says if Gallagher was into that scene, he should have known better than to use liquor with the amyl nitrite. The combination sends blood pressure through the floor. When Gallagher's blood pressure dropped, he must have blacked out. With the veins in his neck compressed from the cord, and the chemical stew from the poppers and the booze sludging his veins, and the hood, he was just too weak to fight for air. It was like drowning."

I felt my stomach lurch. At the Faculty Club that afternoon, Ed's graceful party had seemed to banish the ugliness of Reed's last hours in the rooming house on Scarth Street, but now the horror rushed back. All the show tunes and fond memories in the world couldn't negate the fact that Reed Gallagher had died a terrifying and humiliating death.

Alex put down his coffee cup. As if he'd read my mind, he said, "It's a hell of a way to die." Then he shrugged. "But that is the way it happened. Case closed."

"Alex, you just said this doesn't feel right to you. How can the case be closed?"

"I've told you, Jo. Because there's no evidence to suggest that Gallagher's death didn't happen exactly the way Zimbardo said it did, and the book says you can never prove a positive with negative evidence."

I thought of Kellee Savage. In police parlance, the fact that she hadn't shown up for Reed's memorial service would be negative evidence, but for me it was another piece in an increasingly unsettling puzzle.

"Alex, do you remember telling me that you were going to check out the last twenty-four hours in Reed Gallagher's life?"

"Sure. It's standard procedure. The report's in the file downtown."

"Would it be breaking any rules to let me see it?"

"No. The case is closed. There's public access, and you're part of the public." He raised an eyebrow. "Are you checking up on me?"

"No, I'm still trying to figure out what connection Kellee Savage, that student I told you about, had with all this. I was just curious about whether Reed Gallagher talked to her the day he died."

"Her name wasn't in the report, but Gallagher's secretary did say he had a meeting with a student that afternoon."

"Then the student's name should be in Reed's appointment book."

There was an edge of exasperation in Alex's voice. "Give me a little credit, Jo. I did ask. The secretary said Gallagher told her the meeting was private – the only reason he mentioned it at all was because he was leaving the office."

"Could I look at the report?"

He stretched lazily. "Sure, I'll make you a copy on Monday."

"Alex, could I get a copy tonight? I understand what you said about negative evidence, but there must be times when negative evidence points towards something being seriously wrong."

"You think this is one of those times . . . ?"

"I don't know. All I know is that the last time I saw her, Kellee was miserable, but she also said something like, 'I should have known it was too good to last.' When I tried to get her to tell me what she meant, she wouldn't, but I've found out since that Reed Gallagher chose her for the top internship the School of Journalism gives out. She's an ambitious young woman. If she knew she was in line for that placement, there's no way she'd be jeopardizing it by missing classes for a week. And there's no way she wouldn't have shown up at her benefactor's memorial service. Even if she didn't have feelings for him, there were a lot of important people there."

Alex looked hard at me. "Jo, why are you getting so involved in this now?"

"Maybe because I didn't get involved when I should have."

For a moment he was silent. Then he said wearily, "Bingo! Not getting involved when you should have is the one explanation I'm open to right now."

"Are things worse with your nephew?"

"Yeah," he said. He leaned forward and blew out the candles, but not before I saw the anger in his eyes.

The light was fading as Alex and I walked down towards the Albert Street bridge, but the night was mild, and the hot-shots who drive up and down Albert Street on weekend nights were out in force. When we got to the middle of the bridge, I leaned over the railing to check the ice on the lake. It hadn't started to break up yet, but there were dark patches, and the orange rectangles that warned of thin ice had been placed along the shoreline.

"Look," I said. "Signs of spring."

When Alex and I walked into the police station, some uniformed cops greeted him, but he didn't introduce me, and as we walked down the hall together, I tried to look innocent or at least bailable. I'd been in Alex's office only twice before; both times I had been there on official business, and my mind had not been on the decor. That night as I looked around, I thought how much it was like his apartment: neat, spare, and impersonal. Among the standard-issue furnishings, there were only three personal items. Taped to the inside of the door was a computer-printed sign: "Don't Complain. Expect Nothing. Do Something." A CD player and a case filled with classical discs were within easy reach on the shelf behind the desk, and on the wall facing the desk was a medicine wheel. An elder told me once that the medicine wheel is a mirror that helps a person see what cannot be seen with the eyes. I remembered Alex's anger when he spoke about his nephew, and I wondered what he'd been seeing in this mirror lately.

It didn't take long for Alex to bring Reed Gallagher's file up on his computer. I stood behind him as he hit the print key, and when the machine began printing, I leaned over and embraced him.

Alex put his hands over mine. "One of the first things they teach us at police college is to build defences against the appeal of attractive women."

"You're not on duty right now, are you?"

"No," he said, "I'm not." He stood up and kissed me. "And I'm glad I'm not."

While Alex checked through a stack of papers on his desk, I looked through his CDs: Mozart, Beethoven chamber music, Ravel, Bartok.

"I like your music," I said, "and I like your office. You seem to have figured out how to hang on to what matters and leave the rest behind."

Alex scrawled his initials on the last of the papers in the pile, then he looked up at me. "You're not often wrong, Jo, but you're wrong about this. I don't leave anything behind. And I don't know what matters. All I know is that if I can keep the externals of my life uncomplicated, I can function." He walked over to the coat hook and handed me my jacket. "Time to go," he said. Then he reached behind me and flicked the wall switch.

The wind had come up, bringing with it one of those sudden shifts in the weather that, despite precedent, always seem to come as a surprise. By the time we had walked from downtown to the Albert Street bridge, I was shivering.

"I'm always yelling at the kids about rushing the season," I said. "But I wish I'd worn a heavier jacket. I'm freezing."

Alex put his arm around me. "Better?"

"Much," I said. We were almost across the bridge when a half-ton, travelling in the same direction as we were, slowed down. The window was unrolled, and a beefy man in a ball cap leaned out and shouted something at us.

I felt Alex's arm stiffen.

"Is that somebody you know?" I asked. "I didn't hear what he said."

Alex didn't answer me, but when the light changed and we started across the street, he tightened his grip on my shoulder. The half-ton had stopped for the light, and as we crossed in front of it, the driver yelled again. The words were ugly and racist, but Alex wasn't his target. I was. "Hey, babe," he shouted, "when you're through fucking the chief, maybe you'd like to try it with a couple of white guys."

My reaction was immediate and atavistic. I broke away from Alex's hold and ran across to the sidewalk. In a heart-beat it was over. The light changed; the man in the truck cheered and yelled, "We'll be back for you, baby," and the truck drove off.

When Alex came to me, his eyes were filled with concern, but he didn't touch me. "Are you all right?" he asked.

"I'm fine." I laughed shakily. "Wow! As Mother Theresa would say, 'what a scumbag.'"

Alex didn't smile. I reached for his hand, but he drew away. "Alex, I'm sorry."

"Don't be," he said. "It was just a reflex. Getting out of the line of fire is instinctive."

"You wouldn't have done it."

He smiled sadly. "I couldn't have done it."

"Because you're not a coward."

"No," he said gently, "because I'm not white. That closes off a lot of options. Now, come on. You'd better get back."

He walked me to my door. "Come inside," I said. "I've got a few minutes before I have to get Taylor. I don't want to talk out here."

He came in and I closed the door and went to him.

"Alex, I'm sorry. I don't even know why I did that. I don't care what some idiot in a truck yells at me."

He took me in his arms and kissed me and, for a few moments, I thought I was home-free. Then he stepped away from me.

"That was just the first time," he said. "After a while, you'll care, Jo. Take my word for it. You'll care."

CHAPTER

8

My grandmother's maxim, "Morning is wiser than evening," has helped me through many troubled nights, but that Saturday morning daybreak didn't bring perspective. When the sun came up, I still didn't understand why I had run from Alex on the bridge, and I still had no idea how I was going to make things right between us again.

As the dogs and I started on our morning run, I ached with remorse and regret. The cold wind of the night before had disappeared as suddenly as it had come; the air was mild and the sky was luminous. Once, on a morning like this, Rose and Sadie would have been straining at the leash, but we were all growing older, less anxious to seize the day. As we started across Albert Street, I noticed shards of broken beer bottles at the spot where the half-ton had stopped the night before. I pulled the dogs out of the way, kicked the glass into the gutter, and headed for the lake. "Life's full of symbols," I said, and Rose, our golden retriever, looked up at me worriedly.

As we ran along the shoreline, I worked hard at thinking about nothing, but nature abhors a vacuum, and out of nowhere my mind was filled with images of my first-year Greek class: chalk dust lambent in the late-afternoon sun, muted sounds of traffic on Bloor Street, and a professor's voice, infinitely sad, "Antitheses are always instructive. Take, for example, the pairing of 'symbol,' literally, 'to put together,' and 'diabol,' the root of our word 'diabolic,' 'to throw apart.' Symbol suggests the highest uses of our language and thought; diabol their uttermost degeneration."

The amazing thing was that the diabolical hadn't happened sooner. Alex and I had been going out together since late November; we lived in a city in which racism was a fact of life, and yet this was the first time that a stranger had felt compelled to hurl words at us. November to mid-March. We had, I suddenly realized, been saved by a northern winter. Most of our time together had been spent indoors: at my place, talking, watching movies or playing games with the kids; later, when we became lovers, at his apartment listening to music, making love. When we did go out, for a run with the dogs or to cross-country ski or toboggan with the kids, we were bundled in the layers of Canadian winter clothing that mask distinctions of race, gender, and faith.

Julie and Reed's wedding had been our first real event as a couple, and it had been, in my mind at least, a disaster. For reasons that I would never understand, Julie had decided to make Alex her trophy. She introduced him all around, stumbling over his name, dimpling in mock-confusion and laughter. "Well, it's one of those wonderful native names, but you'll just have to say it yourself, Alex." She'd paraded him through the wedding reception, telling everyone that he was on the police force, cooing over how commendable it was that he was giving his people a role model, someone to look up to. I had been livid, but Alex had been sanguine. "She has to start somewhere, Jo. Maybe knowing me can make the new Mrs. Gallagher more open to the possibilities in the future."

But it hadn't happened that way. In public, Julie may have fawned over an aboriginal police inspector, but in private, when she had needed the services of a cop, she had made it painfully obvious that her personal officer of the law had to be white.

With her smiles and her oh-so-subtle double standards, Julie was the poster girl for polite bigotry, but as comforting as it was to demonize her or dismiss the cretin who had yelled at me the night before as a bottom feeder, they weren't the problem, and I knew it. I had lived in Regina all of my adult life and, to paraphrase Pogo, I had seen the enemy and he was us. I knew the language, and I knew the code: a whisper about the problems in the city's "North Central" area meant native crime; "the people," said knowingly, meant native people. I'd never used the code; in fact, I had prided myself on doing all the right things. Years ago, when an aboriginal couple had wanted to buy a house in our area, a petition had been circulated to keep them out, and I'd gone door to door urging my neighbours not to sign; when racist jokes were told, I walked out of the room; when my kids came home from school talking about "wagonburners" and "skins," I sat them down and talked to them about how words can wound. But until the night before, I had been drawing from a shallow well of liberal decency. In my entire life, I had never once been on the receiving end of prejudice, and the experience had been as annihilating as a fist in the face from a stranger. Alex was forty-one years old. That morning, for the first time, I found myself trying to imagine how it felt to withstand forty-one years of such blows.

When I got back to the house, it was 6:25. I dialled Alex's number. There was no answer, and I didn't leave a message. There was nothing to do but take refuge in my Saturday ritual. I plugged in the coffee, showered, dressed, made pancake batter, brought in the morning paper, and tried to concentrate on the politics of the day. At 7:30, I tried Alex's number again. He picked up the phone on the first ring.

"I was just about to call you," he said.

"Synchronicity," I said. "That has to be a good sign, doesn't it?"

He didn't answer, so I hurtled on. "Alex, I'm sorry about last night. I'm more than sorry, I'm ashamed. I don't know what made me run like that."

I could hear fatigue in his voice. "You didn't do anything wrong. That's what I was trying to tell you last night. There's no reason to blame yourself. You were in a lousy spot, and you reacted."

"But I reacted badly."

"The point is, you wouldn't have been in that spot if you hadn't been with me."

"Alex, I wanted to be on the spot with you. I still do. Come over. Please. Let's talk about this."

"I don't think so. When we're together, it's just too easy to lose sight of the facts."

"What facts?"

"The ones we've been ignoring. Jo, that guy in the truck last night was not an aberration. That's the way it is."

"I know that's the way it is. I just wasn't prepared. Next time, I'll be ready."

"Nobody's ever ready for it. You're talking to an expert witness now. It doesn't matter how many times that kind of crap happens, it's always an ambush. And defending yourself against it changes you."

"Alex, you're one of the best people I know."

For a moment, he was silent. Then he said, "And you're one of the best people I know, but, Joanne, you don't know what you're getting into here. And you don't know what you're getting your kids into. Angus and Taylor are great kids, Jo – so confident, so sure that all the doors are open for them and that when they walk into a room people can't wait to welcome them. I don't think you want that to change."

As soon as he mentioned my children, I felt a coldness in the pit of my stomach. "It wouldn't have to change," I said, but even to my ears, my voice lacked conviction.

"Maybe we should step back for a while," Alex said. "Take a look at where we're headed."

I should have told him that the last thing I wanted to do was step back. I should have said that the direction in which we were headed was far less important to me than the fact that we were headed there together. But those were the words of a brave woman and, once again, I came up short. "Maybe that would be best," I said. And that was it. We told each other to take care, and we said goodbye.

I replaced the receiver slowly. My eyes were stinging. From the moment Alex had called to tell me about Reed's death, it seemed as if everything I'd done had been wrong: I'd failed a student who'd turned to me for help. I'd pushed my best friend so hard that I lost her. I'd been fired from a job that I liked. I'd made a scene in a restaurant. Worst of all, I'd betrayed a man I cared about deeply, and now I'd lost him. When I reached for a tissue to mop my eyes, I knocked over my coffee cup, and then, because I figured I'd earned it, I swore.

"I thought there was a major penalty for using that word." Angus was standing in the kitchen doorway. His face was swollen with sleep, and he was wearing the black silk shorts his sister, Mieka, had sent him for Valentine's Day. He yawned. "What's up?"

My first impulse was to protect him. Then, remembering how much he liked Alex, I decided it would be best to tell him the truth. I poured us each a glass of juice, then my son and I sat down at the kitchen table and I told him about the incident on the bridge, and that Alex and I weren't going to be seeing each other for a while.

He was furious. "That's totally stupid," he said.

"I think so too," I said, "but Alex is worried about us – not just me, but you and Taylor. Angus, has my relationship with Alex ever caused any problems for you?"

"No. Alex is a cool guy. Hey, he taught me how to drive, didn't he? And he lets me drive his Audi." He patted my hand. "C'mon, Mum. Lighten up. And tell Alex to lighten up. If other people are having a problem because you two are going out together, it's their problem."

"And Leah feels the same way you do?"

"She really likes Alex. They're both kind of independent."

"And no one's ever said anything?"

He shrugged. "Some of the guys sort of wondered, but you know me, Mum. I've never cared what people say."

It was true. Of my four children, Angus was the one who cared least about the opinion of others. "Inner-directed" was the term my college sociology book used to describe people like my youngest son. Ian had valued the trait more than I did. For me, Angus's indifference to praise or punishment meant he'd been a difficult kid to raise, but Ian saw it differently. "It means," he'd said, "that when Angus is older, he won't be blown off course by every wind." Ian had been right. Angus wasn't easily blown off course. But he didn't take after me in that, and I knew it.

I picked up our juice glasses and took them to the sink. Angus followed me over, and gave me an awkward one-armed hug. "Mum, don't worry about other people. Do what you want to do." He leaned forward and peered into the bowl of pancake batter on the counter beside the griddle. "Now, is this all for you? Or can I score some?"

In a few minutes, Taylor and Benny joined us for breakfast, and the conversation drifted to Samantha's birthday party. By the time I had scraped the plates and rinsed them for the dishwasher, Taylor's story was still crawling inexorably towards its climax. It was a tale with tragic possibilities. The flashlight had been a hit, but Samantha kept shining it in everybody's eyes, and she refused to relinquish it when her mother asked her to. Finally, Samantha's mother said there'd be no cake until Samantha started behaving, and Samantha said she didn't care. Events at the party had reached a *High Noon* standoff when our phone rang.

As I went to answer it, Taylor called out, "Don't worry, I won't tell any more about the party till you're back."

When I heard Rapti Lustig's voice, my first thought was that somehow I was back on the political panel. Rapti was an assistant producer on Jill's show, and usually she was un-flappable, the calm at the eye of the storm, but that morning she sounded harried.

"Jo, I'm glad I got you. Listen, this is Tina in makeup's last show before the wedding, and we've just decided to have a little party for her after we wrap tonight. I know it's short notice, but we'd really like you to come." Then she added wheedlingly, "Please. For old time's sake."

"Rapti, it's only been a week."

"Maybe," she said, "but a lot of us here are already nos-talgic for the good old days. Jill's new man is a royal pain. Anyway, say you'll come. Tina likes you so much, and we're ordering from Alfredo's. I'll get a double order of eggplant parmesan. I remember you like it."

I thought about Alex and about the empty evening ahead. I hated showers, but I did like Tina. "I'll be there," I said.

"Great," she said. "Now, people are bringing gifts, but don't get anything cutesy. One of the techs had a kind of neat idea. He suggested a tool box and tools. Tina and Bernie are buying that old wreck on Retallack Street. They're going to be fixing it up themselves. What do you think of the idea?"

"I think it's inspired," I said. "No bride can have too many hammers."

"We'll see you at six then."

"But the show starts at six."

"That's why it's our best time to get everything ready so we can surprise Tina. Makeup's through by six, so Bernie's going to take Tina out for a drink and bring her back as soon as the show's over. If you come early, you can help me decorate the green room and stick the food around."

It seemed my penance was taking shape already.

Rapti was buoyant. "We'll have fun," she said. "We can get started on the wine. I have a feeling we're going to have to be totally blitzed to endure Tom's TV debut."

"You don't think he's going to be good?"

Rapti chortled. "I have a premonition that Jill's boyfriend is going to be a twenty-two-karat, gold-plated, unmitigated disaster."

I was smiling when I turned back to Taylor and her narrative. "Okay," I said. "Did Samantha back down, or did her mother have to shoot the cake?"

Our day filled itself, as Saturdays always did, with the inevitable round of lessons and practices and errands. Twice during the day I told myself I should try Kellee's number again; both times, I drew back before I even picked up the receiver. I felt fragile, like someone whose energy has been sapped by a long illness, and I was grateful for the Saturday routine that carried me along in spite of myself. Whenever I thought of Alex and what he must be feeling, I wanted to be with him, but the best I could do was hope that his Saturday had its own pattern of mindless, sanity-saving errands.

In the afternoon, Taylor came with me when I went to Mullin's Hardware in search of something glamorous in a tool box. Then we came home and I made chili while T sat at the kitchen table and worked on her sketches of Nanabush and the Close-Your-Eyes Dance.

After she'd been drawing for about thirty minutes, she called me over. "It's not working," she said. "I'm trying to make it seem real but not real, like the story. But I don't know how to do it." I sat down and looked at her sketch. To my eye, it was amazing. The section Taylor was working on was the one in which the hungry Nanabush tries to convince a flock of plump ducks that if they join him in a Close-Your-Eyes Dance, they'll have the time of their lives.

"See, it's all too real," Taylor said. "Alex's story wasn't like that."

When I looked again, I saw what she meant. "I have something that I think can help," I said. I went into the living room and came back with a book on Marc Chagall that Taylor's mother had given me years ago. I flipped through till I came to an illustration of the painting "Flying Over Town"; in it, a man and a woman, young and obviously in love, float above a village. The village is very real, and so, despite their ability to defy gravity, are the young couple. But the world they inhabit is not a real world; it is a world in which love and joy can carry you, weightless, above the earth. In "Flying Over Town," Chagall had created a fantastic world that transcended physical facts; it was the same world that came to life when Alex told Nanabush stories.

Taylor leaned so close to the book that her nose was almost on the page. Finally, she said, "Nanabush and the birds don't have to be on the ground." Then, without missing a beat, she ripped up the sketches she'd been working on for days, and started again.

Taylor was still at the table when I left for Nationtv at 5:15. I kissed the top of her head. "Chili's on the stove," I said. "Angus promises to dish it up as soon as his movie's over, and I'll be home in time to tuck you in."

For the first time in months, Taylor didn't even turn a hair when I announced I was going out for the evening. "Good," she said absently, and she went back to her drawing. Finally, it seemed I had done something right.

It was strange to walk across the park towards Nationtv on a Saturday evening without feeling a knot of apprehension about the show, but I was grateful that there was no hurdle I had to leap that night. I'd had enough. All I wanted to do was take deep breaths and look around me. In the park, the signs of an early spring were everywhere: the breeze was gentle; the trees were already fat with buds; the air smelled of moisture and warming earth. As I walked, my mind drifted. Once I had heard a poet describe the eyes of Hawaiian men as "earth dark," and I had thought of Alex's eyes. When I told him, he had laughed and said I was a hopeless romantic. Maybe so, but I had still been right about his eyes.

The first person I ran into when I walked into Nationtv was Tom Kelsoe. He was wearing jeans, a black T-shirt, and a black leather jacket. Very hip. My first impulse was to pretend I hadn't seen him, but if I ever wanted to reconcile with Jill, I was going to have to bite the bullet.

I smiled at him. "Break a leg," I said.

Tom Kelsoe looked confused. "What?"

"Good luck with the show," I explained.

"What are you doing here?" he asked. For once, his tone

wasn't rude. He seemed genuinely perplexed; somehow my presence had knocked him off balance.

"It's personal, not professional," I said. "There's a party for the woman who does makeup for the show. She's getting married."

"I guess Jill mentioned it," he said warily.

"Anyway," I said, "I'm glad I ran into you. I didn't get a chance to talk to you and Jill at the service for Reed yesterday."

I could see the pulse in his temple beating. "Who put that display by the door together?" he asked.

"I did," I said. "What did you think of it?"

He flinched. "It was fine." He checked his watch. "I'd better get down to the studio."

"Have you got another minute?" I said. "I need to ask you about Kellee Savage."

"What about her?"

"Apparently, Reed Gallagher had a very high opinion of her work. I wondered if you shared it."

Tom looked at me coldly. "She's a troublemaker," he said; then, without a syllable of elaboration, he headed for the elevators. Apparently I wasn't the only faculty member Kellee had gone to with her charges against Val Massey.

I was the first person at the party. The green room was empty, but somebody had brought in a clear plastic sack of balloons and made an effort to arrange the furniture in a party mode. Two tables had been pulled together to hold the food and drink, and the chairs had been rearranged into conversational groupings. The effect was bizarre rather than festive. All the furniture in the green room had been cadged from defunct television shows, so there was a mix of styles that went well beyond eclectic. I was trying to take it all in when Rapti Lustig came through the door.

Rapti was an extraordinarily beautiful young woman: whip-thin, with a sweep of ebony hair, huge lustrous eyes, and a dazzling smile. But as she looked around the room, she wasn't smiling.

"What do you think?" she said.

"I think it looks like the window of a second-hand furniture store," I said.

Rapti made a face. "A cheesy second-hand furniture store." She pulled a roll of tape out of her pocket and handed me a balloon. "Looks like we've got our work cut out for us."

It didn't take us long to get the balloons up, cover the tables with paper cloths, and set out the paper plates and glasses. Rapti had bought everything in primary colours and, despite its entrenched charmlessness, the room was soon as cheerful as a box of new crayons. At 6:00, Rapti gave the room a critical once-over, pronounced it not half bad, walked to the television set in the corner and turned on our show. When the theme music came up, and I heard the announcer's familiar introduction, I was grateful that I was sitting in the green room with Rapti. In less than a week, I had lost my job and my man. If I'd been sitting home alone, it would have been hard not to feel my life had become a country-and-western song.

Rapti handed me a glass of wine. "To good women and good men. May they find one another."

I pulled a chair closer to the television. "I'll drink to that," I said.

As I looked at the screen, the first thing I noticed was that Tom was still wearing his jacket. Black leather was perfect for Tom's "mad, bad, and dangerous to know" image, but before the show was five minutes old, it was apparent that Tom had given more thought to his outfit than to his homework. He made a lulu of a factual error about the powers possessed by the Senate, but when Sam Spiegel, who was a senator himself, nudged him gently towards the right answer, Tom was adamant. Glayne Axtell wasn't gentle. When Tom misrepresented what the leader of her party had said, Glayne said crisply, "It would help your case if you got at least one of your facts straight."

When the phone-in segment started, Tom's performance went from bad to worse. The callers, sniffing incompetence, made straight for Tom's jugular. As the show ended, and the screen went into its farewell configuration with the host in the centre and the panel members in their respective corners, Sam Spiegel interrupted the host's wrap-up to announce that he wanted to say goodbye to two colleagues who had been on the panel with him from the beginning, and whom he was certain the audience would miss as much as he did. When Sam was through, Glayne Axtell sent what certainly appeared to be genuine good wishes for the future to both Keith and me. Tom Kelsoe, isolated in his box on the lower left of the screen, gave an odd little salute to the camera but remained silent. By the time the credits finally rolled, I almost felt sorry for him.

Rapti jumped up and turned off the set. "That," she said, "was the worst hour of television since 'The Mod Squad' got cancelled. Jill's going to be livid." She shuddered theatrically, "This is going to be one tense little party."

It turned out Rapti was wrong, at least about the party. It was a very merry prenuptial event. No one made a hat with ribbons for Tina, and no one decided to break the ice with games. The wine was plentiful and the take-out from Alfredo's was sensational. The only person happier than Tina was Rapti. As she pushed in the red wheelbarrow that was her gift, Rapti glowed with the effects of good Beaujolais and triumph.

Even I had fun. My improved spirits were, I had to admit, due in no small degree to Tom Kelsoe's pitiful debut. My pleasure might have been mean-spirited, but I was revelling in it until, almost an hour after the party had begun, Jill Osiowy walked in the door. She was pale and tense, and as she picked up a bottle of wine from the refreshments table and poured herself a glass, I saw that her hands were trembling. She drained her glass, refilled it, and walked over to join the group who had clustered around Tina.

I had known Jill for over twenty years, and as I watched her trying to blend in with that carefree crowd, my heart ached for her. I was familiar enough with the structure of Nationtv to know that Jill had spent at least part of the past hour on the telephone being castigated by someone who didn't have half her talent but who picked up a paycheque twice as hefty as hers. I also knew that the most punishing criticism Jill would be subjected to that night would come from herself. She was in a miserable spot. She was passionate about two things: her work and Tom Kelsoe. Tonight the show that she had created, lobbied for, and nursed along had sustained a heavy blow because she had been foolish enough to offer it up to the man she loved.

I had long since stopped trying to fathom the choices other people made in their relationships. Perhaps, as an old friend of Ian's once told me, it was all a matter of luck; if you were born under a benevolent star, your loins would twitch for the right one. In my opinion, Jill's star had led her astray. If that was the case, maybe the time had come for me to stop sulking and let her know she was still very dear to me.

I walked over and put my arm around her shoulder. "How would you like to curl up with a large tumbler of single-malt Scotch?"

She smiled weakly. "That beats my last offer. The vice-president of News and Current Affairs suggested hemlock." Suddenly her eyes filled with tears. In the years I'd known her, I'd seen Jill deal with deaths, betrayals, and disappointments, but until that moment, I'd never seen her cry. "Can

I take a rain check?" she asked. "I think I just want to go home and go to bed."

"Of course," I said. "Any time."

Her voice was low. "Jo, I've missed you."

"Me too," I said.

The clock was striking nine when I walked in the front door. The kids were down in the family room. Taylor and Benny were curled up on the rug listening to the soundtrack from *The Lion King*, and Leah and Angus were huddled together on the couch, doing homework, or so Angus said.

"Fun's over, T," I said. "I'm back."

She rolled over and grinned.

"How's Nanabush?" I said.

"Better," she said, "but I don't want anybody to see it now until it's done."

"How was your party?" Angus asked

"Good," I said.

"How good could it be if you're home by nine o'clock?" Then he grinned. "Alex called."

"And . . . ?"

"And he said he was heading out to Standing Buffalo for a couple of days. He said if we need him, we can get in touch through the band office." My son looked at me expectantly. "Aren't you going to call him?"

"Angus, I think he meant we could call if there was an emergency."

Angus rolled his eyes, but for once he held his tongue. Leah came over and handed me a piece of paper. "You had another call," she said. "I hope you can read my writing."

"Let's see," I said. "Grace from the Faculty Club called. She found the picture. She wouldn't have bothered me at home, except she thought I seemed worried about it the other night, and I can call her at the club until ten p.m." I held the neatly written note out to Angus, who had long been known as the black hole of messages. "This is how it's done, kiddo. Note the inclusion of all pertinent facts."

"Hey," he said. "I've got a life."

I kissed him. "And you're now free to lead it. Thanks for staying with Taylor, you guys. Angus, don't be too late. Church tomorrow. It's Palm Sunday."

He groaned, grabbed Leah's hand, and headed for the door.

I turned. "Okay, Miss, bath-time for you." When he heard my voice, Benny arched his back and hissed. I looked him in the eye. "T," I said, "why don't you throw Benny into the tub, too. I think he's starting to look a little scruffy."

While Taylor ran her bath, I called Grace at the Faculty Club. Her news was unsettling. The cleaners had found the photo of Reed and Annalie when they'd emptied out the receptacle for used paper towels in the men's washroom. Grace had been puzzled. "It was just an old newspaper clipping," she said. "Why would anybody go to all that trouble?"

I told her I didn't know, but as I hung up I thought it would be worth a couple of phone calls to try to find out. On her message to Reed Gallagher, Annalie Brinkmann had said her area code was 416 – that was Toronto. I dialled Information. There was only one "A. Brinkmann" listed and, as the phone rang, I felt my pulse quicken. But it wasn't Annalie who answered; it was her husband.

Cal Woodrow was a pleasant and helpful man. When he told me that Annalie was in Germany attending a family funeral, he must have heard the disappointment in my voice.

"If it's urgent, I can get her to call you," he said. "She'll be phoning here Wednesday night."

"It's not urgent," I said. "But maybe you can tell me something. Did your wife know that Reed Gallagher died?"

"No," he said. "She'd left for Dusseldorf by the time the obituary appeared in the *Globe and Mail*. I didn't see any point in breaking the news to her when she called to tell me she'd arrived safely. Isn't it strange that after all this time . . . ?" He didn't complete the sentence.

"After all this time what?" I asked.

"No," he said decisively. "That's Annalie's story to tell or not to tell."

"Could I leave my number?"

"Of course," he said. "Annalie will be most interested in talking to anyone who knew Reed Gallagher."

It was 9:45 when I tucked Taylor in. She'd brought the Marc Chagall book to bed with her, and she asked me whether her mother had given me the Marc Chagall book because Chagall was her favourite or because she thought he was mine. It was the first time Taylor had talked about her mother openly, and her healthy curiosity about Sally made me optimistic. Maybe Ed Mariani was right in believing that art was the answer.

When I turned out Taylor's light, I went downstairs, made myself a pot of tea, and picked up my briefcase. I was tired, but I was too edgy for sleep. There were a couple of journal articles I had to plough through before class Monday, and this seemed as good a time as any to get started. When I pulled the articles out, I saw Kellee Savage's unclaimed essay, and I felt a sting of irritation. Present or absent, Kellee was a problem that wouldn't go away. On impulse, I picked up the phone and dialled her number. No answer. It was a south-end number, and it suddenly occurred to me that I could stop by her place on the way to church. There were only two weeks of classes left. If Kellee was lying low, watching Oprah and eating Sara Lee, it was time she shaped up and came back to school.

I went over to my desk, took out my box of index cards, and pulled out the section marked Political Science 371 – the Politics and the Media seminar. I flipped through, stopping to smile at Jumbo Hryniuk's. The students filled out their own cards with name, address, and reason for taking the course. Jumbo had stated his reason succinctly: "Because in this day and age, nobody can afford to be just a jock." Fair enough. When I pulled out Kellee Savage's card and checked her address, I felt as if a piece had suddenly dropped into place in the puzzle. Two addresses were listed. One was her Regina address, and the other was the one she called her home address: 72 Church Street, Indian Head, SK.

She had gone home. The obvious answer to her whereabouts had been there all along. I reached for the phone and dialled the Indian Head number. The phone was picked up on the first ring. It was a man's voice. "Kellee?" he said.

"No," I said. "But I'm looking for her. My name's Joanne Kilbourn. I teach Political Science at the university. Kellee's one of my students, but she hasn't been in class for a week. I wanted to get in touch with her; I was afraid that there might be a problem."

"My name is Neil McCallum," the man said. "I'm Kellee's friend, and that's what I'm afraid of, too." He spoke slowly, and there was a slight distortion in his pronunciations, as if he had a speech impediment. He paused, as if giving careful consideration to what he was about to say. Then he cleared his throat and made me an offer I couldn't refuse. "Maybe," he said, "we could help each other."

CHAPTER

9

By 2:00 on the afternoon of Palm Sunday, I was on my way to meet Neil McCallum. After church, I had driven over to Gordon Road and stopped by Kellee's apartment. The building she lived in was called the Sharon Arms. It was a new and charmless building, but it was handy to the university and secure. In the outside lobby, there was an intercom with the usual panel of buzzers opposite the appropriate apartment numbers and name slots. On the information card she had filled out for the Politics and the Media seminar, Kellee had written that she lived in apartment 425. The name slot opposite the buzzer for 425 was empty, but that didn't surprise me. All of Kellee's actions on St. Patrick's Day suggested she was a woman who saw herself surrounded by outside threats; it made sense that she wouldn't advertise her whereabouts. I had pressed Kellee's buzzer long enough to let anyone inside know that I wasn't a casual caller, but there was no response.

By the time I got home, I'd made up my mind. I was going to Indian Head. I called Sylvie O'Keefe and we arranged a double-header for her son, Jess, and Taylor: lunch with me at McDonald's, then bowling with Sylvie at the lanes at the Golden Mile.

As I drove east along the Trans-Canada towards Indian Head, I saw that the fields were already bare of snow. It wouldn't be long before farmers were back on the land, and the cycle of risk and hope would begin again. It took self-discipline not to turn off onto the road that wound through the Qu'Appelle Hills towards the Standing Buffalo Reserve and Alex Kequahtooway. Alex had been a strong and passionate presence in my life for months, and I ached for him. I turned on the radio, hoping to shift my focus. Jussi Björling was singing "*M'appari tutt'amor*" from *Martha*. There had never been a time in my life when I hadn't thrilled to Björling, but as Lionel, his despair as he recalled his former happiness and hopes cut too close to the bone. I leaned forward and turned him off in mid-aria.

For twenty minutes I drove in silence, yearning like a schoolgirl. A few kilometres outside Indian Head, I realized that, before I met Neil McCallum, I had to get a grip on myself. I pulled over on the shoulder, turned off the ignition, got out and looked at the prairie. The sky was clear, and the air was sweet. In the ditch at the side of the road, the first pussy willows were growing, and I broke off some branches to take back to Taylor. The catkins were silky and soft, and the woody, wet smell of the willows filled the car, a foretaste of April, with its mingling of memory and desire. An omen, or so I hoped.

I hadn't hesitated about promising Neil McCallum that I'd drive seventy kilometres to talk to him. His recital of the reasons behind his growing concern about Kellee had been a Euclidean line of facts that pointed in only one direction: something was terribly wrong. Neil and Kellee were the same age; they had grown up next door to one another, and, according to him, they had always been close. The year Kellee graduated from high school, her parents had been killed in a car accident, and she and Neil became even closer. When Kellee went off to university, he had helped pack her things; since then, he had been the one who had made sure her house was ready for her when she came home.

For three years, Kellee's routine, when she was at school, had not varied. She called Neil every Wednesday, she took the 6:20 bus back to Indian Head every other Friday, and she left on the 4:30 bus, Sunday afternoon. But on Friday, February 24, the pattern had changed. She had been home the weekend before; nonetheless, on the twenty-fourth she'd taken the bus back to Indian Head. She'd come home the next two weekends too; then on the weekend of March 17, her birthday, although she had told Neil to expect her, she hadn't shown up. He hadn't seen or heard from her since.

As I turned off the highway and drove over the railway tracks and down the tree-lined streets towards the centre of town, I found myself wondering about Kellee's best friend. The directions he'd given me were a model of clarity, but a certain thickness in his speech and a habit of hesitating before he answered a question and of waiting a beat between sentences made me curious.

Neil McCallum and his dog, a black bouvier who looked like a young bear, were waiting for me on the front lawn of his house. Neil was a little below medium height and stocky. He was wearing blue jeans, a green open-necked sweater, and a Saskatchewan Roughriders ball cap. Up close, I saw that the hair under his ball cap was brown and that he had the small almond-shaped eyes and distinctive mouth of a person with Down syndrome.

He watched as I got out of the car. Finally he took a step towards me. "You're Joanne," he said.

"And you're Neil." The bouvier was watching me intently. I walked over and held my hand out, palm up, for it to sniff. "What's your dog's name?" I asked.

"Chloe," Neil said. "A French name."

Chloe came over and nuzzled me, and I knelt down and stroked her back. "She's beautiful," I said.

For the first time since I'd arrived, Neil McCallum smiled. "I'm going to breed her pretty soon. I'll have puppies at the end of summer."

"Are you going to keep them?"

"Mum says one bouvier is enough. I'm going to sell them. To good homes."

"I always thought that breeding dogs would be a nice job."

He smiled mischievously. "If you breed dogs, you have to have another job. To pay for your dogs."

"I'll remember that," I said. "What's your other job?"

"I have three jobs," he said. "When it's winter, I help at the concession stand at the curling rink. I take care of the ice, too. When it's summer, I help at the concession stand at the ball diamond."

"Must keep you pretty busy."

"Busy's good," he said. "Let's look at Kellee's house."

Neil and Chloe started up the walk between his house and Kellee's, and I followed. The bungalows were almost identical: mid-sized, with white siding, shining windows, and well-kept grounds. On the face of each house were three wooden butterflies, poised as if for flight.

Neil pulled out a key-ring and opened Kellee's front door. The house had a slightly stale closed-up smell, but the living room was pleasant: uncluttered and filled with sunshine. There was a couch on the far wall, a couple of comfortable-looking chairs by the front window, and a television set in the corner. On top of the television were two framed pictures. Neil McCallum picked one up and handed it to me. "That's Kellee's parents."

The photograph had been professionally taken by one of those companies that set up in department stores and malls and offer great prices and your choice of three possible backgrounds. Kellee's parents had chosen spring in the Rockies. As they stood against the cardboard range of improbably pink-hued mountains, the Savages' smiles were open and their eyes were as grey and without illusion as a Saskatchewan winter sky. Good country people.

"Kellee's parents didn't have any other children?"

"Just her." Neil put the family photo back carefully in its place on the television, and handed me the other picture. "That's Kellee graduating from Indian Head High School. I went there too, but in a different class. I have Down syndrome."

"You seem to be having a pretty good life."

He shook his head. "Not any more. I'm too worried. My mum says Kellee's just busy. I don't think so. Something's wrong." Without explanation, he turned and walked away. After a second's hesitation, I followed him past the entrance-way and down a hall that seemed to lead to the bedrooms. Neil stopped in front of the only room with a closed door. The door had a lock, and he pulled out his key-ring and opened it. "Look," he said.

The room was unnaturally dark. When Neil turned on the light, I saw that thick drapes were pulled tightly across the only window. Someone had pushed an old oak filing cabinet and a heavy bookcase in front of the drapes. The result looked less like a decorating decision than a barricade. Flush against the wall to the left of me was the kind of computer table offices use; on top of it were a computer and a printer. Both were state-of-the-art, and both were pricey. To the right of the table was a small metal bookcase. It had three shelves of books, all with Library of Congress numbers on their spines. One shelf contained books I recognized as the reference texts Kellee had used in her essay on how the alternative press had been used to voice the concerns of prostitutes in our city's core area. A second shelf held books on the dynamics of groups, and the third held journals from the J-school library; all of them seemed to focus on the subject of journalistic ethics. Thinking of how old Giv Mewhort would have chortled at that oxymoron, I smiled to myself. I leafed through a couple of the J-school journals, hoping for a bonanza: a bus schedule or travel itinerary. All I could see were yellow Post-it notes marking various case studies and articles.

Neil was watching me with interest. "I don't like it here," he said.

"Neither do I."

Neil frowned. "It used to be nice."

"Before the window was blocked off."

He nodded. "I told her it wouldn't look good. But she said that's the way it had to be. So I put the furniture where she said."

"When did you and Kellee change the room?"

"The weekend she wasn't supposed to come home. That's when she bought the curtains too."

"To close out the light?"

"So nobody could see in." His brow furrowed. "Who would want to see in?"

I looked over at the barricade, and I felt a sense of oppression so overwhelming, I could barely breathe. Suddenly, I wanted to get out of that room. I turned to Neil. "Let's check Kellee's bedroom."

"For what?" Neil asked.

"I don't know," I said. "You might notice that something's out of place."

He looked puzzled. "How would I know? I never go in there."

Neil stayed in the hall while I went into Kellee's room. Everything seemed to be in order. A Care Bear and a Strawberry Shortcake doll rested side by side on a pink satin pillow at the head of the bed, and the girlish pink-and-white bedspread was smooth. A brush and comb were neatly aligned beside a wooden jewel box on the vanity. I opened the box. It was full of barrettes: butterflies, plastic ribbons, beaded sunbursts, feathery combs.

I closed the jewel box and turned back to Neil. "Did Kellee ever talk to you about friends she might want to visit?"

"I'm the only friend," he said gently.

"What about family?"

"She has an aunt."

"Here in town?"

"No, in B.C." Suddenly he smiled. "She sent Kellee a box of apples and I got half."

"Neil, do you think Kellee might have gone to visit her aunt?"

"She wouldn't go away," he said flatly.

I opened the closet door. Inside were clothes that I remembered Kellee wearing in class. Involuntarily, I stepped back.

Neil McCallum was watching my face. "You're scared too," he said.

"A little," I agreed. "But let's not panic. When I go back to Regina, I'll try Kellee's apartment again. I went there this morning, but she wasn't home."

"You should talk to Miss Stringer."

The name was familiar, but I couldn't place it. "Who's Miss Stringer?" I asked.

"Kellee's landlady."

"Neil, it's a brand-new apartment building. Those places don't have landladies."

Neil's voice rose with frustration. "It's not new. It's a dump. Kellee said so. And Miss Stringer lives there."

"On Gordon Road?" I said.

Neil shook his head impatiently. "You went to the wrong place," he said. "Gordon Road is where she lived before." He pulled a small black notebook from the pocket of his shirt, and thumbed through it. "This is where she lives now," he said. "She wrote it in herself. So it's right."

I took the book from him and read:

> Kellee Savage,
> 317 Scarth Street,
> Regina S4S 1S7

For a moment, I didn't grasp the significance of the address. When I did, my pulse began to race. It was the address of the house in which Reed Gallagher had died.

When I drove back to Regina, Kellee Savage's graduation portrait was in a Safeway bag on the seat beside me. I knew the picture would be helpful if I was going to make inquiries about Kellee's whereabouts, but Neil hadn't wanted to part with it. He told me that Kellee didn't like having her picture taken, and that he liked having a photograph of her where he could see it every day. I promised him that I would take good care of it, and he promised me that he wouldn't let anybody else into Kellee's house and that he'd be careful.

Neil and Chloe had walked out to the car with me. Before I left, Chloe gave me a final nuzzle, and Neil reached out as if to hug me, before he drew back and settled for a smile. "One more promise," he said. "No stopping looking until we find her."

"Okay," I said.

He looked at me intently. "You have to say it."

"All right," I said. "No stopping looking until we find her."

It was a little before five when I pulled up in front of the house on Scarth Street, picked up the Safeway bag with Kellee's photograph, and got out of the car. Alma Stringer was out on the porch, knocking down cobwebs with a broom. When Alex had interviewed her the day she found Reed Gallagher's body, he had characterized Alma as a tough old bird. As I watched her darting at the cobwebs with her broom, her arms and legs winter-white and pencil-thin, her scalp pink through her sparse and fading yellow hair, I thought there was something chicken-like about her. When she saw me, she raised her broom aggressively. Alma, it seemed, was more banty rooster than mother hen.

As I introduced myself, I tried to look pleasant and non-threatening. I must have succeeded, because before I had a chance to explain what I was doing on her grassless lawn, she had apparently made up her mind that I wasn't worth her while and gone back to her cobwebs.

I climbed the stairs and stepped in front of her. "I won't take much of your time," I said.

She gave the underside of an eavestrough an expert flick. "You won't take none of my time," she said.

I took the photograph of Kellee out of the bag and held it out to her. "I'm looking for this young woman. She's one of your tenants."

She looked at the portrait without interest. "Number six on the main floor."

"Is she there now?"

"No."

"Do you remember when it was that you saw her last?"

"What's it to you?"

"No one's seen her around for a while. I'm worried."

"You her mother?"

"Her teacher."

"That's a break for you. Popping a kid that ugly wouldn't give a mother much to be proud of." She chuckled at her witticism. Her laugh was a smoker's laugh, and its husky roughness seemed to act as a spur. She reached into her back pocket, pulled out a pack of du Mauriers, and lit up. As the smoke hit her lungs, she closed her eyes in satisfaction. I tried to take advantage of the new and mellow mood.

"Could you just give me a moment of your time, please? If you can't remember when you saw Kellee last, maybe you can remember a visitor she had. Anything, Miss Stringer. What you know may not seem important, but . . ."

She narrowed her eyes. "How did you know my name?"

"I'm a friend of one of the detectives who investigated the murder."

She inhaled deeply, then pivoted on her heel so she could be sure that the smoke she blew out hit me full in the face. "Why don't you get your friend, the detective, to answer your questions?"

"You've lived in the house all along. He doesn't have the perspective you have."

"Yeah, but he also don't have my problem." She looked at me expectantly.

"What is your problem?"

"My problem is that it's almost the end of the month. For your friend on the police force, that's not a problem. Cops can count on getting that monthly paycheque of theirs whether they've earned it or not. I can't count on dick. All I've got is those rents." Alma looked at me craftily. "Maybe you'd like to take care of number six's rent for her."

"No," I said.

Alma took a last deep suck on her cigarette, then, in a movement so effortlessly perfect that I knew she must have done it a thousand times, she drew her arm back and pitched her cigarette so that it sailed across her yard and hit the street beyond her property. "The next time you want to talk to me," she said, "make sure you got a rent cheque in one hand and a damage deposit in the other."

As I walked back to my car, I realized I hadn't eaten since breakfast. I was tired and hungry and discouraged, but Neil McCallum had extracted a promise from me. Police head-quarters were on Osler Street, less than ten minutes away from Alma's; not far at all for a woman who had given her solemn word that there would be no stopping until she found Kellee Savage.

At the station, a downy-cheeked constable directed me to the office that dealt with reports of missing persons. As I turned down the corridor he'd indicated, I caught a glimpse of dark hair and a familiar grey jacket disappearing through an open door. It was Sunday night. Alex might have come back from Standing Buffalo early. Like an adolescent with a crush, I stood in the hallway, watching the door, knees weak with hope, while police and civilians walked by. Finally, the dark-haired man in the grey jacket emerged. I saw that he was a stranger, and I cursed Alex for not being there and myself for being so stupid that I believed he would be.

The name of the officer I talked to in Missing Persons was Kirszner. He was polite, but he pointed out the obvious: many people lived in the rooming house where Reed Gallagher had been found dead, and all of them were free to come and go as they wished. Then, echoing Alex, he sug-gested that the salient fact to consider about Kellee Savage was not that she lived on Scarth Street, but that she was a twenty-one-year-old student who was two weeks away from final exams.

As I walked along Osler Street to my parking place, I tried to buy the officer's explanation. What he had said was both reasoned and reassuring, but he hadn't felt the fear in that barricaded room in Indian Head. I had, and I knew in my bones that his explanation was wrong.

When I got home, Leah and Angus were in the kitchen making a meal that seemed to involve every pot and utensil we owned, but I didn't mind because I was ravenous and whatever they were making smelled terrific.

"What's on the menu?" I asked.

"Pot roast," Leah said. "And a salad and potato pudding and, for dessert, honey cake."

"I didn't know you could cook," I said.

She raised a double-pierced eyebrow. "Actually, what you're getting tonight is my entire repertoire. My grandmother says every woman should know how to cook one meal that will knock people's socks off. This is the one she guarantees."

"Does your grandmother live close by?"

"As close you can get. She lives with us. So does my great-aunt Slava."

"Slava." Taylor said, rolling the word appreciatively on her tongue. "That's a nice name."

Leah wrinkled her nose. "I think it sounds kind of indentured myself, but the Russian meaning is nice – 'glory.' Slava's my grandmother's sister. Anyway, we all live together. It's like something out of Tolstoy."

"You're lucky," I said.

Leah looked thoughtful. "Most of the time, I guess I am."

We made an early evening of it. Leah's grandmother was obviously no slouch; the pot roast knocked our socks off. After we'd cleared away the dishes, Angus walked Leah home, and Taylor and Benny went to the family room to watch television. I poured myself a glass of Beaujolais, sat down at the kitchen table, and thought about the day.

I was deep in the puzzle of the barricaded room in Indian

Head when Julie called. She asked about my family, her house, and her mail. Her questions were perfunctory, and her voice was flat and spiritless. Her lack of interest in my family didn't come as a surprise, but her listlessness about her own affairs was disturbing. Come rain or come shine, the one subject that had always engaged Julie's complete and fervent interest was Julie.

She seemed anxious to get off the phone, but I cut short her goodbyes. "Wait," I said. "There's something I need to know. Did Reed ever mention a student named Kellee Savage to you?"

Suddenly, the torpor was gone, and Julie was hissing, "You mean she was a student?"

I was taken aback. "Yes," I said. "As a matter of fact, she's in one of my classes. Then Reed did mention her."

"No," she said, and her voice was low with fury. "He didn't mention her, but I found out about her."

"What did you find out?"

"For God's sake, Joanne. I thought you were supposed to be so sensitive. You know the answers to these questions or you wouldn't be asking them. My husband was having an affair with that . . . *student*."

"With Kellee? What on earth made you think that?"

"The usual. We hadn't been married two weeks before he started going out nights – no explanations, of course, except when I pressed him, then my very original new husband gave me every cliché in the adulterer's handbook: he had to 'go back to the office' or he had 'a downtown appointment.' The Tuesday before he died, Reed's 'downtown appointment' called our home. We were having dinner, and I answered the phone in the kitchen. He ran down to our bedroom to take the call, but when he picked up the receiver, I didn't hang up. Joanne, I heard that woman telling my husband that she had to see him that night. And I heard him call her 'Kellee.'"

When he left the house, I followed him. Can you imagine how humiliating that was? Married three weeks and following my husband down back alleys, like some slut from a trailer court trying to get the goods on her lover. But I'm glad I did it. I needed to know the truth. I saw him go into that place on Scarth Street. After that, it was easy enough. I just checked the room numbers on the mailboxes in the front hall. The occupant of room six was 'Kellee Savage.' Isn't that just the dearest little name?" Julie's composure broke. "Kellee Savage," she sobbed. "She'd even stuck a goddamned happy-face sticker on her mailbox."

"Julie, listen to me. Please. I just can't believe Reed would have been having an affair with Kellee Savage."

Her voice was sulky. "Why not?"

"Because Kellee has . . . she has these physical problems. I think something must have happened before she was born. Whatever it was, she's terribly misshapen, and her face is . . . it's painful to look at."

"And you don't think Reed could have . . . ?"

"No," I said. "I don't. I don't think Reed could have been involved with Kellee."

"He kept saying he loved me," she said weakly. "I just didn't believe him."

She sounded bewildered, as, of course, she had every right to. In six weeks, fate had cast her in the roles of proud bride, betrayed wife, and embittered widow. It was hardly surprising that she had lost her sense of self.

"Julie, maybe it's time you thought about coming back here," I said. "When Ian died, it helped a lot being in a place where we'd been happy together."

My intention had been simply to give Julie an option, but she pounced on my suggestion. Five minutes later, it was all settled. Julie Evanson-Gallagher was coming home.

The next morning when I got to the university, Ed Mariani was already in my office. He was wearing a white turtleneck and a suede overshirt that I didn't remember seeing before.

"Nice threads," I said. "What do they call that colour."

"Edam," he said gloomily. He patted his belly. "You'll notice that I've graduated to a garment that's designed to cover a multitude of sins. On a brighter note, while I was shopping for my maternity top, I bought us a teapot." He held up a Brown Betty. "I know old Betty here isn't glamorous, but she does the job better than those pricey little beauties at the boutiques. I hope you don't mind."

"I don't mind," I said. "I could use a cup of tea."

"Kettle's plugged in," Ed said. He looked at me closely. "Joanne, is there something wrong?"

"I don't know," I said. "I just know that I'm starting to get scared."

I pulled the student chair closer to the desk and told him everything I'd learned the day before. When I finished, his expression was sombre. "Joanne, are you thinking what I'm thinking?"

"I'm not thinking anything," I said. "I'm absolutely in the dark about this."

Ed sighed heavily. "I wish I was, because what I've come up with isn't very appealing. But I don't know what else it could be. Look at the facts. In the weeks before he died, Reed lied to his wife fairly consistently about where he was. She followed him and discovered him going into Kellee Savage's room. The next thing we knew, Reed Gallagher chose Kellee for the prize internship, a position for which at least a half-dozen people are better qualified than she is."

"Surely, you're not suggesting an affair?"

"No," he said. "When Reed and I went to the Faculty Club the night before he died, he was not a man in love. He was confused and bitter and disillusioned." Ed paused, and when he spoke again, his voice was troubled. "Joanne, I think Kellee Savage was blackmailing Reed. I think she stumbled on something about him, and whatever it was gave her sufficient leverage to get the *Globe and Mail* internship."

"And made Reed so sloppy about his sexual practices that he died," I said.

"Or didn't care if he died. It makes sense, doesn't it?"

"I don't know," I said. "It's all so incredible." But the more I thought about it, the more credible Ed's theory seemed. As well as explaining why Kellee Savage had gone to the top of the internship list when other candidates were better qualified by far than she, it pointed to a logical motive for Kellee's decision to drop out of sight on the night of March 17. It also, I realized with a start, put my promise to Neil McCallum in a troubling new light. If Kellee Savage had dropped out of sight, not because she was embarrassed about getting drunk and making a fool of herself, but because she was a blackmailer who had pushed her victim so hard he hadn't cared whether he lived or died, she might not want to be found.

Ed poured boiling water into the Brown Betty. "Well," he asked, "what are we going to do?"

"I think this may be case of 'she's made her bed, now let her lie in it,'" I said. "Neil McCallum told me Kellee has an aunt in B.C. Kellee's probably out there right now, trying to figure out her next move. I don't think we should do anything."

And that's what I did. My conversation with Ed took place Monday morning. Kellee didn't show up for the Politics and the Media seminar at 3:00, and I had to admit I was relieved. It had been ten days since I'd last seen her, ten days of remorse and anxiety. The possibility that Kellee was manipulator not victim was seductive, and I grabbed it.

I was late picking Julie up from the airport. She was on the 5:30 flight, but when I went to my car, I noticed someone had left the side gate open, and the dogs had made a break for it. Rose and Sadie were of an age where the delights of the larger world had paled, but by the time I found them sunning themselves on the creek-bank and dragged them back to the house, it was 5:35.

When I finally got to the airport, Julie's plane had landed, and she was already at the luggage carousel. As soon as she saw me, she threw her arms around me. The gesture was uncharacteristic, but there was a lot that was uncharacteristic about Julie that day. For one thing, there was a stain on her trenchcoat; for another, her roots were showing. The veneer was chipping away, but, in an odd way, she was more attractive than I had ever seen her. Her eyes were shining, and her cheeks were flushed. It was as if she was feverish with relief that Reed Gallagher hadn't been unfaithful to her after all.

The graduation photograph of Kellee Savage that Neil McCallum had let me take home was still in its Safeway bag on the front seat of the car. Julie had to move it to the dashboard before she could slide into her seat. I told her to take a look, and when she did, she became even more animated. After she'd clucked pityingly over Kellee's deformities, she started floating theories about why Reed might have been visiting Kellee at the rooming house so late at night. All of Julie's scripts cast her husband in the role of the caring and humanitarian professional who was going the extra mile for a needy student. I didn't say a word. Julie was obviously delighted with her fantasies. It seemed cruel to suggest that, asked to rank the possible reasons a forty-eight-year-old man would visit a twenty-one-year-old woman late at night, most sane people would put altruism at the bottom of the list.

When I dropped Julie at her condo on Lakeview Court, she invited me in for a drink. I declined. I was sick of other people's problems. As soon as I got home, I ordered pizza, took a hot shower, and got into my old terrycloth robe. It was Academy Awards night. I had seen three movies that year. Taylor had picked them all, and none of them featured flesh-and-blood actors. All the same, I knew that sitting in the family room with the dogs at my feet, Taylor and Benny sleeping beside me on the couch, and Angus braying loudly at the stupidity of the Academy's choices, beat my other options that night by a country mile.

On Wednesday night, Neil McCallum called. From the time I'd talked to Ed Mariani, I'd been filled with guilt every time I walked by a telephone and thought of Neil. The truth was I simply didn't know what to say, so I had taken the coward's way out and avoided making the call. Now Neil had taken matters out of my hands.

He waited until 6:01 to phone, but even at reduced rates, Neil didn't get his money's worth. As I always do when I'm flustered, I talked too much. I gave him a detailed account of my encounter with Alma Stringer. He laughed when I told him how much Alma reminded me of a cranky old chicken, but he became vehement when I told him about Alma's refusal to give us any information about Kellee unless we paid her.

"We can pay her," Neil said. "I've got money. I can send it on the bus. All you have to do is pick it up and take it to Alma. Then she'll tell us about Kellee. It's simple."

"It's not simple. You can't always trust people to do what they say they're going to do." Remembering the promise I had made to Neil, the words resonated painfully. He deserved to know the truth, or at least Ed Mariani's theory about what the truth might be.

"I need to talk to you about Kellee," I said. "There's a chance she's gone away because she's done something wrong."

"She wouldn't do anything wrong," Neil said angrily. "Kellee's my friend. I don't want to hear this."

For the first time since Neil called, I found myself wishing we were face to face. Over the telephone, it was impossible to tell if he was defending Kellee out of conviction or bravado. In the long run, I guess it didn't matter. Neil believed in Kellee; it seemed both pointless and cruel to disillusion him before disillusion became inevitable.

Before we said goodnight, Neil said he was sorry if he'd been rude and he thanked me for helping him look for Kellee. When I hung up the phone, I felt like hell. Neil's trust in me was absolute, but it seemed that, once again, he'd put his money on the wrong horse. He wasn't having much luck with the humans in his life. I was glad he had Chloe.

Life wasn't all grim that week. The next weekend was Easter, and my daughter Mieka, her husband, Greg, and my son Peter were coming home. Angus and I made up the beds, got out the new bath towels, and brought the leaves for the dining-room table in from the garage. Taylor and I drove out to the nursery and bought lilies and a pot of African violets the colour of heliotrope for Mieka and Greg's room. As I made up the list of food we'd need for the holiday, I could feel, despite everything, the darkness lift. It was Easter, the time, as the Prayer Book says, to be "inflamed with new hope."

When Alex called Thursday morning, I could feel the flames of new hope leaping. It was early when he called, so early, in fact, that I was still in bed. Hearing his voice in my bedroom brought back memories of other mornings:

mornings after the kids had gone to school, when Alex would come over and we'd make love and lie in bed listening to the radio and feeling warm and blessed.

"I'm missing you," he said.

"I'm missing you, too," I said. "The room is full of sunlight, and the paperwhites in the window are blooming. If you give me five minutes, I can put on Mozart, slip into something erotic, and send the kids to school without any breakfast."

"I really do miss you, Jo," he said.

"Then come back."

"It wouldn't work the way I am now." I could hear his intake of breath. "Joanne, I called to tell you I'm going away for a while."

"Why?"

"I don't know. Partly because Eli – my nephew – needs more help than I can give him. There's an elder up at Loon Lake who helped me through a bad patch once. I think he might be able to help Eli." Alex paused, then he said quietly. "And I think he might be able to help me. I seem to have been making a lot of lousy decisions lately."

"Lousy decisions don't need to be carved in stone."

"Maybe Loon Lake will make me as sure of that as you seem to be."

"Alex, I'm glad you called."

"So am I," he said.

After I had showered and dressed, I felt so grateful that I thought it was time to get a few karmic waves going. As soon as I got to my office, I called Jill and invited her for Easter dinner. She said she and Tom had plans, but she sounded friendly, and when she heard Mieka and Peter would be there, she was wistful. "Don't let them go home without seeing me," she said. Jill had known Mieka and Peter almost all of their lives, and they had always enjoyed her as much as she enjoyed them. I promised they'd get in touch. Then I took a deep breath and dialled Julie Gallagher's number. To my surprise, she said she'd be delighted to join us. As I hung up, I sensed that we were, at long last, heading into the final act. If we were lucky, the play that had begun as a tragedy might end up like a Shakespearean comedy, with all past cruelties forgiven, all misunderstandings corrected, and all broken relationships mended.

When I got ready to leave the office late Thursday afternoon, I came upon the copy of *Sleeping Beauty* Kellee Savage had thrust into my hand a thousand years ago. Remembering Kellee's misery that afternoon, I felt a stab of remorse, but if Ed Mariani's reading of the situation was right, wherever Kellee was she should be feeling remorse, not evoking it. I flipped through the book in my hand, and noticed that it had been checked out of the Education library. I might not be able to exorcise Kellee from my consciousness, but at least I could get rid of a painful reminder of her.

The staff at the Education library were in the process of closing up. The next day was Good Friday, and with so many students out of town, there was little reason to stay open. I recognized the young woman on the desk as an old student of mine, Susan something-or-other. Not smart, but pleasant, and very cute: a mop of curly hair, big brown eyes, and a quick smile. She made a face when she saw me.

"You're not going to be long, are you? I'm hoping to get on the road before dark."

"Going home?" I asked.

"You got it," she said. "Three whole days with no texts, no assignments, and no research papers."

"I won't hold you up," I said. "I'm just returning a book." I slid the *Sleeping Beauty* across the desk to her.

She glanced at the cover. "I love fairy tales." She gave me

a sidelong glance. "Do you still believe in happy endings?"

"Depends on which day you ask me," I said. "Today, I do."

"Me too," she said, and she took the book and started to place it on a trolley for re-shelving. Out of nowhere, Kellee's face flashed into my mind.

"Susan," I said. "That book wasn't mine. Actually, I'm not sure who did take it out. Could you check to see whose card it's on?"

She shrugged. "Sure," she said. "That's a real no-brainer – my specialty." She punched something into the computer, watched the screen, and then turned to me with a grin. "Maybe we women aren't the only ones who believe in happy endings. You're not going to believe who checked this book out."

"Who?"

"Marshall Hryniuk."

"Jumbo?" I said.

"The Guzzler himself," she said.

CHAPTER

10

That Easter weekend everything was eclipsed by my daughter Mieka's news that she was expecting a baby in September. She and Greg had planned a dramatic announcement; they even brought down a bottle of Mumms so we could drink a toast to the future. But Mieka had never been good at secrets. Friday night, Greg had scarcely turned off the ignition when Mieka raced up our front walk, burst through the door, threw her arms around me and whispered, "How do you feel about being a grandma?"

Her trenchcoat was open, her dark blond hair was flying out of its careful French braid, and she had a milk moustache from the Dairy Queen shake she was still holding in her hand, but I knew I had never seen my daughter so happy. She was twenty-two. She had dropped out of university in the middle of her first year, taken the money Ian and I had set aside for her education and opened her own catering business. I'd fought her decision hard, and in the way of nettled parents everywhere, predicted that she'd rue the day, but her catering business in Saskatoon was thriving, her marriage was a happy one, and now she was joyfully pregnant. She had every right to say "I told you so." Luckily for both of us, Mieka had apparently decided to bite her tongue.

My son Peter was too thin and too pale, but I knew what the problem was, and I knew there was nothing I could do to help. From the time he was little, he had wanted to be a veterinarian, but he had no more aptitude for the sciences than his father or I had had. The genetic pool he needed to draw from to get a degree in vet medicine was shallow, but Peter was determined, and so year after year he soldiered away. I watched him grab a football and follow his brother outside for a game of pick-up and wished, not for the first time, that babies came with individual sets of instructions: "Teach this one to ease up on himself"; "Give this one the chance to find her own way."

I didn't need a set of instructions to understand Taylor's problem that weekend. As talk about the new baby and about a past that she hadn't been part of claimed our attention, Taylor became first clingy, then bratty. "Pay attention to me," Angus said witheringly as his little sister whirled giddily around the table where Mieka and I were poring through a book of baby names.

We all tried to reach Taylor. Mieka showed her the kiska and dyes she'd brought from Saskatoon and offered to teach her how to make Ukrainian Easter eggs. Peter admired her art and told her that in the summer he'd help her transform the sunroom into a studio where she could get some serious painting done. Angus told her to shape up or ship out. Nothing seemed to help. Saturday night I awoke to discover Benny on my pillow with his purr mechanism on full throttle, and Taylor beside him, eyes filled with tears, lower lip trembling.

I stroked her hair. "T, can you tell me what the problem is?"

She made a sound that was half sob, half hiccup. "No," she said, miserably.

I put my arms around her. "How about building a box and putting that problem in it till the morning?"

"It'll still be there."

"I know, but maybe spending a little time in a box will make it smaller."

"Jo, would it be okay if I stayed here tonight?"

I kissed the top of her head. "Absolutely," I said. "But you and I have a lot to do tomorrow, so you're going to have to ask Benny to put a silencer on that purr of his."

As it always does when life is at its best, the time went too quickly. Easter dinner was planned for mid-afternoon. Julie Gallagher arrived early with two mile-high lemon pies. She was wearing an outfit in jonquil silk, her hair was back in its careful coif, and her makeup was fresh. She looked like the old Julie, but there was uncertainty in her eyes, and as she followed me into the dining room her manner was diffident.

"I thought I'd come early, so I could give you a hand now and leave you and your family to visit after we're through eating."

"You're welcome to stay as long as you want to, Julie."

She set the pies carefully on the sideboard. "I know that, and I appreciate it, believe me. But this is a family occasion, and I'm not family. I'm not even a friend."

"You could be," I said.

"Could I?" she asked. "You'd have to forget an awful lot, Joanne."

"I'm fifty years old, Julie. My memory isn't nearly as sharp as it used to be."

She gave me a quick, dimpled smile. "Thank God for that," she said. "Now what can I do to help?"

Julie was quiet during dinner, but it was obvious she was

enjoying herself. Besides, we'd already had our conversation. When she'd arrived, the big kids were in the park with Taylor, throwing around Frisbees. Julie and I had had twenty minutes alone together; oddly enough, we had used them to talk about love. Our conversation was surprisingly light-hearted, but one of Julie's reminiscences was poignant. She told me that on their wedding night, Reed had said his greatest dream was to grow old with her. Then she had touched my arm and said how grateful she was to me for allowing her to believe again that when Reed died, that was still his greatest dream.

True to her word, Julie left early, but, as I watched her get into her car, for the first time since I'd known her I was sorry to see her go. Peter left early too. He had a lab test the next day, so he caught a ride back to Saskatoon with a friend as soon as we'd finished dessert. After Peter left, Greg started clearing the table.

"It's been great, Jo." he said. "But we'd better take off, too. Mieka's got a lunch for fifty oil guys tomorrow, and I've got a squash game with a client at seven a.m." He grimaced. "Sounds like a page out of Lifestyles of the Young and Upwardly Mobile, doesn't it?"

"Store up those golden memories," I said. "Come September, the oil guys and squash games are going to get nudged aside for a while." I turned to my daughter. "Mieka, I can help Greg get organized for the trip back. Why don't you drive over and tell Jill about the baby? I promised her you'd stop by. You don't have to stay – just a quick flying trip."

Jill's apartment was on Robinson and 12th, an easy five-minute drive from my house, but even so, I was surprised at how quickly Mieka was back, and at how downcast she seemed.

"Nobody home?" I said.

She shook her head. "No, they were home. It just wasn't a good time for a visit." She slipped her coat off and sat down at the kitchen table. "It was so weird. I knocked and knocked, but nobody answered. Finally, a man came to the door. He introduced himself as Tom Kelsoe, Jill's boyfriend, and said she was sleeping. I guess Jill must have heard our voices. Anyway, she came out of the bedroom. Mum, she was a mess. Her face was all bruised and she could hardly talk because her jaw was swollen. She'd been mugged."

"Mugged?" I repeated. "Is she all right?"

"You know Jill. She's tough. She kind of laughed it off – said the most-lasting damage had been to her vanity."

"But she is okay?"

"She says she is."

"Where did it happen?"

"In the parking lot behind Nationtv. Jill was working late. One of the men on her show had offered to walk her to her car, but she turned him down. She says the mugger just appeared out of nowhere. He grabbed her shoulder bag. Apparently, Jill put up a fight, and that's when she got hurt."

"That doesn't sound like Jill," I said. "She always said if somebody was willing to risk jail for a purse full of old Cheezie bags and maxed-out credit cards, she wouldn't stand in their way."

"I guess no one can predict what she'll do in a situation like that," Mieka said. "I'm just grateful it didn't happen to you, too. Tom Kelsoe said there've been several incidents in that parking lot lately. Apparently, there's some sort of a gang – they're after video equipment that they can pawn for drug money, but they'll take anything."

I was beginning to feel uneasy. "It's odd that I've never heard a word about any of this," I said.

Mieka gazed at me thoughtfully. "I guess all that matters is that Jill's going to be all right."

"Of course," I said. "That *is* all that matters." I started for the phone. "I'm going to call her."

"Why don't you wait?" Mieka said. "Tom wanted her to get some sleep. I volunteered your services, but he told me he had everything under control." She rolled her eyes. "He said he was going to find the man who did this to Jill and beat him to a pulp. I must have looked kind of shocked, because he backtracked pretty quickly. When Jill asked me to stay for tea, Tom suddenly became Mr. Sensitive and said he'd make a pot of souchong."

"Retribution and Chinese tea," I said. "He certainly is the Renaissance man."

The sterling flatware we'd used for dinner was on the kitchen table, clean and ready to be put back into the silver chest until what my old friend Hilda McCourt always called "the next high day or holy day." Mieka began sorting through it, placing the pieces back where they belonged. "You don't like Tom Kelsoe, do you?" she said finally.

"Not at all," I said. "And he doesn't like me. But I still think I should go over there."

"Jill seemed fine, Mum. Honestly. And they made it pretty clear they didn't want anybody else around." Mieka aligned the salad forks carefully and dropped them into their slot in the chest. Then she gave me a sidelong glance. "Aren't there times when you and Alex don't want other people around?"

"What do Alex and I have to do with this?"

Mieka reached over and squeezed my hand. "Nothing," she said. "But I'm leaving in ten minutes, and we haven't talked about him all weekend. What's going on there?"

"I told you," I said. "Alex went up north for a few days."

"But you two are still together?"

I didn't answer her. Instead, I turned so I could look out the window into the back yard. Sadie and Rose were lying in what would soon be the tulip bed, catching the last rays of spring sunlight. They were old dogs now, fifteen and sixteen respectively, and I felt a pang thinking about what inevitably lay ahead.

"Penny for your thoughts, Mum," Mieka said.

"You'd be wasting your money," I said.

Greg came in from outside. "No wasting money, Mieka. We've got to act like grown-ups now. Speaking of which, it's time we hit the road."

"Give me five minutes, would you? Mum and I have some unfinished business."

He shrugged. "Sure, I'll go in and say goodbye to the kids." He picked up the plate with the last of Julie's lemon meringue pie. "I might as well take this with me."

When he left, Mieka turned to me. "Are you and Alex having trouble, Mum?"

"Yes," I said. "We are. Something happened." I told my daughter about the incident on the Albert Street bridge. I didn't gloss over the ugliness of the words the driver of the half-ton had hurled at me, and I didn't hold back the fact that I'd run from Alex.

Mieka has the kind of translucent skin that colours with emotion, and by the time I'd finished her face was flushed. "That's just so sick," she said. "How can be people be like that?"

"I don't know," I said. "But I'd give anything to have handled what happened with a little more courage."

"Did Alex go up north because he was angry?"

"No," I said. "He was very understanding. He always is. I don't think what happened that night would have been a huge problem except it was so obviously a sign of things to come. Alex is afraid that having to deal with that kind of bigotry day after day would change me, change all of us."

"Is it that serious between you two?"

"I don't know how serious it is, Mieka. I think that's part of the problem. For a long time, Alex and I were just going along, enjoying each other's company, doing things with the kids. He's so good with them. When they talk, he really listens to them, and he tells Taylor all these terrific Trickster stories."

Mieka raised an eyebrow. "And, of course, he did teach Angus to drive. It must be love if he let a fifteen-year-old with a learner's permit drive his Audi."

"Alex would do that for any fifteen-year-old who wanted to get behind the wheel as much as Angus did. That's the kind of man he is – generous and decent. And he's an amazing lover."

Mieka reddened and looked away.

"Sorry," I said. "I forgot that mothers aren't supposed to have sex."

Mieka gave me a small smile. "They can have it; they're just not supposed to tell their daughters about it." Her face grew serious. "Alex isn't much like Daddy, is he?"

"Does that bother you?"

"Not as long as Alex makes you happy."

"He does. And I make him happy. But there are things that have to be considered."

"Such as . . . ?"

"Such as the fact that he's nine years younger than I am and his experience of life has been very different from mine."

"And those things matter?"

"I don't know, Mieka. In the long run they might. I guess that's what Alex and I have to figure out."

When Greg and Mieka left, Taylor and Benny and I walked out to the car with them. We watched the car drive towards the Lewvan Expressway; as it disappeared from sight, Taylor tugged at my sleeve.

"Are you going to love that new baby, Jo?"

"You bet," I said. "And I'm going to keep on loving you." I knelt beside her. "Taylor, when you first came to live with us, I didn't really know you, but I wanted you with us because I loved your mother. Now I know you, and I want you with us because every single day in this house is better because you're a part of it."

I didn't call Jill that night, but the next morning after I came in from my run with the dogs, I phoned her at home. There was no answer, but I left a message on her machine. When I got to work I called her office at Nationtv. Rapti Lustig answered and said Jill was working at her apartment that day.

"Isn't that kind of unusual?" I said.

Rapti sighed. "Tell me one thing that's usual around here these days."

Jill phoned me at the university around noon. I'd just come back from a particularly rancorous department meeting, but when I heard her voice, I forgot about my colleagues' crankiness.

"How are you?" I asked.

"I'm okay," she said.

"You don't sound okay," I said.

"My jaw's sore. It's hard to talk."

"Is there anything I can bring you?"

"I'm fine."

"Mieka said Tom was taking good care of you."

"He's right here," she said. "That's wonderful news about the baby, Jo. Congratulations."

"Thanks," I said. "Jill, are you really all right?"

She tried a laugh. "You should see the other guy."

"I'd like to do more than see him," I said. "But I guess that's why we have a legal system. Look, I don't have any classes around lunchtime tomorrow – why don't I bring you over a crême brulée? That's easy to eat, even with a hurt jaw."

"Good old Jo. Food for every occasion. But something sweet and soft does sound tempting, and it would be great to see you." Despite the painful jaw, Jill sounded warm and welcoming.

"I'll be there at noon," I said, and as I hung up, I felt as if I'd scored a major victory.

When Kellee didn't show up for the Politics and the Media seminar at 3:00, I knew the time had come to do what I should have done at the outset: find her and give her a chance to tell her side of the story. Neil McCallum had been vague about the name of Kellee's aunt, but if his family had lived next door to Kellee's all those years, his parents might remember hearing something about Kellee's relative in British Columbia. As soon as class was over, I'd call him, but first I had the seminar to get through.

It was no easy task. The tension in the room was palpable. Ed Mariani had told me once that everyone who taught this particular group had been struck by their cohesiveness. Kellee Savage hadn't been one of the elect, but her absence seemed to change the balance for the others. They were unusually quiet and uncharacteristically tentative in proffering their opinions. The minutes seemed to crawl by, and I was relieved when my watch finally indicated that it was time to go.

Val Massey and Jumbo Hryniuk were the last to leave. Beside Jumbo's cheerful bulk, Val looked both slight and vulnerable. As they passed me, I reached out and touched Jumbo's sleeve.

"I need to talk to you for a minute," I said.

Val looked at me questioningly. "Should I wait for him in the hall or is it going to take a while?"

"It might take a while," I said.

A flicker of concern pass across Val's face, but he didn't ask me anything else. He mumbled something to Jumbo about meeting him at the Owl, then he left.

Jumbo looked puzzled. "What's up?"

"It has to do with a book. Did you check out a copy of *Sleeping Beauty* from the Education library?"

He grinned. "One of the guys got you to ask me that, right? Very funny." He frowned. "Except I don't get it."

"It's not a joke," I said. "Actually, it might be pretty serious."

"Then seriously," he said, "I didn't check out *Sleeping Beauty*."

"Did you lend your library card to anybody?"

Jumbo was no poker player. It was clear from his expression that my question had hit a nerve. "Why would I do that?" he asked.

"I don't know," I said. "Why would you?"

For the first time, the gravity of the situation seemed to strike him. "Professor Kilbourn, can you tell me what this is about?"

"Of course," I said. "But why don't you sit down. I'm getting far too old to get a crick in my neck from looking up at a football player."

The joke seemed to relax him, but as I told him about Kellee and the book and the note that had been left in her place at the seminar table, Jumbo's amiability vanished, and he looked first confused, then frightened.

"I didn't write any note," he said. "I give you my word."

"I believe you, but there's still a problem. Jumbo, that book was taken out on your card. I know that because I had somebody at the Education library check it on the computer."

I could see him mulling over the possibilities. He was not what they call in football a thoughtful player; nonetheless, that afternoon, Jumbo Hryniuk called the right play. "I'll talk to the person involved," he said.

"Make sure the person knows how serious this is."

"I will," he said.

Neil McCallum was happy to hear from me. Chloe had been running in the fields and come home full of burrs. It had taken him all afternoon to get them out of her coat, and as he worked, he had worried about Kellee. As it turned out, Neil was way ahead of me. He'd already asked his mother if she remembered the name of Kellee's aunt. She didn't, but she knew someone who she thought might be able to help. Neil said his mother was doing her best, and he would call me as soon as he heard anything.

Tuesday morning when I got back from taking the dogs for their run, the phone was ringing. It was Margaret McCallum, Neil's mother. She was as affable as her son, but her news was disappointing. The woman she was counting on for help was a widow named Albertson who had spent the winter in Arizona. When Margaret had finally tracked down the woman's number in Tucson, she learned that Mrs. Albertson, like many other snowbirds at the beginning of April, was on her way home. Echoing her son, Margaret McCallum told me that as soon as she had any information, she'd let me know.

I thanked her, wrote her name next to Neil's in my address book, then went into the kitchen to hunt up my recipe for crême brulée. The kids were on Easter holidays, so I doubled the quantities and left a dish for them and put the one for Jill in a cooler and took it to the university with me. I had some newspaper articles I wanted to track down in the main library, so it was close to 11:30 when I got back to my office. Ed Mariani was sitting at the desk, marking papers.

"Finally," he said theatrically. "I was just about to send out the bloodhounds."

"Does this mean I'm grounded, Dad?" I said.

He grimaced. "Sorry, I guess that did sound a little paternalistic. It's just that Jill Osiowy called, and she wanted to make sure you got her message before you headed off to her place."

"What message?"

"Jill can't be there for lunch. She had to fly to Toronto – Nationtv business. They're apparently experiencing a crisis."

"They're always experiencing a crisis," I said. I thought of Jill having to fly to Toronto when she was feeling lousy and looking worse. In the days of cutbacks and takeovers, corporate hearts were hardening. I started to pack up to go home, then I remembered the cooler sitting in my car. "How do you feel about crème brulée, Ed?" I asked.

"Love it," he said.

"Good. Then let me snag us some bowls and spoons, and I'll buy you lunch."

Just as I was dishing up the dessert, Angus called. "Some of the guys are going over to play football on the lawn in front of the legislature," he said.

"Is one of those guys you?"

He laughed. "Well, yeah, Mum. Why else would I call? Anyway, Leah wants to know if it's okay for her to take Taylor over to her house to have tea with her Aunt Slava."

"I guess so," I said. "Have you met Leah's aunt?"

"Yeah. She's about a hundred years old, but she's cool."

"That's certainly a ringing endorsement."

"Whatever," said my son. "I'll be home at the usual time."

After we'd eaten, Ed started gathering his books together for his 12:30 class. "Dynamite crème brulée, Jo. Jill's loss is my gain."

"That'll teach her to go to Toronto," I said. "Actually, I'm just relieved she was well enough to go."

Ed looked at me anxiously. "Was she ill?"

"No, worse than that. She was mugged the other night. That's why I made the crême brulée. Her jaw was bothering her."

"My God, that's terrible. You never think of that happening to someone you know. Did the police catch the mugger?"

"I don't know any of the details. I haven't seen Jill. My daughter went over there Sunday night. Mieka said Jill was pretty banged up, but when I talked to her on the phone, she seemed to be in good spirits."

"So she *is* all right?"

"She must be if she's well enough to travel. Didn't she say anything when she called?"

"Just that she was in a rush." He leaned towards me, his moon face creased with concern. "Joanne, Jill's a kind of hero to me. The truth is she saved my life once – at least the part of my life that I value the most."

It was a line that cried out for elaboration. Ed didn't offer any, but his obvious affection for Jill gave me the opening I needed.

"Jill's a hero to a lot of people," I said. "This shouldn't be happening to her."

"You mean the mugging."

"If it was a mugging." I took a deep breath and plunged ahead. "Ed, I haven't said anything to anyone about this, but I'm not sure I buy the story that Jill was attacked by a stranger. Since I started doing the political panel, I've walked through that parking lot every Saturday night. It's a safe area: a lot of security lights and a lot of traffic. Nationtv vans are in and out of there all the time. Another thing – Jill would fight the good fight for a story, but I've never known anyone who's as indifferent about possessions as she is. If someone tried to take her purse, she wouldn't have turned a hair."

Ed gave me a searching look. "What do you think happened?"

"I think it was Tom," I said.

"You think he hit her?"

"I think it's possible," I said. "And as soon as Jill gets back, I'm going to talk to her. I won't let her put me off, Ed. Unless she can convince me that I'm way off base about this, and Tom is innocent, I'm going to go to the police."

Without a word, Ed picked up his books and moved heavily towards the door.

"Will you be in tomorrow?" I asked.

Ed looked at me oddly. "I don't know," he said. Then he was gone.

I thought about the afternoon ahead. Angus and Taylor were accounted for, so it was a good chance to get some marking done. I tried, but it was a profitless exercise. All I could think about was Jill. When I realized that I'd read an entire essay without retaining even the faintest hint of its content, I decided to go home. On my way out of the office I spotted the dishes I'd borrowed from the Faculty Club; I dropped them into a plastic grocery bag and headed out.

Grace Lipinski, the Faculty Club manager, was at the entrance to the bar arranging some dazzling branches of forsythia in a Chinese vase the colour of a new fern.

"I brought back the dishes," I said, "with thanks."

"Anytime," she said. "And while you're here, you can take back the picture that the cleaning people found. It was just in with the paper towels, but I wiped down the frame and glass with disinfectant to be on the safe side."

"You're a wonder," I said.

"Tell the board," she said. "I'll be right back. Enjoy the forsythia."

Grace disappeared, but I wasn't alone for long. Old Giv Mewhort was standing at the bar and, when he spotted me, he picked up his drink and started over. He moved with great precision, careful not to spill so much as a single drop of gin in the glass in his hand. It was mid-afternoon, but Giv had already reached the orotund stage of drunkenness.

"My dear," he said. "I haven't had a chance to tell you how distressed I was to see that young Cassius has taken your place on that political show. Did you step aside or were you pushed?"

"I was pushed," I said, "by young Cassius."

Giv sipped his drink and sighed. "'Such men as he be never at heart's ease/Whiles they behold a greater than themselves,/And therefore are they very dangerous.'"

I smiled at him. "Thanks for the warning," I said. "But I think Tom Kelsoe's done about all the damage to me that he can."

Giv leaned forward and whispered ginnily. "Don't bet the farm on it, Joanne." He pointed towards the back of the bar and roared dramatically. "'Yond Cassius has a lean and hungry look. . . .' See for yourself." I turned and glanced into the bar. On the couch in the far corner, two men were deep in conversation. They were so close together and so intent on their conversation that they seemed oblivious to everything around them. One of the men was Tom Kelsoe, the other was Ed Mariani. I felt the way I had in high school when I'd poured my heart out to my best friend and discovered her ten minutes later, laughing and intimate with the one girl in school I considered my enemy.

Grace came back with the photograph and handed it to me. "It's all yours," she said.

Giv Mewhort leaned across me and gave the picture of Reed Gallagher and Annalie Brinkmann the once-over. "So he gave it back," he said. "The Human Comedy never fails to surprise, does it? Although I must say that I never understood why he nicked that photo in the first place."

"You know who took this?" I asked.

Giv waved his glass towards the recesses of the bar. "Young Cassius." He laughed. "I warned you, my dear. 'He thinks too much: such men are dangerous.'"

When I slid behind the steering wheel of the Volvo, I realized how badly the scene in the Faculty Club had shaken me. Like Giv, I didn't understand why anyone would want to take an old newspaper photograph. But while the news that Tom Kelsoe was a thief was unnerving, it was the sight of Ed Mariani cosying up to him that had jolted me.

They were colleagues. There were a half-dozen innocent reasons for them to have a quick meeting in the Faculty Club. But in my heart, I knew there was nothing innocent about their meeting. For reasons I couldn't fathom, Ed had run to Tom as soon as I'd told him my suspicions. For a moment, I thought I was going to be sick to my stomach. It had never occurred to me not to trust Ed. I had told him everything: first about Kellee, and now about Jill.

I put my head down on the steering wheel and tried to think. At the moment, there was nothing I could do about the situation with Jill. She was in Toronto. I couldn't get to her, but neither could Tom Kelsoe. For the time being, she was safe. I didn't have that assurance about Kellee Savage. I'd already failed her twice, but there was still time to make amends. It was April 5. If Kellee Savage hadn't paid the rent for her room on Scarth Street, Alma Stringer might be interested in showing me the room.

When I got to Scarth Street, Alma was hammering a piece of laminated poster-board to the wall next to the mailboxes in the front hall. "I thought you and me did all the business we were going to do," she said.

I pulled a twenty-dollar bill from my wallet and held it up. "I want to see room six. I just want to look at it; I promise I won't touch anything. You can stand in the doorway and watch me if you like."

Alma's fingers took the twenty so quickly the act seemed like sleight-of-hand. Then, without a word, she turned and walked into the house. I followed along behind. She had an old-fashioned key-ring attached to the belt of her pedal pushers and she stopped in front of number 6 and leaned into the door to insert the key in the lock.

I don't know what Alma had expected to find on the other side of the door, but it was obvious from her shriek of fury that she hadn't anticipated being confronted by a room that seemed, quite literally, to have been torn apart. Whoever had destroyed Kellee's room had been as mindlessly destructive and as efficient as the vandals who had attacked the Journalism offices at the university. Bureau drawers were pulled out and overturned; the sheets had been ripped off the bed; the mattress had been dragged to the floor. The table had been upended and the drawer that held utensils had been flung across the room.

Alma looked at the mess, and said, "If shit was luck, I wouldn't get a sniff."

"Are you going to call the police?" I asked.

She laughed derisively. "Sure. That's what I'm gonna do. And have them all over the place, tracking in mud, leaving the door open, runnin' up my heating bill. No, little Miss Goody Two-Shoes, I'm not gonna call the police. I'm gonna hand the rummy in the front room a ten and get him to clean this up, so I can rent it." She started down the hall.

"Wait," I said. "When was the last time you were in here?"

"You know, that's quite a mess in there," she said innocently. "That rummy's probably gonna want at least twenty bucks."

I opened my wallet and pulled out my last twenty. Alma bagged it in a snap. "The last time I was in number six was the day she moved in, and that was January. As long as my tenants don't bother me, I don't bother them. We both like it like that."

"But Kellee hadn't paid her rent for April."

"I figured I'd let her use up her damage deposit." She smoothed her thin yellow hair. "I try to be decent. Now, unless you got the wherewithal to keep the meter running, get outa here. I got work to do."

When she left, I stood for a moment in front of the locked door of number 6. I hadn't had much time to look around, but even a quick glance had revealed there wasn't much in the room that was personal. There were a few items of lingerie near the overturned bureau drawers and a flowery plastic toilet kit had been flung into the corner, but there didn't seem to be nearly the quantity of personal effects you'd expect to find in a room someone actually lived in. It was apparent that Kellee had pretty well moved out by the time her intruder had trashed the room.

I walked back up the hall. Alma's laminated sheet was a bright square against the faded wallpaper. It was headed "Rules of This House," and a quick glance revealed that Alma had a an Old Testament gift for conjuring up activities that could be proscribed. Beside the list was the rack of mailboxes Julie had told me about. Sure enough, Kellee had placed a happy face sticker beside her name; I looked at her box more closely. There was no lock on it. I opened the lid and pulled out her mail. There wasn't much: what appeared to be a statement from the Credit Union, the May issue of *Flare* magazine; a couple of envelopes addressed to "Occupant," and the cardboard end flap from a cigarette package. On the flap, someone had pencilled a message. "I've moved. #3, 2245 Dahl. B."

I stuck the cigarette flap in my bag. It was a slender thread, but it was all I had. I walked back to the Volvo, slid into the driver's seat, and headed for Dahl Street.

CHAPTER

11

As I walked up the front path of 2245 Dahl Street, the building cast a shadow that seemed to race towards me, and I knew I'd had enough of sinister rooming houses with their emanations of despair and of hard-lived lives. This place was even worse than Alma's. The paint on the Scarth Street house might have been peeling and the porches might have been sagging, but it was still possible to spot vestiges of the building's former elegance and coquettish charm. There were no suggestions of past glory here. The apartment on Dahl Street had been a squat eyesore the day it was built, and sixty years of neglect hadn't improved it.

Someone had propped the front door open with a brick, and I thought I was in luck, but inside the vestibule there was a second door, and this one was locked tight. I pounded on the door, but when no one came I could feel the relief wash over me. I'd done my best, but my best hadn't been good enough. I was off the hook. As I turned to leave, a tortoise-shell kitten darted in from the street and ran between my legs. It was wet and dirty, but when I reached down to reassure it, it shot back out the door. My fingers were damp from where I had touched its fur and when I raised my hand to my nose, I could smell kerosene.

I hurried down the steps, eager to put some distance between me and this neighbourhood where horrors that should have been unimaginable were part of everyday life. I'd parked across the street, and before I opened the door of the Volvo, I took a last look at 2245 Dahl Street. The fire escape on the side of the building zigzagged up the wall like a scar. In case of fire, it would have been almost impossible to get down those metal steps. The life of the tenants had spilled out onto them, and the steps had become the final resting place of beer bottles, broken plant pots, and anything else small enough and useless enough to be abandoned. On the step outside number 3 someone had propped a statue of the Virgin Mary. According to the message on the cigarette flap, number 3 was B's flat. It seemed that Kellee's friend was a person with a faith life. I looked up the fire escape again. The door on the third floor was open a crack. It didn't look inviting, but it did look accessible. My time off the hook was over.

Climbing the fire escape was a nightmare. Picking my way through the litter meant watching my feet, and that involved peering through the metal-runged steps at the ground below. The effect was vertiginous, and by the time I'd reached the landing outside the door to number 3, my head was reeling, and I had to hold onto the Virgin's head to get my balance.

Inside, a television was playing; I could hear the strident accusing voices of people on one of the tabloid talk shows.

I leaned into the opening of the door. "Anybody home?" I asked.

There was no answer. I pushed, opening the door a little more. "Can you help me?" I called. "I'm looking for someone who lives here."

On the television, a man was shouting, "you ruined my life . . . you ruined my life," as the studio audience cheered.

Nobody home but Ricki Lake. I turned to go back down, but when looked at through three flights of metal staircase, the ground seemed a dizzying distance away. It didn't take me long to decide that slipping into the house and leaving by the front door made more sense than plummeting to my death. I pushed the back door open and stepped inside. The kitchen was small and as clean as it would ever be. The linoleum had faded from red to brown, and it was curling in the area in front of the sink, but the floor was scrubbed, and the dishes on the drainboard were clean. The refrigerator door was covered with children's drawings and an impressive collection of the cards of doctors at walk-in medical clinics.

The curtains in the living room were drawn; the only illumination in the room came from the flickering light of the television. Still, it was easy enough to pick out the front door, and that's where I was headed when my toe caught on the edge of the carpet. As I stumbled, I caught hold of the back of the couch to break my fall. That's when I saw the woman. She was lying on the couch, covered with a blanket, but when our eyes met, she made a mewling sound and tried to raise herself up.

"I'm sorry," I said. "I was looking for someone."

She stared at me without comprehension. She was a native woman, and she seemed to be in her thirties. It was hard to see her clearly in the shadowy room, but it wasn't hard to hear her. As she grew more frantic, the sounds she made became high-pitched and ear-splittingly intense.

I tried to be reassuring. "It's okay," I said. "I'm leaving. I'm not going to hurt you." I reached the door, but as my hand grasped the knob, the door opened from the outside.

The woman who exploded through the door was on the

183

shady side of forty, but she had apparently decided not to go gently into middle age. Her mane of shoulder-length blond hair was extravagantly teased, her mascara was black and thick, and her lipstick was a whiter shade of pale. She was wearing a fringed white leatherette jacket, a matching miniskirt, and the kind of boots Nancy Sinatra used to sing about.

She was not happy to see me. "Who the fuck are you?" she rasped. "And what the fuck are you doing in my living room?"

"My name's Joanne Kilbourn, and I'm trying to find Kellee Savage."

She reached beside her, flicked on the light switch and gave me the once-over. "Social worker or cop?" she asked.

"What?"

She narrowed her eyes. "I asked you if you were a social worker or a cop."

"Neither. I'm Kellee's teacher."

"Well, Teacher, as the song says, 'take the time to look around you.' This isn't a school. This is a private residence."

I reached into my pocket and pulled out the cigarette flap with the address. "I found this in Kellee's mailbox. It has your address on it. Are you B?"

She took a step towards me. Her perfume was heavy, but not unpleasant. "Teacher," she said, "let's see how good you are at learning. Listen carefully. This is my home, and I want you out of it."

"I just wanted to ask . . ."

She wagged her finger in my face. "You weren't listening," she said. She grabbed my arm and twisted it behind my back. As she propelled me through the door, she gave me a wicked smile and whispered, "Class dismissed."

It was almost 5:00 when I got home. The dogs came to greet me, but the house was silent. The kids would be barrelling through the front door any minute, but for the time being I was alone. I was also miserable and hungry and tired. I decided I would meet my needs one at a time. I poured myself a drink, took it upstairs, ran a bath, dropped a cassette of Kiri Te Kanawa singing Mozart's *"Exsultate, jubilate"* into my cassette player, and shut out the world. By the time I got out of the tub and towelled off, I wasn't quite ready to "rise up at last in gladness," but I had improved my chances of getting through the evening. As I pulled on fresh sweats and a T-shirt, I sang along with Kiri, but even Mozart couldn't block out the images of the kerosene-soaked kitten and the native woman's terrified face. The memories of that afternoon were a fresh bruise, but I was no closer to Kellee Savage. It seemed that, like the Bourbons, my destiny was to forget nothing and learn nothing.

When I went downstairs to start dinner, I discovered the cupboard was bare. I thought about take-out, but I'd given Alma my last twenty dollars. What I had on hand was half an onion, a bowl of boiled potatoes, a pound of bacon, and eleven eggs. Wolfgang Puck could have whipped these homely staples into something transcendent, but Wolfgang had never paid a visit to Dahl Street. I pulled out the frying pan and started cracking.

Angus had been outdoors all afternoon, and once again proving the adage that the best sauce is hunger, he inhaled everything I put in front of him. Taylor was finicky. Slava had spoiled her.

"She gave me tea with milk and sugar in a little cup that was so thin you could see through it, and cakes with pink icing, and we talked about art and her house when she was a little girl."

"Would you like to invite Slava for tea some day?"

Taylor's eyes lit up. "Do we have any of those little cups?"

"Of course," I said. "It'll take some digging to find them, but I distinctly remember getting some when I got married."

"When you got married," Taylor said dreamily. "Did you have a big dress?"

"The biggest," I said.

"I'd like to see that dress," Taylor said.

"I'm afraid the dress is long gone, T, but I do have some pictures. I'll hunt them up for you when I've got a bit more time."

"Good," she said, "because I'd like to draw a picture of you dressed as a bride."

Julie came just as I was clearing off the dishes. Before our sisterly reconciliation at Easter, I would have cringed if Julie had spotted yolk-smeared plates on our table at 6:00 p.m., but our relationship had entered a more equitable phase. I smiled at her. "One of those nights," I said.

She shrugged. "I ate the first two things I found in the freezer: a Lean Cuisine that I think was a pasta entrée and a pint of strawberry Haagen Dazs."

"Then we're both ready for coffee," I said. I poured, and Julie and I sat down at the kitchen table. She was wearing jeans and a sweatshirt and, for the first time since I'd known her, no makeup. She asked about my kids and about Alex and then finally she began to talk about Reed. As she remembered their life together, her brown eyes danced, and she smiled often. I recognized the syndrome. I'd felt that warmth, too, when someone let me talk about Ian in the months after he'd died.

Finally, the memories grew thin, and Julie returned to the present. "I've got to know what happened the night he died," she said simply. "When we were at the conference in Hilton Head, he gave the most wonderful speech, and he ended it with a quotation. He said it was just an old chestnut, but I can't get the words out of my mind. 'The journalist's job is to comfort the afflicted and afflict the comfortable.' That's what he said. Joanne, the more I think about it, the more I'm convinced that my husband's death was connected to his work."

"Do you mean at the university?"

She shook her head vehemently. "No, not there. Downtown. On Scarth Street. Joanne, I think Reed had discovered something in that house that someone didn't want brought to light."

"You think he was murdered?" I asked.

"It sounds so melodramatic when you say it out loud. But it's the only explanation that makes sense. Joanne, Reed and I hadn't been married long, but we'd been together since the first week he came here. I knew him. He was a healthy man. I don't mean just physically, but psychologically. He didn't have dark corners, and" – she smiled at the memory – "he was a very ordinary lover. Nothing kinky. Just lights-out, garden-variety sex. Don't you think I would have known if he had those tendencies? There was nothing, nothing in the man I knew that would connect him to that . . ." Her voice was breaking, but she carried on. "To that nightmare I walked in on."

"Did you tell the police this?"

"Not when he died. I wasn't thinking clearly. I was so humiliated. Seeing him like that. Try to put yourself in my place, Joanne. We'd been married five weeks. I loved him, and I thought he loved me. But after I followed him to Kellee Savage's room, anything seemed possible. Now . . . Jo, so many things don't add up, and I told the police that."

"You've talked to them recently?"

"Yesterday. They say the case is closed. They were civil enough, but I know they were thinking I was just a neurotic

widow." She laughed ruefully. "They don't have your perspective, Joanne. If they did, they'd see that I'm less neurotic now than I've been in years. Not that that's saying
much."

"You're doing all right," I said.

"Am I?" she asked, and her voice was thick with tears. "I
can't even remember the last time I slept for more than two
hours. And when I'm awake, all I do is think about everything I've done wrong in my life. Joanne, I've made so many
mistakes. I set up expectations for everyone I loved, and
when they didn't meet those expectations, I walked away.
I've walked away from so many people: my first husband,
my son, my daughter-in-law, my grandchildren." The tears
were streaming down Julie's face, but she didn't seem to
care. "And at the end, I walked away from Reed. But I'm not
walking away any more. Reed was a good man, and I'm going
to find out what happened to him."

"What are you going to do?"

She took out a tissue and wiped her eyes. "I thought I'd
start by talking to the superintendent of the building where
Reed died." She looked at me hopefully, seeking approval.

I thought of Alma Stringer saying that if shit were luck,
she wouldn't have had a sniff. Finding another middle-aged
matron in search of truth on her doorstep wasn't going to
make Alma feel any luckier. I reached out and touched
Julie's hand. "I've already talked to the landlady," I said. "So
have the police. I don't think you're going to get very far
there. But if you think Reed's death is connected with his
work, why don't you go through his papers?"

She blew her nose. "I can't go through his papers," she
said. "They're gone. I went up to the university the morning
after I got back. I couldn't even get into his office. There was
a work crew there. They said the office had been vandalized.
Apparently, somebody from the School of Journalism tried

to retrieve what they could, but there wasn't much that was salvageable."

Julie ran her fingers through her hair in a gesture of frustration. "Everything Reed was working on was at the university. He didn't believe in bringing work home. He always said if you have to bring work home with you, your job needs redefining or you need retooling."

"Would the people in his department know that everything he was working on was at the university?"

Julie nodded. "Everybody knew."

The only association I'd made between the chaos in Kellee Savage's place on Scarth Street and the scene at the J school had been the fact that both places had been an unholy mess. The vandalism at the university had so obviously been the work of gay-bashers that I hadn't connected it with what I'd seen in Kellee's room.

Julie leaned towards me. She was frowning. "You look as if you're a million miles away," she said.

"Sorry," I said, "I guess I was wool-gathering. I'm back now." But I wasn't back, not really. I was still in room 6 of the house on Scarth Street, assessing the holes that were appearing in Ed Mariani's theory that Kellee Savage had been blackmailing Reed Gallagher. The possibility that whoever had wrecked Reed Gallagher's office had vandalized Kellee's room on Scarth Street had ceased to be a long shot.

I thought again about Reed's destroyed papers, and about Kellee's fortress in Indian Head. Another possibility was beginning to seem less remote; there was a strong chance that the vandalism I'd seen had been a smoke screen thrown up to camouflage two coolly deliberate missions of search and destroy. If that hypothesis were true, there was an adversary out there who was far more deadly than a pack of hate-filled kids.

But who was that adversary? No matter how much I

wanted to turn from the thought, one name kept insinuating itself into my consciousness. From the beginning, Ed Mariani had been front and centre. He had been Reed's rival for the position of head of the School of Journalism. He had been with Reed the night before he died. Suddenly, there were troubling memories: of Alex, perplexed by the presence of amyl nitrite at Reed's death scene because amyl nitrite was most often used by gay men; of Ed seeking me out the night of Tom Kelsoe's book launch; of Ed, Johnny-on-the-spot with a dinner invitation the day I'd been at the J school and seen the vandalism. He'd been there all along, offering explanations, shaping my perception of Reed Gallagher, and, finally, conjuring up the blackmail scenario that I'd seized on with such alacrity.

I'd been wrong about the blackmail. I was convinced of that now. But if I'd been mistaken about the blackmail, it was possible that my perception of other events had been faulty, too. I had to go back to the beginning, try to look at everything afresh. If Julie was right about Reed Gallagher's sexual style, it was possible that the bizarre sexual scene the police had found when Reed Gallagher died was staged. And if Reed's death scene were bogus, where was the truth?

When Julie left, I told her to take care of herself, and it wasn't just a pleasantry. Something was very wrong. Remembering Kellee's room in the house in Indian Head, I decided Julie wasn't the only person who needed a reminder about being careful.

Neil McCallum answered the telephone on the first ring, and he sounded so sane and cheerful he seemed like a citizen of another planet. He and Chloe had been for a walk on the prairie, and they'd found crocuses.

"I wish I could see them," I said.

"You can," he said. "Just come out here. I'll show you where they are."

"It's not that easy," I said.

"Sure it is," he said. "People always make easy things hard. I don't get it."

I laughed. "Neither do I. But Neil, I didn't just call to talk. I wanted to ask you to keep a specially close watch on Kellee's house. Make sure the front door and the door to her office are always locked."

"I always do that." He paused. "Have you heard something bad about Kellee?"

"No," I said. "I haven't heard anything. Honestly. But Neil, you've got to promise me you'll be careful. If anyone you don't know comes around, make sure you've got Chloe with you, and don't tell them how sweet she is. Make them think she means business."

"Like on TV," he said.

"Yes," I said. "Like on TV."

For a moment, Neil was silent. Then he said, "But this isn't TV, and I'm getting scared."

That night I couldn't sleep. I was getting scared, too. For the first time since Alex had gone up north, I wanted him with me not because he was a man I cared about, but because he was a cop and he'd be able to put together the pieces. He had told me once that police investigations involved a lot of what he called mouse work. He'd pointed to the medicine wheel on his wall and talked about the Four Great Ways of Seeking Understanding. One of them was Brother Mouse's: sniffing things out with his nose, seeing what's up close, touching what he can with his whiskers. Alex had told me that when a police officer had a treasure trove of facts and information, it was time for him to stop seeing like a mouse and start seeing like an eagle. As I tossed and turned, mulling over my accumulation of fact and theory, only one thing was certain: as far as insights were concerned, I'd never been more earth-bound in my life.

The next morning when I got to the university I went straight to Physical Plant. The cheerful woman who'd given me the extra key to the office for Ed Mariani was moving a tray of geranium slips in peat pots from a window on the west side of the office to a window on the east.

"Caught me," she said, and the lilt of her native Jamaica warmed the room. "There's so much light here, and I want my babies to get a good start. When spring comes, that garden of mine is my life. Now, don't tell me, let me guess. You lost your extra key."

"No," I said. "It's something else, but, in a way, it's connected to the key. The man who's sharing my office now is from the School of Journalism. I wondered if you'd heard how things were shaping up about that vandalism case."

She looked fondly at her sturdy little geranium plants, then she turned back to me. "I'm afraid you're going to have to be a Good Samaritan for a couple more weeks," she said. "The vandals really did a job on that place."

"Did the police catch them?"

She shook her head. "No. It's scary too, because it looks like it might have been an inside job. We've put a security officer in there all night now and a surveillance camera, but, if you ask me, we're closing the barn door after the pony's gone."

"What makes you think it's an inside job?"

"Whoever did it had to get through the outside doors somehow, and the lock wasn't forced. They must have had keys. There were no fingerprints, but that's hardly a surprise since they used gloves." She flexed her fingers. "Latex gloves. Ours. The gloves were traced to the Chemistry department, as were the lab coats."

"Lab coats?"

"To keep the paint off their clothes, I guess. Anyway, we got the gloves and the lab coats back, and the computer they took. It was a Pentium 90 – cost five thousand dollars. And they just pitched it in the garbage bin back of the Owl."

"When did you find it?"

"Last Friday. It hadn't been there long. Whoever took it must have decided it was too hot to keep around. Those Pentiums are great little machines. The one in the garbage was still functioning, but the memory on the hard drive had been reformatted."

"Who would go to all that trouble?"

She chuckled. "Somebody who had big plans, then got cold feet."

"Do you know who the machine belonged to?"

She went over to her computer, tapped in the serial number, and shook her head sadly. "Reed Gallagher. Well, I guess he won't be missing it now."

"No," I said, "I guess he won't."

When I went back to my office, Ed Mariani was there. The sight of him pouring boiling water into our Brown Betty disarmed me. How could I suspect such a gentle and giving man of . . . of what? I couldn't even articulate in my own mind what I suspected Ed of doing.

He opened his arms in welcome. "You must have smelled the tea," he said.

"I guess I did," I said. I took off my coat, sat down in the student chair, and buried myself in my lecture notes.

"Anything new on Kellee Savage?"

I shook my head. "Nothing significant."

Ed was watching me carefully. "Joanne, correct me if I'm wrong, but have I overstayed my welcome?"

"I just have to get ready for class, Ed." When I glanced up, he looked so wounded, I found myself thinking I must be crazy. But I had to be careful, too. I'd never been good at subterfuge. For the first time since we'd started sharing the office, the atmosphere between Ed and me was strained, and I was relieved when he finally picked up his books and headed out the door.

Val Massey appeared so quickly after Ed left that it was obvious he'd been waiting until I was alone. Like everyone who teaches these days, I'm careful about leaving the door open when a student is in the room, but when Val pulled the door closed behind him, I didn't move to open it.

He looked terrible. He was pale, and there were deep shadows under his eyes. It was apparent he'd been through more than a few sleepless nights. I invited him to sit, but he went over and stood at the window as he'd done the day he'd come to my office and asked me if any of my children had ever got into a real mess. I bit my lip, remembering how I had jumped to what I believed was the heart of the problem, and how quickly I had assured him that I didn't believe the charges that Kellee Savage was levelling at him.

But I was through being impetuous. Like Freudian analysts and good interviewers, I was going to count on the power of silence. It was an uncomfortable wait. If the silence between Ed and me had been awkward, the tension as I waited for Val Massey to talk was painful.

When he finally turned to face me, he didn't waste time on a preamble.

"I was the one who borrowed Jumbo's library card," he said. "And I was the one who left the book for Kellee." He lowered his voice. "I wrote that letter inside the book, too."

It was news I was expecting, yet hearing the words was a blow. "Whatever made you do it, Val?"

"I don't know," he said miserably.

Suddenly I felt my resolve harden. "That's not good

enough," I said. "You don't do something that cruel without a reason."

He flinched, but he didn't offer an explanation.

I got up from the desk and walked over to him. "Damn it, Val, I thought I knew you. I had a pretty good idea about what kind of person you were. For one thing, I thought you believed what you said in our seminar about the journalist's obligation to protect the powerless."

"She wasn't powerless," he said quietly. "She had her lies, and she was using them to destroy a decent human being."

"But, Val, you started it. You just said you were the one who wrote that letter, and Kellee said there were incidents before that."

Val laughed derisively. "Oh yes, there were other incidents, but I'll bet she didn't tell you about her part in them. Professor Kilbourn, whatever you may think, Kellee Savage is no victim. I know that what I did was wrong, but what she was threatening to do was worse. She was prepared to ruin someone's career, even their life. All I was trying to do was muddy the waters."

"Muddy the waters," I repeated. "I don't understand."

Val averted his eyes. "Kellee was threatening to make her charges against . . . against this other person public. The things she was saying were crazy, but you have no idea how terrible the consequences would have been if people had believed her. We had to make sure people wouldn't take what Kellee was saying seriously. It was like that story of the boy who cried wolf. We had to make certain that when Kellee talked, no one listened."

"It got a little out of hand, didn't it?" I said. "Kellee's disappeared, Val."

"And I've spent the last week trying to find her. I've tried to call her and I've talked to everybody who might have seen her. I feel sick about this whole thing. You've got to believe me. I didn't want Kellee to quit school. I just wanted to teach her a lesson. I couldn't just sit by and let her destroy a person's life, could I?"

"Whose life was she going to destroy?" I asked.

He shook his head vigorously. "No," he said. "I can't tell you that."

"Was it another student, or someone on faculty?"

"I've told you everything I can," he said. "If you have to take some sort of action against me, I understand, but please don't involve Jumbo in this any more. He really was just doing a favour for a friend."

"The way you were," I said.

"Yes," he said. "The way I was."

I came home to a crisis. Taylor had sliced her hand with a knife. The cut was a real bleeder, and she was wailing. Angus was holding a wad of paper towels against the wound with one hand and dialling my number at the university with the other.

I took a peek at the cut, reassured Taylor, and ran upstairs to the bathroom to get a sanitary napkin to act as a pressure bandage.

When I came back, I handed the napkin to Angus. "Wrap that tightly around the cut," I said.

He looked at me in horror.

"It'll stop the bleeding," I said. "And it's sterile." Suddenly I realized the problem. "Angus, nobody has ever died of humiliation from holding a Stayfree. Now do it."

An hour later, Taylor was wearing a button that declared, "Hospitals Are Full of Helpers," her wound was sewn up, and we were on our way to Kowloon Kitchen for Chinese take-out: Won-ton soup and a double order of Taylor's favourite almond shrimp. The cut had been nasty, but it had also been on Taylor's right hand, and as she was left-handed, the injury had already become an adventure rather than a catastrophe.

The phone was ringing when we got in the door. I picked it up, and heard a man's voice, not familiar. "Is this Joanne Kilbourn?"

"Yes," I said.

"Regina Police, Mrs. Kilbourn. You were in last week and talked to Constable Kirszner about a missing person."

"He didn't think there was cause for alarm," I said, but my heart was already starting to pound.

"He may still be right," the voice said. "However, we just picked up the body of an unidentified female. A farmer outside Balgonie found her in one of his fields. She's not carrying any identification, but the age and the general description seem to fit the woman you were concerned about."

At the kitchen table, my children were laughing, doling out the won-ton soup, sniping at each other about who would get the extra shrimp.

"How soon will you know?" I said.

"That depends on you. I wonder if you could come down to Regina General and have a look."

"Isn't there anyone else?" I said.

"If you'd rather not come down, we can go to the media."

I thought of Neil McCallum, having his supper, watching television and hearing about the discovery of a body that might be Kellee's.

"I'll be right there," I said.

"We'll have a uniformed officer meet you at the doors to the emergency room. Do you know the place I'm talking about?"

"Only too well," I said. "Only too well."

CHAPTER

12

The uniformed officer who met me was female, and she was good at her job: cool and perceptive. Angus would have said her energy was very smooth. She introduced herself as Constable Marissa Desjardin, and as she walked me to the elevator, she began to explain the identification process. All I had to do, she said, was look at the body long enough to make an identification, positive or negative, then I could be on my way. It was, she added briskly, important to keep my focus and not let my imagination run away with me. As I walked beside her through the maze of surgical-green corridors, I willed myself to heed her words; nonetheless, when we came to the double doors marked "Pathology," my heart began to pound.

Constable Desjardin gave me a reassuring smile and pointed to a room across the hall. "That's the staff room," she said. "Why don't you wait in there while I make sure they're ready for us inside?"

The staff room was small, with furnishings that were hearteningly ordinary: an old couch, a kitchen table and four chairs, a microwave oven, a small refrigerator, a sink with a drainboard on which mugs were drying. There was an acrid smell in the air; someone had left an almost empty pot on the burner of the coffee maker. I gulped in the familiar odour hungrily. Despite Constable Desjardin's sensible advice, my imagination was in overdrive. From the moment I'd seen the doors marked "Pathology," I was certain the air I was breathing carried with it a whiff of the charnel house.

I didn't have long to look around the coffee room before Marissa Desjardin was back. "All set," she said. "We might as well get it over with."

Hours of watching "Quincy" and other crime shows on television had prepared me for the harshly lit, sterile room behind the doors. I was even ready for the pathologist in the lab coat and for the gurney with its plastic-shrouded but unmistakable cargo. But nothing could have prepared me for the horror that was exposed when, at a signal from Constable Desjardin, the pathologist reached over and pulled back the heavy plastic sheeting. A quick glance, and I knew that the dead woman was Kellee. However, it wasn't Kellee as I had known her. Two weeks of exposure to weather had taken its toll. Her body was swollen and her skin had blistered and split; in places, her flesh looked as if it had been eaten away. Her green wool sweater had darkened and begun to rot as if it, too, was returning to its elemental state. Only the plastic shamrock barrettes in her hair remained unchanged. They were as sunnily cheerful as they had been on the morning when Kellee had chosen them, out of all the others, to anchor her hair on her twenty-first birthday.

I turned to Constable Desjardin. "That's her," I said. "What happened to her skin?"

Marissa Desjardin looked away. "Insects," she said tightly. "We've had an early spring."

I couldn't take my eyes off the ruin that had once been Kellee Savage's face. "She didn't live long enough to feel the insects doing that to her, did she?" I asked, and my voice was edged with hysteria.

"We won't know exactly what happened until we have the autopsy results," Constable Desjardin said quietly. Then she squared her shoulders. "Mrs. Kilbourn, I promise you that as soon as we know how Kellee Savage died, we'll tell you. Now, I really do think it's time we got out of here."

I didn't put up an argument. When Constable Desjardin went to get the forms I had to sign, I wandered back into the staff room. It hadn't been five minutes since I'd left, but everything about the room now seemed surreal. On the wall beside the sink was a poster, black with bubble-gum-pink lettering. I read and reread it numbly, trying to comprehend its message:

No means NO. Not now means NO. I have a boy/girlfriend means NO. Maybe later means NO. No thanks means NO. You're not my type means NO. $#@!!! off means NO. I'd rather be alone right now means NO. You've/I've been drinking means NO. Silence means NO. NO MEANS NO.

After I'd signed the forms, Constable Desjardin gave me a quick assessing look. "I don't think you should be driving," she said. "I'll take you home."

"I'm fine," I said, and I thought I was, but when I went to stand, my knees buckled. Marissa Desjardin leaned forward and slid a practised arm around me.

"Let's get you some air," she said. She steered me down another corridor and onto a ward. To our immediate left was a small room with some cleaning equipment and a window that Constable Desjardin cranked open. "Take some deep breaths," she said.

I did as she told me and immediately felt better. After the

stale antiseptic air of the hospital, the oxygen was tonic. "I'm okay now," I said. "It was just a shock."

"It always is," she said.

"Even for you?"

She smiled. "How do you think I found out about this room?"

When we got to my car in the parking lot, I handed Marissa Desjardin the keys and slid gratefully into the passenger seat. We drove in silence. I was fresh out of words, and Constable Desjardin, mercifully, was not a person who saw silence as a vacuum waiting to be filled.

She pulled up expertly in front of my house. "There'll be a squad car picking me up here," she said. "It shouldn't be long." Then she added kindly, "You did fine."

"Do you know what happened to Kellee?" I asked.

She shook her head. "They'll be doing the autopsy tomorrow. If you'd like, I can call you when we have the report."

"Thanks, I'd appreciate that."

"Mrs. Kilbourn, there's something you might be able to help us with. You told Officer Kirszner that early in the evening of March 17, Kellee Savage called you several times from the Lazy Owl Bar at the university."

I nodded.

"Her body was found thirty-two kilometres east of the university. Do you have any idea what she was doing out in that field?"

I thought of Kellee's bedroom in Indian Head: the girlish pink-and-white bedspread, the Care Bear and the Strawberry Shortcake doll positioned so carefully on the pillows. "I think she was trying to go home," I said.

Constable Desjardin sighed. "You'd be amazed at how often they are," she said. She reached over and touched my hand. "If you don't mind my saying so, Kellee Savage was lucky to have a teacher like you."

I tried a smile. "Thanks," I said. "But you couldn't be more wrong about that."

After the squad car came for Marissa Desjardin, I sat in the Volvo, taking deep breaths and trying to shake off the existential horror that gripped me. It was an impossible task, and when the clock on the dashboard showed that ten minutes had elapsed, I gave it up as a bad job and headed for the house. Taylor met me at the front door. She was in her nightie, and I noticed she'd pinned her "Hospitals Are Full of Helpers" button to its yoke.

"How's your hand?" I asked.

"It's okay," she said. "I was brave, wasn't I?"

I put my arm around her. "Very brave."

She moved closer to me. "It was nice of them to give me the button, but I hate hospitals, Jo."

"Me too," I said. "Let's do what we can to stay away from them for a while."

When Taylor wandered off to find Benny and take care of his final needs of the day, I went into the kitchen. There was a note in Taylor's careful printing on the kitchen table. "Anna Lee called." It took me a minute to connect Anna Lee with Annalie Brinkmann, but when I did I started for the phone.

As I picked up the receiver, the memory of Kellee's ravaged face hit me like a slap, and a wave of dizziness engulfed me. I leaned against the wall. I wasn't hungry, but I knew I had to eat. I poured the last of the won-ton soup into a bowl and stuck it in the microwave. The soup was good, and after I ate it, I felt better. Still, I knew that all the won-ton soup in the Kowloon Kitchen couldn't make me strong enough for the task at hand. Annalie Brinkmann would have to wait. I rinsed my bowl and put it in the dishwasher, then, with limbs that felt like lead, I walked to the phone and dialled Neil McCallum's number.

Like many people confronted with brutal news, Neil's first refuge was disbelief. "You could have made a mistake," he said, "or the police could have. Everybody makes mistakes."

When, finally, I'd convinced Neil that there was no mistake, that Kellee Savage was the woman in the photographs I'd seen, he grew quiet. "I'm going to hang up now," he said. "I don't want you to hear me cry."

I didn't try to dissuade him. Neil had announced his decision with great dignity. He knew what he was doing; besides, I was fresh out of what Emily Dickinson called "those little anodynes that deaden suffering."

That night I couldn't sleep. For hours, I lay between the cool sheets, watching the shifting patterns of the moonlight on my ceiling, breathing in air scented by the narcissi growing in pots in front of my open window, and wondering what kind of fate could decree that a twenty-one-year-old woman should die before she had known a lifetime of nights like this. When, at last, I drifted into sleep, the room was dark and the air had grown cold, but I still didn't have an answer.

The first voice I heard the next morning came from my clock radio. The newsreader was intoning the final words of an all-too-familiar litany: "name withheld, pending notification of next of kin," she said, and I knew my day had begun.

When the dogs and I set off for our run, the city was thick with fog. As we started across Albert Street, there wasn't a car in sight. Obviously, most of Regina's citizens were smarter than I was. While we were waiting for the light to change, I reached down and rubbed my golden retriever's head. "Looks like we've got the world all to ourselves, Rosie," I said. She looked at me with disdain; apparently, that morning, she regarded the world with as little enthusiasm as I did.

Our progress through the park was slow. There were patches of muddy leaves on the path that curved around the shoreline. The leaves were slick and we had to travel carefully to avoid a misstep. As we rounded the lake, Sadie began to whimper with weariness. I reassured her and slowed our pace even more. And so we headed home: a woman in middle age and her two old dogs, trying to find their way through the fog. It was a metaphor I could have lived without.

By the time I'd taken the dogs' leashes off and fed them, I knew I was running on empty. It was time to shut down. I didn't have classes that day, and there was plenty of work on my desk at the university that could just as easily be done at home.

When I looked into my closet, the prospect of selecting something to wear to the university suddenly became as daunting as a run in the Boston Marathon. Anyone I ran into that day was just going to have to take me as they found me. Unfortunately, the first person I ran into was Rosalie Norman.

When I came into the Political Science offices, she looked at my jeans and sweatshirt assessingly. "Are we having Casual Friday on Thursday this week?" she asked.

"I've decided to work at home today."

Since the advent of her fatal perm, Rosalie had taken to wearing a series of hand-knitted tams. The tam *du jour* was the colour of powdered cheese and, as she framed her response to me, Rosalie tucked a wiry curl back under its protection.

"Must be nice to be able to work at home whenever you feel like it," she said.

"I'm hoping it'll be productive, too," I said.

"I suppose you'll want me to handle your calls."

"If you don't mind."

"What do you want me to tell them?"

"Tell them I'll call them tomorrow," I said. "Or tell them to go hell, whichever you prefer."

I walked out of the office, warmed by the pleasure of meanness. For the first time since I'd become a member of the Political Science department, I had rendered Rosalie Norman speechless.

One of the realities of university teaching is that mindless tasks are never in short supply, and it didn't take me long to fill a file folder with work that demanded less than my complete attention. I had my jacket zipped up and I was on my way out the door when I saw Kellee's tape-recorder on my shelf, waiting to be claimed. From the time she had asked permission to tape my lectures so she wouldn't miss anything, I had never seen her without it. The tape-recorder had seemed an extension of Kellee, ubiquitous and imbued with her plodding, mechanical determination to complete the task at hand.

When she'd telephoned me from the Owl on the last night of her life, Kellee had bragged about getting "proof." She hadn't mentioned the tape-recorder, but Linda Van Sickle had.

I went to my shelf and took down the tape-recorder. Linda had said there'd been some sort of blowup when Kellee's classmates had discovered she was taping their private conversations. I rewound the tape and pressed *play*, hoping, I guess, for some sort of revelation, but all I got were the sounds of a student bar on a Friday night: music; a burst of laughter; a drunken shout; more laughter. The first voice I was able to recognize belonged to a young woman named Jeannine who was in the Politics and the Media seminar, and who had told me on at least three separate occasions that I was her role model. As it turned out, she was talking about me again.

"If I'd known Kilbourn was such a bitch about not letting people express their own ideas I wouldn't have taken her fucking course. You know what she gave me on my last paper? Fifty-eight per cent! Just because I didn't use secondary sources! I showed that paper to my boyfriend and a lot of other people. Everybody says I should've got an A."

Unexpectedly, it was Jumbo Hryniuk who jumped to my defence. "Kilbourn's all right," he said. "She's kinda like my coach – tough, but generally pretty fair."

The conversation drifted to other subjects: exam schedules; a new coffee place downtown; the most recent movie at the public library. Then Jeannine was back, whispering sibilantly to Linda. "Doesn't it piss you off," she said, "that even though your marks are better, Val Massey's probably going to get that *Globe and Mail* placement? And he's only getting it because he sucked up to you-know-who. I know everybody brown-noses, but I hate the ones who get their nose right in there."

Linda's voice was mild. "Val's not a brown-noser," she said. "There's no reason he can't be friends with somebody on faculty."

"If you ask me, I think it's more than that," Jeannine hissed. "I'd have too much pride to do what he's doing, but it's going to pay off. Wait and see."

Someone whose voice I didn't recognize joined the group, and the topic changed. I listened until the tape ended, but there were no more references to the *Globe and Mail* placement, and there were no more references to Val Massey.

As I walked to my car, Jeannine's sour little discourse on brown-nosing was still on my mind. She had been wrong, at least in part. Not all students saw sucking up to professors as the surest route to academic success. Still, a surprising number did, and an equally surprising number of faculty members fell for student blandishments, hook, line, and sinker.

It was an old game, but Val Massey had never struck me as a player. The only faculty member Val had ever seemed close to was Tom Kelsoe, and that relationship was more complex than a simple friendship. At twenty-one, Val was a little old for hero worship and, to my mind at least, Tom didn't fit the job description, but there was no mistaking Val's unquestioning adoration. It had puzzled me until the day the kids and I had stopped at Masluk's Garage in Regina Beach. Given Val's father's performance the day we saw him, it wasn't surprising that Val had been desperate for someone to look up to.

All things considered I had a pretty good day. By mid-morning the fog had moved off and the sun was shining. I bundled up and took my work and my coffee out on the deck. Just before noon, Taylor called me into the house to show me her mural. Nanabush and the Close-Your-Eyes Dance was taking shape. Most of the time there wasn't much I could do to help Taylor with her art, but giving her the Chagall book had obviously been an inspiration. I'd hoped Chagall's "Flying Over Town," with its magical mix of reality and myth, would help Taylor paint the picture she wanted to paint, and it had. The world she'd created with her poster paints seemed to me to be very like the world Alex Kequahtooway had conjured up for us on those winter evenings when we listened to the wind howl and felt the darkness come alive with his tales of the Trickster.

Taylor was eyeing me anxiously. "Do you think it's any good?" she said finally.

"It's terrific," I said.

"Do you think Alex will like it?"

"I know he'll like it. As Angus would say, it's the smokingest."

She didn't smile. "Jo, when is Alex coming back?"

"Soon, I hope."

"But you don't know for sure."

"No," I said, "I don't know for sure."

After lunch, Taylor and I went to the mall to see the movie that was required viewing for everyone under the age of twelve that Easter. As I sat in the dark, smelling the wet-wool smell of little kids, watching the endless procession of parents and children moving up and down the aisles, slopping drinks, spilling popcorn, heading for washrooms, I felt my nerves unknot. The holiday matinee was familiar turf, and it was a relief, for once, just to sit back and watch the movie.

When we pulled up in front of the house after the movie, Angus and his friend Camillo were in the driveway, shooting hoops. I dropped Taylor off and went to pick up our dry cleaning.

Taylor was all smiles when I got back. "Guess who called?"

"I don't know. You're the one who was here. Why don't you tell me?"

"Alex. He said to tell you he's sorry he missed you and he'll call again Saturday night. He and Eli . . ." She scrunched her face. "Who's Eli?"

"Alex's nephew. He's the same age as Angus."

"Anyway, Alex and Eli are going to some island up there. He says he'll bring me a fish when he comes back."

"Did he say when that's going to be?"

"No, but guess what, Jo? I invited Alex to the Kids Convention to see the mural and he says wild horses couldn't keep him away. That's good, eh?"

"That's more than good," I said. "The Kids Convention is on the tenth – not long at all."

Angus and I were upstairs looking for the shorts to his basketball uniform when Annalie Brinkmann called. As soon as I heard her pleasant contralto, I felt a twinge. "I'm sorry," I said. "I meant to get back to you. But when I got your message, I'd just had some bad news. I teach at the university here, and one of our students died."

I could hear her intake of breath. "Not the one who was being harassed?" she said.

I felt as if I'd been kicked in the stomach. "How did you know about that?"

"Then it was her?"

"Yes," I said. "The student who died was Kellee Savage."

"Kellee Savage," she repeated dully. "Reed didn't tell me her name. And now he's dead too."

"Ms Brinkmann, how are you connected to this?"

"Through history," she said heavily, "and through Reed Gallagher. I have to know – did that young woman – did Kellee Savage commit suicide? Because if he drove her to that . . ." Her voice broke. When she spoke again, it was apparent she was fighting for control. "I'm not an hysterical person, Mrs. Kilbourn, but this case has a special resonance. Twenty years ago, what happened to Kellee Savage happened to me."

"Ms Brinkmann, you're going to have to . . ."

She cut me off. "I'm sorry," she said. "I know I'm being elliptical." Her pleasant voice had gone flat. "I was in J school here in Toronto. Reed Gallagher was my instructor. Charges were made." Unexpectedly, she sobbed. "Without ever seeing her, I can tell you what Kellee Savage was like. She worked hard. She took journalism seriously, and . . ." Annalie Brinkmann hesitated. "And she was ugly."

"What else did Reed tell you?"

"Not much. He just left a message on my machine – said he was having a problem with a student, that she was accusing another student of harassment, and he was afraid there might be some truth to her charges. Then he said he thought, because of my history, I might be able to help him get to the truth."

"Why would he drag you into this after twenty years? Did he just want your advice because what Kellee was going through was similar to what you'd gone through?"

Annalie laughed, not pleasantly. "It wasn't similar; it was identical. I was the prototype: the ugly girl who worked hard and came up with something the handsome young man wanted; the ugly girl who couldn't make anybody believe her when she said the handsome young man was pursuing her sexually. Mrs. Kilbourn, Reed Gallagher called me because he was suddenly facing the possibility that twenty years ago, when he believed the handsome young man instead of believing me, he'd put his money on the wrong horse."

I thought of Tom Kelsoe taking the picture of Reed and Annalie and shoving it into the paper-towel receptacle in the Faculty Club washroom. Suddenly, in the midst of all the questions, there was one answer. "The man who did that to you was Tom Kelsoe, wasn't it?" I said.

"Yes." Annalie's voice was low with anger. "It was Tom, and I'll tell you something else. Without knowing any of the circumstances of Kellee's death, I can assure you that when the facts come to light, you'll discover that that bastard Kelsoe might as well have been holding a pistol to her head."

After that, Annalie's account of her relationship with Tom Kelsoe tumbled out. Twenty years had passed, but the pain of what Tom Kelsoe had done to her was still acute.

Like so many tragedies, Annalie's grew out of an act of misplaced altruism. When Annalie left her home town and moved to Toronto to study journalism, she was lonely and homesick. Working on the premise that one way out of her misery might be to help someone whose problems were larger than her own, she became a volunteer at a private hospice for children with incurable diseases. The place was called Sunshine House, and it didn't take Annalie long to realize that it was an institution with serious problems: administrative staff had thin credentials and fat expense accounts; the personnel charged with the care of the children were incompetent or indifferent; the children themselves were casually ignored or abused. Despite the conditions, Annalie stayed on for two and a half years – in part because she felt the children needed an ally, and in part because she was patiently building up a dossier on the mismanagement at Sunshine House.

By the time Annalie Brinkmann and Tom Kelsoe were thrown together in an investigative journalism class, two things had happened: the dossier on Sunshine House was bulging, and Annalie had been fired as a volunteer. She'd been caught in the director's office photocopying a particularly damning file. Sunshine House was about to launch a major fundraising campaign, and they had put together a series of heartbreaking pictures of dying children; the problem was the children had all been recruited from a modelling agency, and they were all healthy as horses. The director of Sunshine House had been brutal in his internal memorandum justifying the expense of hiring professionals: "a picture of any of the kids here would make Mr. and Mrs. John Q. Public throw up. We're not going to get our target group to write big cheques if they've got their eyes closed."

Even without the modelling-agency file, Annalie knew she had a story, but the director's letter was dynamite, and she wanted it. When a fellow student in the investigative journalism class confided that he hadn't come up with a subject for his major report, Annalie thought she'd found a perfect fit. No one at Sunshine House would suspect a connection between her and Tom Kelsoe. Tom could copy the relevant file and dig up whatever other dirt he could find. He would come out of the experience with enough material for a term paper, and she'd have a shining bauble to dangle in front of the Toronto media.

It was, in Annalie's mind, a fair exchange, but after agreeing to her plan, Tom Kelsoe decided not to trade. After he'd photocopied the modelling-agency file, he told Annalie he'd unearthed some material that was even more damaging, and that he needed time to bring it to light. When she objected, he surprised her by making a crude but unmistakable pass.

The pattern continued. Every time she pressed him about the file, he fondled her and murmured about their future together. Annalie was, by her own assessment, both plain and naive. She had never had a date in her life. A more experienced young woman would have seen through Tom Kelsoe's ploy, but Annalie didn't. She believed the lies and she enjoyed the sexual stirrings. She created a fantasy in which she and Tom were journalists, travelling the world together, famous and enviable. She knew the Sunshine House story was their entrée into the glittering media world. So complete was her belief in the fantasy that, on the day she passed a newsstand and saw the Sunshine House exposé on page one of the evening paper, her first thought was that Tom had surprised her by getting their story published. When she saw that the only name on the by-line was Tom Kelsoe's, she fell apart.

By the time she pulled herself together enough to go to Reed Gallagher, Tom Kelsoe had beaten her to the punch. Tom's version of the story had enough basis in truth to be credible. He acknowledged that Annalie had been a volunteer at Sunshine House, but he said she'd been fired before she had anything more solid than suspicions. He acknowledged that Annalie had suggested that he volunteer his services at Sunshine House, but he said the story he dug up was all his own.

Then Tom Kelsoe made a pre-emptive strike. He confided to Reed that he had a terrible personal problem. Annalie had, Tom explained, become obsessed with him. She was phoning him at all hours of the night, following him on the street. He was, he told Reed, afraid for her sanity, but he was also afraid for himself.

Annalie said Reed had been very compassionate with her, very concerned. He heard her story, then he suggested she seek counselling. When she objected, he talked gently to Annalie about the importance of a journalist's good name. When that didn't work, he talked less gently about the possibility that, if she kept harassing him, Tom might be compelled to seek legal redress against her. By the time she left Reed's office, Annalie knew that Reed Gallagher hadn't believed a word she'd said. She also knew she had no alternative but to withdraw from J school.

She'd been lucky. She'd got a job at a small FM station that played classical music, and had been there ever since. She had married. Her husband didn't want children. He didn't like confusion. It had been, Annalie said, a very quiet life.

"But a good one," I said.

She laughed. "Yes," she said, "I've had a good life, but then so has Tom Kelsoe."

The first item on the 6:00 news was Constable Desjardin's announcement that the name of the woman whose body had been found in the farmer's field was Kellee Savage. When I made the identification of the body at the hospital, I had thought the worst was over, but the official announcement of Kellee's death hit me hard. There were no surprises in the way the television story unfolded; nonetheless, as Marissa's image was replaced by shots of the area in which the body had been found, and as the death scene faded into the inevitable interview with the finder of the body, I started to shake.

I turned off the television. I didn't need TV images to underscore a truth that seemed more and more unassailable: Reed Gallagher's death hadn't been accidental. I didn't know who killed him, and I didn't know why, but I was sure of one thing: as soon as I knew what had happened to Kellee in the hours before she started her final, fatal walk home, a giant piece in the puzzle of Reed's death would slide into place. A theory was starting to gather at the edges of my mind, but a theory without substantiation wasn't enough. I needed proof. Annalie Brinkmann's story had been compelling, but if I was going to prove that Tom Kelsoe was behind Val Massey's harassment of Kellee, I had to have more to go on than a twenty-year-old story from a woman I didn't know. I needed to come up with some solid reasons why Kellee Savage had been worth attacking.

There was another reason I needed proof. If I was going to blow Tom Kelsoe out of the water, I had to make sure Jill was ready for the blast. She deserved to know the truth, and that meant waiting until I was absolutely certain what the truth was. I called Rapti Lustig to see if she knew when Jill would be back from Toronto. Rapti said Jill had called her to say she had a meeting Saturday morning, but she'd be back in time for the show. That meant she'd be on the late-afternoon flight. I started to ask Rapti for Jill's number in Toronto, but decided against it. If I phoned Jill to tell her I wanted to pick her up at the airport, she'd have questions, and, at the moment, I didn't have enough answers.

I ran through a mental list of what needed to be done before I confronted Jill with my suspicions. I had to go back to Dahl Street. I wanted to talk to Marissa Desjardin and I wanted to talk again to some of the people who'd been closest to Kellee in the Politics and the Media seminar. But the first piece in the puzzle was Val Massey's. I picked up the phone, called Information, got the number of Masluk's Garage and began to dial.

CHAPTER

13

There was no answer at Masluk's Garage the first time I called, and there was no answer any of the other times I dialled the Regina Beach number that night. The next morning, before I left for the university, I made a final stab at getting in touch with Val, but I came up empty again. It was puzzling. Val's father had struck me as the type who wouldn't shut his business for anything short of the Second Coming.

When I got to the university, Rosalie Norman was waiting for me. Today's knitted tam was a pretty shade of chestnut.

"That's a nice colour on you," I said. "It brings out your eyes."

She looked at me suspiciously. After my performance the previous day, I could hardly blame her. "I'm sorry about yesterday," I said. "The police had called me the night before to go downtown and identify Kellee Savage. I guess I was still pretty shaky when I came in here."

"Next time, if you're having personal problems, mention it," she said.

"I will," I promised meekly.

She handed me an envelope. "Professor Mariani asked me to give you this."

I looked inside the envelope. It was Ed's key to the office. "More coals upon my head," I said.

Rosalie's blackberry eyes were bright with interest. "Did you two have a fight? It's never a good idea to share a work space. That's what they told us at our ergonomics seminar."

"I guess they were right," I said, and my tone was so bleak that I startled myself. The sight that greeted me when I opened the door to my office didn't improve my spirits. On my desk were a florist's vase filled with irises and a gift beautifully wrapped in iris-covered wrapping paper. I opened the box. It was a paella pan with Barry Levitt's recipe, and a note in Ed's neat hand: "For Taylor and for you, with thanks and affection, E."

I called Ed's home to thank him, but there was no answer. I called Masluk's Garage. No answer there, either. Apparently, it was not my day to reach out and touch someone. Just as I was hanging up, Linda Van Sickle and Jumbo arrived.

Linda's glow had dimmed. Her face was pale and her eyes were dull. "I feel so awful," she said. "I can't stop thinking about Kellee. I keep replaying that evening, thinking about all the points where I could have acted differently."

"Me too," I said.

"There's no use retrospecting," Jumbo said sagely. "That's what my coach tells us and he's right. You've got to focus on what's ahead."

"What's ahead doesn't look all that terrific, either," I said. "But you're right. Going over what might have been is a pretty profitless exercise. Was there something special you two wanted to talk about?"

"The funeral," Linda said flatly. "Do you know when it's going to be? Jumbo and I think we should be there."

"I agree," I said. "You should be there. So should a lot of other people – Val, for instance. Have you seen him today?"

Jumbo and Linda glanced at one another quickly.

"No," Jumbo said. "We haven't seen Val. He wasn't in class yesterday and he wasn't at our eight-thirty seminar this morning."

Linda hugged herself as if she were cold. "I'm worried about him," she said. "The news about Kellee is going to devastate him."

Jumbo frowned. "Well, at least he's got nothing to feel guilty about. That night at the Owl when Kellee left, he was the only one who – "

Linda touched his arm, as if to hold him back.

Jumbo turned to her, perplexed. "Val tried to do the right thing. Why shouldn't I talk about it?"

Linda started to respond, but I cut her off. "Jumbo, what did Val do that night?"

"When Kellee left the bar, he went after her. I guess he knew she was in no shape to be out there alone."

"Why didn't he stay with her?"

Jumbo shrugged. "I don't know. I didn't see him again that night. Neither did anybody else. He never came back."

After Jumbo and Linda left, I went down to the library. The silent rows of books and journals were balm to my raw nerves. It was a relief to have concrete proof that ultimately all information and speculation can be catalogued neatly by the Library of Congress. By the time I got back to my office, the late-afternoon sun was pouring through my window. I put on my coat and packed up my books, then I caught sight of the telephone and decided to give Val's number one last try.

The voice that answered was male and as wintry as a Prairie January.

"I'm trying to get in touch with Val Massey," I said.

"He's not here."

"You're not Mr. Masluk, are you?"

"I'm the neighbour."

"Do you know when the Masluks are expected back? This really is important. I'm one of Val's teachers at the university, and there's something I have to talk to him about."

"They're at the hospital."

"What?"

The voice was kinder now, patient in the way of someone giving road directions. "Herman had to take young Val into the General this morning. I don't want to say any more than that. It's not my business."

"Is Val all right?"

"He's gonna be, but he gave everybody a scare. Now, I think you'd better save the rest of your questions for Herman or for Val when he's able."

I called Regina General and asked for Val's room number. The operator told me it was 517F – the psychiatric unit. The nurse at the charge desk told me that Val wasn't allowed visitors yet, but that his father was putting together a short list of people who could see Val the next day.

When I turned the Volvo onto the parkway, I was deep in the puzzle of Val Massey's connection with Kellee's death. I didn't see the city bus until it was almost upon me. I hit the brake, and the bus sped on. As it passed me, I saw Tom Kelsoe's picture on its side panel. He was wearing his stressed-leather jacket, his black hair was tousled, and his eyes burned with integrity. Under the photo, in block letters, was the word "KELSOE!" Then, in smaller letters, "Saturdays at 6:00, only on Nationtv." There were no pictures of Glayne Axtell or Senator Sam Spiegel. Just of Tom. He'd moved quickly. As I pulled up in front of our house, I knew it was time that I moved quickly, too.

When I walked into the living room, Taylor was kneeling at the coffee table drawing and Angus and Leah were sitting on the rug, drinking tea and playing Monopoly. Angus was in the middle of his usual Monopoly cash-flow problem, and he waved at me absently. "There's a message from Constable somebody-or-other, but it's nothing to worry about. You're just supposed to give her a call. Her number's on your desk."

Marissa Desjardin sounded weary. "There are no surprises in the pathology report," she said. "Death due to a combination of acute alcohol poisoning and exposure. In other words, Kellee Savage drank enough to shut down her major systems, and the weather did the rest."

I thought of the wicked storm we'd had on the night of March 17. It made sense and yet . . . "Constable Desjardin, if Kellee was that drunk, how did she get so far?"

"That occurred to us too, and we're looking into it. The most likely explanation is that once Kellee hit the highway, somebody picked her up and gave her a lift. I'll bet whoever picked her up regretted it. They'd probably have to fumigate their car. Even after two weeks in the open air, her clothes smelled like a brewery."

Something about what she said nagged at me. "You mean Kellee's clothes smelled of beer?"

"They were soaked in it. There was an empty beer bottle beside her when they found her, and a full bottle in her book bag. Do you have any other questions?"

"No," I said. "Thanks. That's all I needed to know."

As soon as I hung up, I realized why Marissa Desjardin's reference to the smell on Kellee's clothes had nagged at me. When Linda Van Sickle described Kellee's drinking that night, she said she'd been struck by the fact that Kellee had been drinking Scotch. The beer-soaked clothes were another puzzle piece that just didn't fit. I was more anxious than ever to talk to Val Massey.

It was close to 8:30 when I finally got through to Herman Masluk, and he was ready for me. It seemed that during his time at the hospital, Herman had figured out that the blame for everything that had gone wrong with his son could be laid on the doorstep of the university, and that night the closest he could get to the university was me.

Between the accusations and the invective, a few facts emerged. Sometime during the previous night, Val had tried to commit suicide. Herman Masluk had found his son parked in an old garage they sometimes used for storing vehicles. The door to the garage had been closed, and the motor of Val's Honda Civic had been running. Val had attached a length of hose to the exhaust and run it through the window on the passenger side into the car's interior. Mr. Masluk had been out looking for his son all night. It was just good luck that he noticed that the door to the garage hadn't been closed properly.

The ferocity of Herman Masluk's anger rocked me; so did the depth of his love for Val. It was apparent from what he said that he felt he'd been engaged in a battle for Val's soul. The university and all it stood for was anathema to this man who had worked for a lifetime to give his son a profitable business. Val's suicide attempt had terrified his father, but it had been proof that he was right, that nothing but trouble came from those alien buildings on the plain.

As he talked about Val, I found myself warming to Herman Masluk, and when it seemed his tirade had run its course, I told him about my daughter, Mieka, and the struggle we'd had when she decided to quit university. He listened intently, and soon the two of us moved into a discussion of that age-old topic: the struggle between a parent's experience and a child's hope. I told him that when I felt I was floundering with our kids, I'd often found my bearings by remembering C.P. Snow's line that the love between a parent and a child is the only love that must grow towards separation. He was silent for a moment, then he asked me to write out what I'd just said and bring it along with me to the hospital when I visited Val. Before he said goodbye, Herman Masluk told me that Val had never known his own mother, and that maybe what his son needed was a lady's perspective. I told him I'd do my best.

After I hung up, I dialled Ed Mariani's number. I knew Ed would want to know about Val; more selfishly, I welcomed any excuse that would allow me to get my relationship with him back on solid ground. There was no answer at Ed and Barry's, but I left a message on the machine, thanking them both for the paella dish and telling Ed I'd be in touch.

By the time I got to Taylor's room to tuck her in, she'd fallen asleep. In the crook of her right arm was the Marc Chagall book; in the crook of her left arm was Benny. When I reached down to move the book, he shot me a look filled with reproach.

"I've learned to live with your displeasure, Benny," I whispered, and I turned out the light and went downstairs. I made myself a pot of tea and put Wynton Marsalis's recording of Haydn's Concerto for Trumpet and Orchestra in E-flat Major on the CD player. I had plans to make, and I needed an infusion of clarity. As they did surprisingly often, Haydn and Marsalis did their stuff, and by the time I went to bed, I had the next day pretty well mapped out. The last thing I did before I turned out the light was drop Tom Kelsoe's book, *Getting Even*, into my bag.

If I had believed in omens, I would have found plenty to reassure me in the weather on Saturday morning. The sky was blue, the sun was bright, and I could feel the possibilities of birdsong and wildflowers in the air. Even the house on Dahl Street looked less grim.

As it had been on Tuesday, the front door was propped open with a brick, but this time when I pounded on the inside door, a girl about Taylor's age opened it and let me in. Flushed with good luck, I ran upstairs and knocked on the door to number 3. A good-looking native kid with a brushcut answered, and as he gave me the once-over, I was able to look past his shoulder and get a glimpse of life in apartment 3 on a Saturday morning. The television was blaring cartoons, and a boy, who judging from his looks was the older brother of the boy who had answered the door, was sitting on the couch. Beside him was the woman I had frightened so badly when I'd come in unannounced on Tuesday. Today, she had a pink ribbon tying back her long dark hair, and, as I watched, the boy reached up and smoothed it with a gesture of such tenderness that I felt my throat catch.

Across the room was the blonde who'd thrown me out. Today she was in blue jeans, a denim jacket, and her Nancy Sinatra boots. She was wholly engrossed in the television. Apparently, she'd been expecting a delivery, because when I came in, she gestured towards the door without looking up. "My purse is on the table, Darrel," she said. "Give the kid a nice tip."

"It's somebody else," Darrel said. As soon as she heard his words, the blonde woman's head swivelled towards me. She might have looked like a superannuated superstar Barbie, but she moved like the wind. Within seconds, she was so close to me that our noses were almost touching. "Teacher," she said in a voice heavy with exasperation. "This is Saturday. No school today. Go home."

I stood my ground. "I want you to listen to something," I said. "If you decide you don't want to hear what I'm saying, stop me. I'll leave and, I promise you, I won't bother you again."

Without waiting for her answer, I pulled *Getting Even* out

of my purse and started to read the story of Karen Keewatin and her sons. I didn't get far before the blonde reached out and took the book from me.

"Let's go out in the hall," she said. "My name's Bernice Jacobs, and you and I got things to talk about."

Half an hour later, I was back on the sidewalk outside the apartment on Dahl Street. I was edgy but exhilarated; Bernice Jacobs had not only confirmed my theory about what had happened to Kellee Savage, she'd come up with some theories of her own.

When I saw the little girl who'd let me into the building throwing a ball against the side wall of the apartment, I called out and thanked her. What I had learned from Bernice Jacobs was terrible, but knowledge is a sturdier weapon than ignorance, and I was grateful I didn't have to go into the battle ahead unarmed.

I was halfway down the block when I heard the kitten's thin mewing. I almost kept walking. Taylor was the cat person in our family, and I had enough on my plate. But the image of the kerosene-soaked animal I'd seen the first time I'd come to Dahl Street was a powerful spur. I turned and retraced my steps.

The little tortoise-shell had crawled in between two garbage cans in the alley beside the apartment building where Bernice lived. When I moved one of the cans to get a closer look, the kitten struggled to get away. It didn't get very far. It was dragging its right front leg and, as I watched, it collapsed from the effort. I went back to my car and got the blanket we kept in the trunk in case we got stuck in a blizzard. After I'd wrapped the cat up, I went back to the building on Dahl Street. The little girl was still throwing her ball against the side wall. I could hear her voice, singsonging through the same ball chant I'd used forty years earlier:

"Ordinary, moving, laughing, talking, one hand, the other hand, one foot, the other foot." When she dropped the ball just before "clap in the front," I made my move. I pulled the blanket back so she could see the kitten's face.

"Do you know who this belongs to?" I asked.

She glanced at it without interest. "It don't belong to nobody."

"Are you sure?"

She sighed heavily. "It lives on the street," she said, and she turned away and threw her ball against the wall. "Ordinary, moving . . . ," she began. I covered the cat again and headed for the Volvo. It was 10:30; our vet stayed open till noon on Saturday mornings.

Dr. Roy Crawford had been our vet for more than twenty-five years. He was a gentle, unflappable man, but he winced when he looked at the cat I'd brought in.

"Can you do anything?" I asked.

He looked at me hard. "It depends."

"On what?"

"On whether this animal has a home to go to when I'm finished. That leg's going to need surgery. There's no point operating on this animal if it's going to be euthanized in a couple of weeks. Your decision, Mrs. K."

"It'll have a home," I said.

He raised an eyebrow. "With you?"

"Where else?" I said. "Incidentally, is it a male or a female?"

Roy Crawford leaned over and checked out the cat's equipment. "Male," he said. Then he smiled. "There's going to be hell to pay when Benny has to abdicate the throne."

"Benny won't abdicate," I said. "He believes he's there by divine right. But he is going to have to learn to share the crown."

By the time I'd signed the papers at Roy's, it was past

11:00. Herman Masluk had said that since the only two names on Val's visitors' list were his and mine, I could go to the hospital whenever it suited me. Eleven o'clock seemed as good a time as any.

I parked in the lot beside the General, made my way past the inevitable cluster of patients and practitioners huddled around the doorway smoking, and headed for the elevators. When I stepped out on the fifth floor, I was facing a desk and a nurse who looked like a defensive lineman. He had a lineman's professional warmth, too, but when I'd finally satisfied him that my name was on his list, he looked almost cordial. "Can't be too careful," he growled.

"You're telling me," I said, and I walked down the hall towards room 517.

It surprised me that Val was in his bed. At first, I thought he must be sleeping, but when I called his name, he turned. Then, reminding me of just how young twenty-one really is, he dived under the pillow.

I pulled a chair up and sat by the side of the bed. "We have to talk, Val," I said, "but I can wait till you're ready."

Waiting for Val to decide when to face the inevitable gave me far more time than I needed to check out his room. It was small and relentlessly functional; the only non-institutional touch was a soothing landscape of a pastel boat in which no one would ever sit, drifting serenely on a pastel lake which no ripple would ever disturb. Prozac art.

I'd just begun to wonder if I'd erred in letting Val take the initiative when he sat up, swung his legs over the side of the bed, and faced me. He was wearing a blue-striped hospital gown that seemed designed to strip the wearer of dignity, but Val managed to give even that shapeless garment a certain style.

"It's my fault she's dead," he said, and there was an edge

of hysteria in his voice that frightened me. "I didn't mean for any of it to happen, but she's still dead, isn't she?" His face crumpled, and he buried it in his hands.

I reached out and touched his shoulder. "Yes," I said, "Kellee's dead. But, Val, if you can tell me what really happened between you and her, I think we can get at the truth."

"And the truth will set me free," he said bitterly.

"No," I said, "you'll never be free of this. But the truth might help you put what you did into perspective. Start at the beginning."

"You know the beginning," he said. "She was telling lies about . . ."

"About Tom Kelsoe," I said.

Val sighed with relief. "I'm so glad he finally decided to talk to somebody about it. Tom always puts other people first. Even when Kellee was trying to destroy him, he protected her. The night he called and told me that she was accusing him of sexual harassment, I said he should go to Professor Gallagher. But you know Tom. All he thinks about is his students. He said that Professor Gallagher would have to expel Kellee, and he didn't want that." Val's voice was filled with the fervour of the acolyte. "But Tom said that for Kellee's own good she had to learn that a journalist's reputation for truth must be beyond reproach."

"So he got you to put Kellee in a position where everyone would believe she was lying."

Val leapt up from the bed and began pacing. "She was lying about him. Can you imagine anybody lying about a man like Tom Kelsoe? You were at his book launch. You heard what he wrote about Karen Keewatin and her sons. That's the kind of journalist he is. He sees the dignity in every one, and Kellee was going to destroy him." Val's voice broke with emotion. "All I was trying to do was protect the finest man I've ever known, but everything went wrong."

He was close to the edge, but I had to keep pushing. "Val, what happened at the Owl that night?"

He came back and sat on the bed. "It all happened so fast. I'd been over at Tom's office, so I was late getting to the Owl. When she saw me, Kellee went crazy. Somehow she'd figured out why I'd been . . . bothering her. She was very drunk and very hostile. She said she couldn't trust anybody at the university, so she was going to the media. She started hitting me, and then somebody – I think it was Meaghan Andrechuk – said Kellee had her tape-recorder going. By that time a lot of people had had too much to drink and there was a kind of scene. Then we heard that they'd just announced on TV that Reed Gallagher was dead. Kellee was standing in front of me. It was awful. All the blood just went out of her face. At first, I thought she was going to pass out, but she just grabbed her bag and left."

"Did she take any beer with her?"

Val looked at me curiously. "Beer? No. Why? Did somebody say she had?"

"No," I said. "I'm sorry. Go on."

"There's not much more to tell. I went after Kellee. She was over the edge. I was afraid she really was going to go to the media. When I got outside, I saw that she was walking in the direction of the J school, so I followed her." Val shook his head. "I watched until she went inside. Believe it or not, I thought the worst was over. I figured she'd just go into the cafeteria and drink coffee until she'd sobered up."

"And that was the last you saw of her."

"Yes, I was pretty much out of the party mood by then, so I just drove home."

"And people saw you there?"

"Friday's my Father's poker night. All the real men in town were sitting in his living room drinking rye and smoking Player's. I sat in the game until three in the morning."

"But you didn't go to bed after that, did you? You went back to the campus to make sure there was nothing on Reed Gallagher's computer that would incriminate Tom Kelsoe."

"Tom phoned me at home. He laid the situation out for me. No one knew what Kellee Savage had told Professor Gallagher. And now that he was dead, there was no way we could explain the truth to him. Tom said the last thing Professor Gallagher would have wanted to leave behind was a legacy of lies." Val raked his hands through his hair. "Dr. Kilbourn, I know it's hard to understand the vandalism, but Tom said that this was a case of doing the wrong deed for the right reason."

"And that made sense to you?"

"Yes," he said. "It did. I really screwed up, didn't I?"

"I guess the important thing right now is that you don't compound the error. Val, you do know that what you tried to do Thursday night didn't make anything better. You're not going to try that particular exit again, are you?"

He blushed. "No, that was stupid."

"Good, because you've got a great life ahead of you."

"Yeah, right."

I took his hand. "I am right, Val. Check it out. After I go, why don't you ask the nurse if you can take a little walk around the hospital. Try to find one person in this whole place who has as much going for him as you do."

I opened my purse, took out the paper with the C.P. Snow quote, and handed it to him. "Your father asked me to bring this for him," I said. "You can read it if you like."

He unfolded the paper. "'The love between parent and child is the only love that must grow towards separation.'" Val looked at me uncomprehendingly. "Why would my father want this?"

I squeezed his hand. "Maybe because he knows you're not the only one who screwed things up."

Jill's plane wasn't coming in till 4:30, so after lunch I took Taylor and her friend Jess over to the Marina for ice cream. It was a bright, windy day, and on the lawn in front of the museum, people were flying kites. After the kids and I got our ice cream, we took it back to the museum lawn, found a bench in the sunshine, and gave ourselves over to the pleasures of banana splits and watching a sky splashed with diamonds as brilliantly hued as the colours in Taylor's first paint box. All in all, it was a four-star afternoon, and by the time I dropped the kids off at Jess's house I knew that, as difficult as it was going to be to tell Jill what I'd learned in the last forty-eight hours, I was ready to talk.

The problem was that Jill wasn't there to listen. My nerves were taut as I watched the passengers from the Toronto flight file into the reception area at the airport. A lot of travellers got off the plane, but I didn't spot Jill. My first thought was that, because she wasn't expecting me to pick her up, I'd simply missed her. I went over to the luggage carousel and watched as passengers grabbed their bags and headed for home. When the last bag was taken, I watched the carousel make its final revolution, then I went to the bank of phones by the doorway, dialled Nationtv, and asked for Rapti Lustig.

Rapti sounded tense, too, but it was only an hour and a half to airtime, so I wasn't surprised.

"I know you've got a million things to do," I said, "so I won't keep you, but I'm at the airport. I thought you said Jill was coming in from Toronto this afternoon. Did I get my wires crossed?"

There was a three-beat pause, then Rapti said, "Somebody's got their wires crossed. Jill called this morning to tell me

I'd have to produce the show tonight because she was delayed. We talked for ages, trying to cover all the bases. As soon as I hung up, I realized I'd forgotten to ask her what she wanted to go with as a lead-in. I tried the hotel we all use when we're in Toronto, but she wasn't registered. Then I called our Toronto office. They didn't know anything about it, Jo. As far as they knew, Jill hadn't been in the city at all this week."

"Then where is she?"

"Your guess is as good as mine."

As I hung up, I felt the first stirrings of panic. I tried to tell myself I was overreacting. Rapti had talked to Jill that morning, and she'd been all right then. Obviously, there'd just been some sort of misunderstanding. Nonetheless, as I left the terminal, I was uneasy.

I was so preoccupied that I walked right by Ed Mariani. He called after me, and when I turned, I saw that he was carrying an overnight bag and was dressed for travel. I also saw that I'd hurt him.

"If you'd rather just keep on going, you can forget you saw me," he said. "But I did want you to know how pleased I was to hear your voice on the message-minder last night. I'm glad you liked our gift."

"I don't want to forget I saw you, Ed," I said. "It's just that I have a lot on my mind."

He put down his bag and came over to me. "Is something wrong?"

"I hope not," I said. "But there are some things I'd like to talk to you about. Do you have time for a drink before your plane?"

Ed shook his head. "As usual, I've left arriving at the airport till almost the last moment. But if it's an emergency, I can change my plans."

His generosity brought tears to my eyes. "Ed, I'm sorry if I've been cool to you lately."

I could see the relief on his face. "Don't give it a second thought. I know I can be a bit overwhelming in close quarters."

"It wasn't that. It had to do with Tom Kelsoe."

Ed's eyes were wary. "What about him?"

"I saw you with him in the Faculty Club on Tuesday. It was just after I'd told you that I suspected him of abusing Jill."

"And you thought I was warning him about your suspicions."

"Ed, what were you talking to him about?"

Ed picked up his bag. "I don't want to lie to you," he said.

"Then tell me the truth. I'm going around in circles here. First Reed, then Kellee, now Jill . . ."

He took a step towards me. "Jill! Nothing's happened to her, has it?"

"No, she's fine. It's just that Tom Kelsoe is the man in her life, and suddenly everything about Tom scares me."

"It should," Ed said quietly. "Tom Kelsoe is a violent man. That's what I was talking to him about at the Faculty Club when you saw us. After what you'd told me, I had to make certain that Jill really had been mugged."

At first, the implication of what he'd said didn't hit me. When it did, my knees turned to water. "What did Tom say?"

"He was very forthcoming. He gave me all the details of the mugging. Then he told me to call Jill and ask her myself."

"And you did?"

Ed nodded. "She gave me the same account, thanked me for my concern, and told me, very politely, to mind my own business."

"And that was the end of it?"

"Yes." Ed looked at his watch. "Joanne, I really do have to get in there. My flight is boarding."

I stepped in front of him. "Ed, what made you think Tom Kelsoe was capable of violence?"

I could see he wanted to bolt, but he stayed his ground. Then, unexpectedly, he smiled. "I guess the confessional moment has come. As it inevitably does." He took a deep breath. "Okay, here it is. Last year, Barry and I were having troubles: my mid-life crisis, I guess. I started cruising again, looking for younger men." Ed looked straight into my eyes. "I'm deeply ashamed of what I did, Joanne. It was stupid and dangerous and a terrible betrayal of Barry. Of course, this being Regina, my sin did not go undetected. Nationtv was doing an investigation of male prostitution in the downtown area, and I, apparently, stumbled into camera range. When Jill saw the tape, she killed it; she also phoned me and told me . . ." He winced at the memory. "She told me that I had a good career at the university, and a great relationship with Barry, and I 'should smarten the fuck up.'"

"But you didn't."

"No, I didn't. I don't know if you've ever been close to someone who's decided to self-destruct, but our instincts to be obtuse are quite breathtaking."

"So you kept on."

"Yes, I kept on, and this time it was Tom Kelsoe who saw me on Rose Street, cruising." Ed chewed his lower lip. "Tom didn't have Jill's scruples about protecting me from myself."

"And that's why you withdrew your name from the competition for head of the J school."

"And why I shook that bastard's hand the night of his book launch. I couldn't risk him telling Barry."

I was confused. "Ed, I'm missing something here. What's the connection between Tom blackmailing you and what you said about him being violent. Did he threaten you physically?"

Ed shook his head. "No. That's not where he gets his pleasure. Jo, during my walk on the wild side last year, I heard a few things, too. Tom Kelsoe is pretty well known to the prostitutes downtown."

"Male prostitutes?"

Ed smiled sadly. "No, at least we've been spared Tom Kelsoe. As they say on 'Seinfeld,' he doesn't play for our team. Tom's a red-blooded heterosexual, but I don't think that gives women much to celebrate. Rumour has it that he's into some pretty brutal sex."

My mind was racing, but I had to acknowledge Ed's trust. "Thanks for telling me," I said. "I know it wasn't easy."

"You were the easy one, Jo. In two hours, Barry's going to meet me at the Minneapolis airport. We've got tickets for *Turandot*. It's an anniversary celebration. We've been together eight years today. I hope after I tell him, we'll still have something to celebrate."

I leaned forward and kissed his cheek. "You will," I said.

I watched as Ed Mariani plodded heavily towards the terminal. When he reached the door, he turned back. "I'll call you from Minneapolis," he said. "In the meantime, tell Jill to be careful."

"I will," I said.

Fifteen minutes later, I pulled up in front of Jill's apartment on Robinson Street. There was a moving van parked outside, and as I ran up the front steps I almost collided with a burly young man who was carrying out a love seat. "Hope you get there," he yelled after me as I pushed past him and entered the building.

By the time I got to Jill's apartment on the third floor, the adrenaline was pumping. I was prepared, if necessary, to smash the door in, but Jill surprised me by answering after my first knock. She was wearing a jacket and dark glasses, and she'd tied a scarf around her head. She'd covered as much of herself as she could, but I could still see the bruises. Without a word, I reached over and lifted her dark glasses. One of her eyes was almost swollen shut, and the bruise under the other one was fresh. But there were other marks too: bruises that had faded and cuts that were healing.

"How long has Tom been beating you up, Jill?" I said.

Her voice was surprisingly strong. "Too long," she said. "But it's over. You'll notice that I'm dressed and on my way out."

"Are you going to the police?"

"Eventually," she said. "But first, I've got a television program to produce." She looked at her watch. "Twenty minutes to air."

I put my arm around her shoulder. "You'll make it," I said. "You always do."

CHAPTER

14

Tom Kelsoe had taken Jill's car, so we drove over to Nationtv in the Volvo. When I saw the pain on Jill's face as she climbed into the passenger seat, I was filled with rage. But anger had to wait. During the ten-minute drive to the studio, I told Jill everything. She listened in silence, but near the end of my account, when we stopped for a light, she pulled the cellular phone out of her briefcase and made a call.

"Rapti," she said. "It's me. I'm fine. Yes, Jo did find me. We haven't got much time, so you're going to have to take this one on faith. I want you to tell Sam and Glayne that we're changing the lead story tonight to a discussion of journalistic ethics. They're both pretty quick on the uptake, so they'll be okay with the change."

Jill paused. Rapti had asked her the obvious question. When she answered, Jill's voice was steely. "No," she said, "Tom isn't to know anything about this till we're on the air. You'll have to fill Toronto in on the change of focus, and you'll have to fax Cam a new intro: something about how journalists who use composite characters in their stories are violating the audience's trust. You'd better define what we mean by 'composite characters.' Nothing too technical – just something like 'composite characters are what you get when some journalist who doesn't know his dick from a dildo rolls three or four people together and presents the new creation as a living, breathing human being.' Throw in the Janet Cooke case. You remember that one from J school, don't you?"

As soon as Jill mentioned Janet Cooke's name, another piece in the puzzle fell into place. An article about the Janet Cooke case had been on Kellee Savage's bookshelf in Indian Head. Cooke was a young journalist who had worked for the Washington *Post* in 1981. She won a Pulitzer for a story about child heroin addiction, but had to give the prize back when her paper learned that Jimmy, the eight-year-old addict Cooke had written about with such passion, didn't exist. The story must have had a particular resonance for Kellee after she discovered that Karen Keewatin, the heartbreakingly determined hooker and mother in *Getting Even*, didn't exist, and that, like Janet Cooke, Tom Kelsoe had used the lives and stories of a handful of people to create a character who would tear at the reader's heartstrings and advance his journalistic career.

That morning, when Bernice Jacobs began leafing through my copy of *Getting Even*, it hadn't taken her long to figure out that she was holding concrete proof that the story Kellee Savage had been putting together when she died was true. The tragedy of Bernice's friend, Audrey Nighttraveller, a woman who'd been so severely beaten by a john that she was incapable of caring for herself, had simply been material for Tom Kelsoe. He had used Audrey's life and the life of her sons as he had used the lives of countless unknown women and their families to create a book that would enhance his reputation. What he had done was, in Bernice Jacobs's words, "worse than the worst thing the worst bloodsucker of a pimp ever did to any of us."

And Kellee Savage was going to expose him. I thought of the Post-it notes in the journals stacked on the shelf in the barricaded office in Indian Head. Each one of them had signalled an article on a reporter's use of a composite character. Dogged to the end, Kellee Savage had been preparing the foundations for her story. Now it was up to Jill and me.

It was Saturday, so I didn't have any problem finding a parking place outside Nationtv. Kellee's graduation portrait was in its Safeway bag on the dashboard. After I'd helped Jill unsnap her seatbelt, I handed the picture to her. "This is Kellee Savage, the student who discovered what Tom did," I said.

Jill took the picture from me. "How old was she?"

"Twenty-one."

"Let's take this with us," she said. "I want him to see it."

Jill shook me off when I offered to help her get out of the car. She said she could do it on her own, but as she began her methodical, agony-filled ascent of the stairs outside Nationtv, I had to look away. I had watched her bound up those steps a hundred times; she had always seemed invincible.

Nationtv was deserted. Jill used her security card to get us in, and we didn't see a soul as we headed across the cavernous lobby. When we got to the elevator, Jill checked her watch and turned to me. "We have five minutes," she said. "I'm going to go to the control room. You'd better stay out of the way till we're on the air."

"But you *are* going to call the police, aren't you?"

"Of course I am, but not until every viewer who tunes in tonight has a chance to watch that bastard twist in the wind. Jo, if we hand Tom over to the police right now, the story will be page one here, but I have to make sure that what he did ends up on the front page of every newspaper in this country. I owe it to Reed , and I owe it to Kellee Savage."

"I'll wait in the green room," I said. "I can watch the show from the monitor in there."

"When it looks like the time's right, come into the studio," Jill said. "If you sit on that riser behind the cameras, he'll have to look at you. Be sure to bring the picture." She ran her fingers through her hair. It was a gesture she often made when she was on edge, but this time, as she touched the back of her skull, she winced. "Sonofabitch," she said softly.

I put my arm around her shoulder. "When the show's over, let's find ourselves a bottle of Glenfiddich and crawl in."

Jill gave me a grim smile. "Promises, promises." She pushed the elevator button, and we stepped in. "Let's go," she said. "It's showtime."

At some point within the past twenty-four hours, there had been a birthday party in the green room. Soggy paper plates, dirty coffee cups, and used plastic wine glasses littered the end tables and window sills, and on the coffee table in the middle of the room a big cardboard box leaked crumbs from the remains of a bakery birthday cake. I removed a plate full of half-eaten angelfood from the chair nearest the monitor and sat down.

The screen was already picking up images of the members of the political panel, taking their places, smoothing their clothes, adjusting their earpieces. Tonight, Glayne and Sam were both in Ottawa. Behind them I could see the shot of the Peace Tower Nationtv always used for its Ottawa segments. Usually, in the minutes leading up to airtime, there was laughter and nervous kibitzing, but tonight Glayne and Sam were all business. They might not have known exactly what was coming, but their tense silence was evidence that they foresaw trouble.

When Tom Kelsoe's face appeared on the screen, my pulse quickened. His microphone was turned on, and I could hear him chewing out the young woman who'd attached it to his jacket. She'd apparently caught the leather in the mike clip and he was berating her for her carelessness. The second hand of the clock on the wall behind the monitor was sweeping; in sixty seconds, the state of his leather jacket would be the least of Tom's worries. The young woman disappeared from the shot. Tom settled in his chair, caught his likeness in one of the monitors, and assumed his public face. "Canada Tonight" was on the air.

The host of the show, Cameron McFee, was an unflappable Scot with an easy manner and a ready wit that made him a natural for live television. He couldn't have had time to do much more than glance through the new introduction, but he read Rapti's lines about the immorality of journalists who pass hybrids off as truth with real conviction.

Until Cam began to describe the Janet Cooke case, Tom looked alert but not alarmed. However, when Cam started to give details about how Janet Cooke had entrapped herself with her lies, Tom's chest began to rise and fall rapidly, and sweat appeared on his upper lip. As the awareness hit him that Cam's homily about unethical journalists was a prelude to real trouble, I could see the panic rise sharply. Attentive as a lover, the camera moved in for a tight shot of Tom's face, found the desperation in his eyes, and moved closer.

At that moment, I could think of few activities more rewarding than watching Tom Kelsoe's persona crumble, but I had a part to play too. I picked up Kellee's photograph and started towards the studio. There were no police in the corridor, and I felt a tingling of apprehension. From what I'd seen on the monitor, Tom was close to the edge, and I would have welcomed the presence of some officers in blue. When I walked into the studio, Troy Prigotzke, a member of the crew on "Canada Tonight," was standing in the shadows near the door.

I moved close enough to him so I didn't have to raise my voice. "Troy, did anyone tell you that the police are supposed to show up here tonight?"

"Rapti did," he said. "That's why I'm here, but she didn't elaborate. She just told me that it was Jill's call, and that, when the cops arrived, I should make sure they got in."

"Well, as long as you're watching . . . ," I said, and I started towards the riser.

"Jo!" Troy's whisper was insistent, and I turned. "All the outside doors to the lobby are locked," he said. "Nobody can get in without a security card. Did Jill send somebody to let the cops in?"

"I don't know," I said.

"I'd better get up there and check," Troy said.

I went to the riser and sat down. When he saw me, Tom was in mid-sentence, but the sight of me seemed to derail his train of thought. He stumbled through a few more words, then fell silent. Our eyes locked. I pulled Kellee's photograph out of the Safeway bag. Then I leaned forward and held it out to him.

I'd expected that the sight of his victim's face would rock Tom. It demolished him. The photograph seemed to shatter whatever vestiges of ego were keeping him in front of the camera. I wasn't ready for what happened next. He bolted out of his chair and started to run off the set. In a moment straight out of a sitcom, the wire on the lapel mike Tom was still wearing jerked him back. He ripped it off, then darted past me towards the door that led out of the studio. My most fervent hope was that he would collide with Troy and the Regina City Police, but I couldn't take that chance.

I was on my feet in a split-second. By the time I got out of the studio, Tom had already made it past the green room and was heading towards the stairs. He spotted the two uniformed police officers emerging from the stairwell before they caught sight of him. It took the police a moment to get their bearings, and by then Tom had doubled back and was running towards me. When he turned left at the corridor that led to the elevators, I was right behind him. So were the police and so was Troy Prigotzke. As I ran, I could hear their shouts and their footfalls behind me. On the wall facing us at the end of the hall was the same poster that I had seen the day before on the side of the city bus. Tom's likeness, poised, ironic, eyes burning with integrity, hovered over us all as we raced along. I caught up with him in front of the elevators. As he reached over to punch the button, I jumped in front of him. "Oh no, you don't," I said. "You're not going anywhere."

My intention was simply to block his way until Troy and the police reached us, but events spun out of control. It happened in a flash. I heard the mechanical groan of the elevator approaching; I felt the doors open behind me; then Tom Kelsoe pounded his outstretched hand against my collarbone and shoved me into the elevator. The police got there just as the doors were closing. My grandmother would have said they made it just after the nick of time. As the elevator started its ascent, Tom Kelsoe took a step towards me. He was panting with exertion, filling the small space with the smells of leather and fear.

I was breathing hard too. "Don't make it any worse for yourself," I said. "There are police all over this building."

Tom laughed and punched the stop button on the panel

beside the doors. The elevator lurched to a halt. "There are no cops in here," he said.

For the first time since I'd fled the studio, I was afraid. I ran through my options. There weren't many. For a woman of fifty, I was in good shape, but Tom Kelsoe was forty, and he had spent a lot more hours in the gym than I had. In the close confines of an elevator, I wouldn't have a chance against him. I couldn't even appeal to Tom's highly developed sense of self-interest. He had already killed twice. He had nothing to lose by battering me. All I had going for me was the possibility that, like all egotists, Tom would be unable to resist the chance to tell his tale.

I tried to keep my voice steady. "I've always told my kids there are two sides to every story," I said. "Maybe it's time I got your perspective on everything that's happened."

His fist seemed to come out of nowhere. I jumped aside, and the punch he'd aimed at me landed on the elevator wall. The pain goaded him. He pulled his fist back and struck again. This time, he connected. My head snapped back, and my nose gushed blood. I cried out. As soon as he saw that he'd hurt me, Tom Kelsoe was transformed. The fear and confusion went out of his face. He looked like a man who had come to himself. "Don't patronize me, bitch," he said. "And don't you ever underestimate me."

"Is that what Reed Gallagher did?" I asked, and my voice sounded small and beseeching.

"He thought I needed help," Tom said, spitting out the word *help* as if it were unclean. "But Reed Gallagher was the one who was weak. When Kellee Savage came to him with her accusations, he should have thrown her out of his office. If he'd shown some balls then, the problem would have solved itself. But Reed said he had 'an obligation to the truth.'" Tom shook his head in wonder. "The truth. As if anybody gives a rat's ass about the truth any more. I tried to tell Reed that nobody cared if the characters in the book were composites. All people wanted was a chance to get their rocks off reading about a whore with a heart of gold. And they sure as hell didn't care if I used Kellee's interviews to give them their little catharsis."

I could taste the blood in the back of my mouth. I swallowed. If I didn't want to get hit again, I had to keep Tom talking. "But Reed didn't see it that way," I said.

"No," Tom said. "Reed didn't see it that way. Kellee Savage was useless, a total waste of skin, but Reed decided she needed an advocate. That's how I got him to come to Scarth Street that night. I told him I'd had a change of heart, that I was ready to accept the conditions he and that little toad had decided upon."

"What did they want?" I asked.

"Not much at all," he said bitterly. "Just a public admission that Karen Keewatin was a created character and that Kellee Savage had been an invaluable colleague in researching the book. Can you conceive of anybody obtuse enough to cave in to those conditions?"

Thinking the question was rhetorical, I remained silent, but silence seemed to be the wrong response. Tom took a step towards me. "Well?" he said.

"No," I said meekly, "I can't imagine anybody that obtuse."

Tom punched the air with his forefinger in a gesture of approbation. "Right," he said. "I know you've got a somewhat negative opinion of me, Joanne, but even you will have to admit that I'm not stupid."

"No," I said, "you're not stupid."

"Well, apparently Reed lost sight of the fact. When I told him I'd decided to apologize publicly for what I'd done, he fell for it. In fact, he was *thrilled*. He said that he knew all along that I'd do the right thing, and that he'd stand by me and help me salvage my career. As if there would have been any career left to salvage after I'd gone through that charade." Tom's eyes burned into me. "He didn't leave me any choice. I didn't enjoy what I had to do, but it had to be done."

My head was pounding. I thought of Reed Gallagher telling Julie that his greatest dream was to grow old with her. The words seemed to form themselves. "Why did you have to humiliate him like that?" I asked. "Why couldn't you just kill him?"

Tom looked at me incredulously. "Because I had a plan," he barked. "What the police found when they walked into that room on Scarth Street was a scene perfectly calibrated to divert their attention away from all the questions I didn't want asked."

"But Kellee would have asked the right questions."

Tom's tone was almost dreamy. "She would have, and from the moment I heard that they'd found Reed's body, I knew she'd be a problem. That's why I was in my office that night – trying to come up with a solution. I hadn't thought of a thing, then that stupid cow just came lumbering in." As he remembered the night of March 17, it was apparent that Tom's focus had drifted from the present. Wherever he was, he wasn't in the elevator with me. I calculated the distance between me and the panel beside the doors. The buttons that would restart the elevator were seductively near. I moved closer.

"What did Kellee want?" I asked.

"Justice," Tom said in a mockingly declamatory voice. "Revenge. Who the fuck knows? She was drunk, and she was half out of her mind because she'd just heard about Reed. It was so easy. There were some cases of beer in the Journalism lounge. I offered to get us a couple of bottles to drink while we talked things over. When Reed and I had had our meeting on Scarth Street, I'd added some secobarbital to the Dewar's I'd brought for him to sip while we discussed my rehabilitation. There was enough left over to make Kellee's beer a real powerhouse. It hit her like a bag of hammers. She started to cry. Then she asked me to take her home."

I backed along the wall of the elevator till the panel of buttons was within striking distance. "But you didn't take her to Indian Head," I said. "You dumped her in that farmer's field."

Tom shrugged. Suddenly he seemed bored by the turn the conversation had taken. When he dropped his glance, I shot my hand towards the panel of buttons. I thought Tom had lost interest in my movements, but I was wrong. As my finger touched the button for the mezzanine, Tom chopped my forearm with the edge of his hand in a gesture so violent it brought tears to my eyes.

"You knew Kellee would die if you left her there," I said.

He brought his face close to mine. "And I couldn't have cared less," he said. "Because I'm not like Reed Gallagher. I *do* have balls."

"And that's where you found the courage to kill a man who thought of you as a son and a twenty-one-year-old woman who was too drunk and too drugged to find her way home." I leaned toward him and whispered, "You really are piece of work, Tom." Then I raised my knee and caught him square in the crotch. He yelped in pain, and fell to the floor. I reached past him and hit *M* for mezzanine. This time Tom Kelsoe was too busy moaning to rip my finger from the button. All the same, it wasn't until the elevator began to move that I felt safe enough to cry.

My memories of the next few minutes are fragmented: sharp and separate vignettes as distinct as stills from a movie.

The elevator doors opened, and Jill and Rapti were there. So were five members of the police force, and a lot of people from the show. I was glad to see that one of those people was Troy Prigotzke who, in addition to being a nice guy, was a body builder. Beside me, Tom Kelsoe was struggling to his knees. When Troy saw him, he reached down, grabbed Tom's jacket collar and dragged him into the lobby. Then in a smooth and effortless move, he lifted Tom up and handed him to one of the cops. "I believe you have some interest in this piece of shit," he said.

Rapti had a sweatshirt tied around her waist; she took it off and draped it around my shoulders. Then she took the sleeve and mopped at the blood on my face. "Poor Jo," she said.

"I'm okay," I said, but my tongue felt thick, and my words didn't sound right.

As the police put the handcuffs on Tom Kelsoe, he shot Jill a pleading look. "You've got to help me, baby," he said. Jill gave him a glance that was beyond contempt, and turned to me. "Let's get out of here," she said.

Before the police left, they offered to radio for someone to take Jill and me to the hospital to get checked out and then bring us downtown to make our statements. I asked if Constable Marissa Desjardin was on duty, and they said they'd see.

While we were waiting, I went over to a pay phone and called Sylvie O'Keefe to ask if Taylor could stay the night. After Sylvie and I made our arrangements, Taylor came on the line. I started to ask what she'd been up to, but she cut me off. "You sound funny," she said.

"I have a nosebleed," I said.

"But you're okay." I could hear the anxiety in her voice.

"I'm fine," I said. "I'm just trying to be as brave as you were when you cut your hand. Now, you have fun, and I'll pick you up tomorrow morning."

Marissa Desjardin shuddered when she saw my face, but after the doctor in emergency had checked me over, he said nothing was broken and I'd live to fight another day. He said the same thing to Jill. When he went off to write a prescription for painkillers, Marissa Desjardin rolled her eyes and whispered "asshole" at his retreating back.

We were out of police headquarters in twenty minutes. Marissa Desjardin was a whiz at taking statements, and, as she said, she knew Jill and I were fading fast. It was a little after 8:00 when we walked through my front door.

After I'd helped Jill off with her coat, I said, "We can't combine painkillers and Glenfiddich. Which would you prefer?"

"The Scotch," she said. "And Carly Simon. Have you still got those old tapes of hers? The ones we used to listen to when we'd stay up and talk all night."

"Of course," I said. "I was just waiting for our next pyjama party."

While Jill went after the Scotch, I got out the glasses and ice and checked the messages. The first one was from the Parents' Committee at Taylor's school, wondering if I could bring a pan of squares to the Kids Convention Monday night. The second one was from Angus. He and Camillo had gone to Sharkey's to play pool, and he'd check in later. The third message was from Alex. It was a bad connection, and I could only catch snatches of what he said. But I heard enough to know that he had had car trouble somewhere outside of Meadow Lake and was waiting for parts. When I heard Alex's voice, I instinctively raised my fingers to my face, wondering what he would see when he looked at me.

Jill came into the room just as the tape played its final message. It was Dr. Roy Crawford. "Your new kitten came through the surgery with flying colours," he said. "You and Benny can pick him up on Monday."

Jill looked at me quizzically.

"Don't even ask," I said.

I dropped a tape in my cassette player. As Carly Simon began to sing "Two Hot Girls on a Hot Summer Night," Jill handed me a drink and raised her glass. "Life goes on," she said, but there was a bleakness in her tone that made me wonder whether she was wholly convinced that life going on was a good idea.

Jill and I listened to all my Carly Simon tapes twice that night, and we went through a fair amount of Glenfiddich. The combination seemed to help. Jill needed to talk, and I needed to hear what she had to say. The truth of the matter was I didn't get it. I didn't understand how a woman as smart and as competent as Jill could make herself believe she was in love with a manipulator like Tom Kelsoe, and I didn't understand how, once the beatings began, she didn't simply report him and walk away.

Every situation Jill described that night was a perfect fit for the pattern of abuse. Tom's father had been a batterer whose frequent absences only served to underline the horror of his presence. When Tom's father was away, the Kelsoe home was a happy one, but when he returned he was, by turns, demanding and cold. Tom could never measure up to the ever-shifting standards his father set for him, and he came to see his mother as his only anchor in a violent and unchartable sea of threats and violence. After enduring years of cruelty at her husband's hands, Tom's mother ran away with the first man who promised her safe haven. Tom was left with his father. He was devastated. As soon as he was old enough, he left home and began the search for his ideal: a woman who would never desert him, no matter what.

The first time Tom hit her, Jill had been dumfounded. She and Tom were, as Tom frequently asserted, the perfect match, complementary halves of a whole, logos and eros. Tom's remorse when he saw Jill's bruises the morning after the first beating had been so intense, Jill had feared he would harm himself. He'd come to her apartment that night with a bottle of expensive bath oil and a silk peignoir. As he bathed Jill's bruised body, he had tearfully offered up his excuse: he was obsessed by the fear that his new book would fail and that Jill would abandon him the way his mother had, the way everybody he'd ever counted upon had. And so she had forgiven him.

As Jill told me about her relationship with Tom Kelsoe, I tried hard to make some sense of it. I couldn't. In my heart, I didn't believe Jill could either. That night, as we talked, she was filled with guilt. She felt that, if she had acted, Tom could have been stopped before two lives had been lost. Her anguish about what might have been allowed me to ask the question I'd been haunted by. "If you didn't want to involve the police," I said, "why didn't you come to me?"

She shook her head. "I don't know. I felt so cut off. It was as if I was living on the other side of a glass wall." Her eyes were miserable. "Jo, believe me, it's not easy to let people see that you've allowed yourself to be victimized."

After I showered the next morning, I flinched at the sight of my face in the bathroom mirror. When Angus and Taylor saw it, they were going to need a lot of reassuring. Before I took the dogs for their walk, I smoothed makeup over my bruises, swathed my head in a scarf, pulled up my jacket collar, and put on my largest dark glasses. As I gave my face a last anxious check before I left the house, the light began to dawn. Jill was right. It wasn't easy to face the world as a victim.

When it was time to pick up Taylor, I let Angus drive. Before she'd taken a cab home to her apartment, Jill had made me promise that I wouldn't get behind the wheel until I'd had a chance to recover. Besides, I didn't want to face Taylor alone. Angus had done exactly the right thing when he saw my bruises. He had put his arms around me without saying a word. When we got to Sylvie O'Keefe's house, Angus went to the door to get Taylor. As they walked towards the car, I could see him preparing her for what she was about to see. She looked scared, but she managed a smile when I told her there was nothing to worry about. As soon as we got home, I gave Taylor a short but honest account of what had happened. After I'd finished, she asked me two questions: the first was, did I hurt; the second was, did the doctor think my face would ever look the way it used to look. I told her the answer to both questions was yes.

I spent Sunday recuperating. The most vigorous activity I undertook was to find my old bridal picture so Taylor could draw a portrait of me in my big dress to cheer me up. Jill arrived at dinnertime with two pizzas from the Copper Kettle: spinach and feta for the grown-ups, and everything but the kitchen sink for the kids. By the time I slipped between the sheets, I felt I was on my way to recovery, but when the dogs and I set out on Monday morning, it soon became apparent that one day of rest hadn't been enough. I was bone-tired and we only made it part way around the lake before I gave it up as a bad job and came home. Rosalie Norman was sympathetic when I called in sick. She hadn't seen the political panel Saturday night, but she'd certainly heard about it. News travels fast on a university campus.

When I hung up, the day stretched before me. There were a hundred things that needed my attention, but only two jobs I had to do. I called Roy Crawford and told him the kids and I would be in after school to pick up the new kitten;

251

then I got down my cookbooks and began searching for a recipe for Nanaimo bars.

I deep-sixed Taylor's plan to have Benny join us when we went to the vet's, but she was too excited to put up more than a token protest. From the moment she saw the tortoise-shell, Taylor was filled with plans. "He and Benny will be best friends," she said. "When I'm at school, they'll play all the time."

Angus rolled his eyes, but remained silent.

"Don't expect too much of Benny, T," I said. "His nose may be a little bit out of joint at first."

"Not Benny," she said confidently.

When we were leaving, the receptionist smiled at Taylor. "What are you going to call your kitten?"

Taylor didn't miss a beat. "Bruce," she said, and she headed for the car.

Benny's reaction to Bruce surprised me. Apparently, there were depths of feeling in Benny that had been unplumbed. From the moment Taylor undid the blanket and placed the new kitten in front of him, Benny was devoted to Bruce. It was clear that I had seriously underestimated Benny, and every glance he gave me let me know it.

It was still light when Taylor and I set out for the Kids Convention. As we walked towards Lakeview School, we spotted other parents with other kids and other pans of Nanaimo bars. Taylor was buoyant with the combined excitement of Bruce's arrival and of being out after supper on a school night. But as we crossed Cameron Street, she scrunched up her nose. "I wish Alex had got here in time for us to all go to school together."

"Taylor, I wish you wouldn't count on Alex making it tonight. Meadow Lake's a long way from here, and it takes time to get car parts."

Taylor's gaze was untroubled. "He'll be here," she said. "He promised."

The front hall of Lakeview School was hung with construction-paper stars. Inside each star was a student's picture. In case we didn't get the message, there was a sign in poster-paint script: "At Lakeview School, every student is a S*T*A*R!" After Taylor and I found her star, and Jess's and Samantha's and those of her seven other best friends, I said, "Let's go see your Nanabush mural."

"No," she said. "It wouldn't be fair. We have to wait for Alex. There's other stuff."

For the next half-hour, we looked at stuff: a fisherman's net filled with oddly coloured papier-mâché fish made by the grade ones; First Nations masks made by the grade threes; family crests made by the grade sixes; poems about death and despair written by the grade eights.

We ended up in front of a collage called "Mona and the Bulls"; in it, the Mona Lisa was wearing a Chicago Bulls uniform and looking enigmatic. "I can only take so many high points, Taylor," I said. "I think 'Mona and the Bulls' is going to have to be my last stop before the mural. I promise I'll enjoy it all over again when we look at it with Alex."

The Nanabush mural had been mounted in the resource room, and it had attracted quite a crowd. At the edge of the gathering, just as Taylor had predicted, was Alex Kequahtooway. When she spotted him, Taylor said, "There he is," and her tone was matter-of-fact.

She went over to him and tweaked his sleeve. He knelt down and talked to her for a moment, then he stood up and started towards me.

I put my hand up to cover my face. "I had an adventure," I said.

He reached over and took down my hand. "Marissa

Desjardin left a message for me at the garage in Meadow Lake. I was on the next bus home." Alex reached out to embrace me; then he noticed, as I had, that we were attracting more than our share of sidelong glances. He stepped back.

I moved towards him. "Alex, I really could use someone to lean on right now."

He slid his arm around my shoulder. "Are you sure you're all right, Jo?"

I closed my eyes and lay my head on him. "No," I said, "but for the first time since all of this happened, I think maybe I'm going to be."

It rained the morning of Kellee Savage's funeral, but by the time Jill and I were on the highway, the sky was clear and the sun was shining. Alex had offered to drive to Indian Head with me, but Jill had been anxious to go. "It's the least I can do for another journalist," she said simply.

The United Church was full, but the only people I recognized were Neil McCallum and Kellee's classmates from the J school. There were flowers everywhere. Ed Mariani, who'd come back from Minneapolis with a terrible cold and Barry's forgiveness, had sent the white roses that were on the table with the guest book, and the air of the church was sweet with the perfume of spring. The service had the special poignancy that the funeral of a young person always has. There were too many young faces in the pews, and the minister had the good sense to admit that the reasons for the death of a person who has just begun life were always as much a mystery to him as they were to any of us.

Afterwards, the congregation was invited down to the church hall for lunch. It was a pretty room: warm with pastel tablecloths and bowls of pussy willows splashed with afternoon light. Neil McCallum was surrounded by people, so I went over to the table where Linda Van Sickle and Jumbo Hryniuk were sitting. When he saw me, Jumbo leaped up and helped me with my chair.

"This is the first funeral I've ever been to," he said. "I almost lost it up there. Do they get any easier?"

"No," I said. "They don't. But I'm glad you're here." I turned to Linda Van Sickle. "I'm glad you came, too. I never had a chance to ask you the results of that ultrasound you had."

"I'm going to have twins," she said. "Two little boys."

"That must be so exciting," I said.

"It is," she agreed, but her voice was flat. Physically, Linda looked better than she had the last time I'd seen her, but she'd lost the serenity that had enveloped her during so much of her pregnancy. When she spoke again, I could hear the strain in her voice. "Is it true about Tom Kelsoe? That he killed Kellee and Professor Gallagher?"

"It's true," I said.

"The worst part," Jumbo said, "was the way he dumped Kellee in that field – just like she was an animal."

"Less than an animal," I said.

Linda chewed her lower lip. "What's going to happen to Val?" she asked.

"He's still in the hospital," I said. "I guess the first thing he's going to have to do is come to terms with what happened. His dad has a lawyer working on the legal questions."

Jumbo looked puzzled. "Val always thought his dad hated him."

"Val was wrong about a lot of things," I said.

Linda shook her head sadly. "I guess we all were."

I looked across the room. Neil McCallum was motioning to me to come over. I stood up, shook hands with Jumbo and gave Linda a hug. "There's someone over there I want to talk to," I said. "I'll see you in class on Friday."

Neil's eyes were red-rimmed and swollen, but he smiled when he saw me.

"How are you doing?" I asked.

"Not very good," he said. "I miss Kellee. I hate wearing a suit, but Mum says you have to for a funeral."

"Your mum's right."

"I know," he said. Then he brightened. "Are you ready to go?"

"Go where?" I asked.

"To see the crocuses," he said. "Don't you remember? When I told you Chloe and I saw the crocuses, you said you wanted to see them." He held out his hand to me. "So let's go."

I followed Neil outside, and we walked down the street to his house to get Chloe. As we headed for the edge of town, the dog bounded across the lawns and ran through every puddle on the street. When we hit the prairie, and started towards the hill where Neil had seen the crocuses, a breeze came up and I could smell moisture and warming earth. Neil and Chloe ran up the hill ahead of me.

Suddenly he yelled, "Here they are."

I followed him to the top of the hill and looked around me. For as far as I could see, the ground was purple and white. It was an amazing sight.

Neil bent down, picked a crocus and handed it to me. "They're nice, aren't they?" he said.

"They're beautiful," I said. "There's a story about where crocuses came from."

Neil sat down on the ground and began to take the burrs out of Chloe's coat. "Do you want to tell it?"

I sat down beside him. "Yes, I think I do," I said. "It's about a woman named Demeter who had a daughter named Persephone."

Chloe yelped, and Neil leaned over to reassure her.

"Persephone was a wonderful daughter," I continued. "Very sweet and thoughtful. Her mother loved her a lot. One day Persephone decided she had to go to the underworld to comfort the spirits of the people who had died."

"Like Kellee," Neil said.

"Yes," I said. "Like Kellee. But in the story, once Persephone was gone, her mother missed her so much that she decided that nothing would ever grow again." Chloe leaned over and put her muddy head on my lap.

"She likes you," Neil said.

"I like her too," I said. "Anyway, one morning when Demeter was missing Persephone so much she thought she herself might die, a ring of purple crocuses pushed their way through the soil. The flowers were all around her, and they were so beautiful Demeter knelt down on the earth so she could see them up close. Guess what she heard?"

Neil shrugged.

"She heard the crocuses whispering, 'Persephone returns! Persephone returns!' Demeter was so happy she began to dance, and she made a cape out of white crocuses to give to her daughter when she came back from comforting the spirits of the dead."

Neil lay down on the ground. For a while he just lay there, looking up at the sky with Chloe panting beside him. Finally, he turned to me and smiled. "I heard them," he said. "I heard the crocuses whisper."